VICTORIOUS VICE

BELLAMY BROTHERS SIX

HELEN HARDT

HARDT & SONS

VICTORIOUS VICE

BELLAMY BROTHERS SIX

Helen Hardt

WWW.HELENHARDT.COM

PRAISE FOR HELEN HARDT

Wow! Mind just blown! A complete mindf**k...
    ~**GoddessWithanAttitude** on *Spades*

"Literally perfection."
    ~**Read with Aimee** on *My Heart Still Beats*

"Helen Hardt is a master at making you fall for the bad boy."
    ~**Words We Love By** on *Savage Sin*

"Hardt spins erotic gold..."
    ~*Publishers Weekly* on *Follow Me Darkly*

"22 Best Erotic Novels to Read"
    ~*Marie Claire* **Magazine** on *Follow Me Darkly*

"Intensely erotic and wildly emotional..."
    ~*New York Times* **bestselling author Lisa Renee Jones** on
Follow Me Darkly

"Christian, Gideon, and now...Braden Black."
    ~**Books, Wine, and Besties** on *Follow Me Darkly*

"This red-hot tale will have readers fanning themselves."
    ~**Publishers Weekly** on *Blush*

"Scintillating..."
    ~**Publishers Weekly** on *Bloom*

"Helen's intelligent writing style and skills have made this story a must-read."
    ~**FireSerene Reads** on *Bloom*

"It's hot, it's intense, and the plot starts off thick and had me completely spellbound from page one."
    ~**The Sassy Nerd Blog** on *Rebel*

"This book was fantastic! It was steamy, funny, romantic, and just about any other emotion you can think of..."
    ~**Steamy Book Mama** on *Lily and the Duke*

"*Craving* is the jaw-dropping book you *need* to read!"
    ~*New York Times* **bestselling author Lisa Renee Jones** on *Craving*

"Completely raw and addictive."
    ~**#1** *New York Times* **bestselling author Meredith Wild** on *Craving*

"Helen Hardt has some kind of skill I don't have the words to describe. Her writing is addictive. She sucked in my mind and I just don't want to read anything but her right now!"

~**OMGReads Blog**

"Helen Hardt...is a master story teller."

~**Small Town Book Nerd**

In memory of Russell A. Staab

I have a feeling that the Bellamy ranch shrouds more secrets than perhaps even Austin Bellamy himself knows.

"I believe Falcon is a good man," I say.

"I do as well. Otherwise I wouldn't have saved his ass."

"What about his brothers?"

Dad shrugs. "I wasn't able to find out too much about them before I had to go to prison. The older one, Hawk, seems good. But I sense that the younger one is a bit of a loose cannon."

My father has no idea.

"I'll look into all of them," I say. "I'll make sure Savannah is safe."

He gives a weak smile. "I know you will, Vinnie."

"I should've been here, Dad." I run my hands through my hair, sighing. "If I had been, Mikey would still be alive."

"I'll never stop mourning your brother," he says. "Just as I'll never stop mourning your mother." He looks at me, a small glimmer of light in his eyes. "But I have you, and I have

Savannah. I trust Falcon to keep Savannah safe. And you know what I need you to do."

"I'll do it, Dad. You have my word."

I drop him off at the prison, and when I get back to my mother's home—now *my* home—my grandfather is waiting for me at the front door.

"I have nothing to say to you." I brush past him, opening the door.

"Check your email," he says. "You're back on that flight to Colombia. Leaving tonight."

"Send someone else." I take a step inside the house.

"Nope. I'm sending you." He grabs my arm. "You want to be my second-in-command? That's who I need on this mission. You'd be there now if your mother hadn't had that heart attack."

I grit my teeth. "Don't even talk about my mother."

He frowns, laying a hand over his heart. "You think this isn't killing me? She was my child."

"Yes. Your only child."

His lips twitch.

And I cock my head.

"My mother was trying to tell me something before she died. Something about you. Something about my father."

He raises an eyebrow. "You mean you haven't guessed?"

I whip my arm out of his grasp. "Stop playing games with me, old man. If there's something I need to know about my father, you need to tell me."

"All you need to know about Vincent Gallo Senior is that he's a weakling." Grandfather scowls.

"Weak men don't kill a man to save their daughter from marriage to a degenerate."

He says nothing.

"So don't ever tell me my father's a weak man again."

"To the contrary," he says, "your father is the strongest man I know."

"But you just said—"

My flesh goes cold as ice.

Oh my God.

What my mother was trying to tell me...

What my grandfather just said...

I feel my blood draining from my face.

There's a reason I look so much like my mother, so much like my grandfather.

And my father doesn't know. *He doesn't know.*

And all mafia brides are supposed to be virgins...

Nausea grips me, but I resist the urge to double over and retch.

"You fucking bastard," I grit out.

A wicked grin crawls across his wrinkled face. "Now, Vincent," he sneers. "Is that any way to speak to your *father?*"

I grab his shoulders violently. "You raped your own daughter?"

"And that surprises you?"

"Wasn't she supposed to be a virgin?"

He shrugs. "She was. Until about a month before her wedding. I waited until I knew she was ovulating." His grin widens. "I suppose one could say I invoked the right of *prima nocta.*"

My stomach is twisting into a pretzel. "And you knew... You knew she was pregnant..."

"Yes, I lucked out." He smirks. "Your grandmother

couldn't give me any more children, but I knew *I* wasn't the problem. I had to make sure my line continued."

"My father..."

He clasps his hands together, frowning. "Do you know how difficult it's been, Vincent? Letting you take *his* name?"

"Oh my God..."

"So you see—"

I cut him off. "You knew I was your son this whole time. You still raped me with that billy club."

He raises a finger. "As my father did to me."

Vomit threatens to erupt from my throat. "This is over, old man. It's over now."

I reach for my gun, and out of nowhere, two goons who work for the family leap into action. They must have let themselves in before I got home. They charge forward like twin shadows. The first goon lunges at me, slapping the gun out of my hand. It skids across the marble floor, stopping under a side table.

I duck as the second goon swings a fist at my head, and counterattack with an uppercut to his jaw. The man staggers back, but before I can get back to my gun, the first goon grabs me from behind in a bear hug, lifting me off the ground.

I grit my teeth and slam my head backward into the goon's face. I can hear the crunch of his nose breaking. He drops me, and I pivot on my heel and throw an elbow into the man's throat for good measure. He gags in response.

The second goon recovers and charges like a bull, tackling me into the staircase. The impact sends a painful jolt up my spine, but I wrap my legs around the goon's waist and flip him into the other one. They both crash to the floor, and I slam my fist into the goon's temple once, twice—until he goes limp.

My grandfather—correction, my *father*—remains calm, almost amused, as I stand, panting. He slowly brings his hands together in mock applause.

"Impressive, Vinnie. Now tell me, *son*, what's your next move?"

I wipe a smear of blood from my lip and dart to the side table, diving for my gun, but my father steps forward, drawing his own weapon just as I get mine. We're faced off, our guns aimed at each other's chests. The room falls into a tense silence.

The man who sired me smirks.

"You won't do it. You don't have it in you."

I tighten my finger on the trigger. "I killed Puzo."

"Indirectly." He crinkles his forehead. "I'm not so sure you have the balls to get your own hands dirty."

"I have nothing left to lose, old man."

I fire the gun. The bullet slams into my father's chest, and he stumbles back, a stunned expression crossing his face. He looks down, his hand clutching his suit jacket.

But then I notice.

No blood.

I go to him, rip open his shirt.

Sure enough, a bulletproof vest.

He lets out a cold, dark chuckle. "I'm afraid you'll find this old man still has a few tricks up his sleeve." He stares daggers into me from the floor. "I *own* you, Vincent. Your name should be Mario Bianchi, Junior. But I'll let you keep his name. Consider it a gift from the man who fathered you." He looks down at his vest, chuckling lightly. "And I won't punish you for this. In fact, I'm proud of you. I would've probably done the same thing in your shoes, which is why I was prepared."

Rage.

Pure rage. The kind that blurs your vision and roars in your ears, demanding action, any action, just to release the fury burning inside. It's the kind that makes your hands shake, your body tense, and your thoughts spiral out of control, searching for something—anything—to destroy.

But I hold it in.

I hold it fucking in.

I will never concede.

But at this point, I have to let my grandfather think that I am.

"All right, Grandfather."

He clears his throat, glaring at me.

I draw in a breath. "*Father*," I say. "I'll be on that plane tonight."

"Good," he says. "Your life begins tonight, Vincent. You will see what awaits you."

1

RAVEN

everal hours earlier...

The service for Vinnie and Savannah's mother is over. Jared, my bodyguard, and I walk out of the church. We awkwardly dogleg to avoid the receiving line. I don't want to look at Vinnie. I'm only here because my brother is engaged to the daughter of the deceased.

As we reach the parking lot, I hear a buzz from my purse.

I reach in, but it's not my normal phone that vibrated.

It's the burner.

I've been carrying it around with me just in case the Uber driver—or whoever is on the other end—needs to get in touch with me.

Jared's eyebrows rise when I pull it out. "What did they say?"

I pull up the text. Three simple words send my heart into violent tremors.

You're in danger.

"What does it say?" Jared asks again, this time with more of an edge to his voice.

I hand him the phone.

His eyes widen. "Who sent this?"

I gulp. "I don't know. I've had this phone since I took that Uber ride home from Austin. When the driver pulled over, scared the hell out of me, and told me I needed to invite Vinnie over for dinner that Friday night."

"So this is *his* phone?"

"It's the phone he gave me."

Jared snatches the phone out of my hand. "I need to take this. See if we can trace the phone number."

"It's a burner phone," I say.

"Yeah, most likely. But I have to do my job, Raven." He examines the phone's screen. "If you're in danger, as this text indicates that you are, then I—"

"You need to protect me," I finish for him. "Yes, I know the drill."

He frowns. "You need to take this more seriously."

"Believe me, Jared, I take it very seriously. I just..." I shake my head. "I just attended a funeral for a woman. A woman who seemed to be in perfect health only days ago when I saw her and ate dinner at her house. A woman who meant the world to Vinnie and Savannah. Before that, my brother and Leif found surveillance equipment in my home. My *home*, Jared. And yes, I know that's why you're here. Why I need you to be here. Why I need a freaking bodyguard." I sit down on the curb, rubbing at the sides of my face. "My life for the past several years has been surreal. Nightmarish, truly. I was sick, wondering if I'd even live. But I'm alive, Jared. I'm alive, and I feel good. At least I *should* feel good. I kicked cancer's ass, and I fell in love. But I don't feel good. I feel bad. Someone's watching me. The man I love is in danger. Belinda, his eleven-year-old bride-to-be, is in danger. I can't help either one of them."

Jared sits down next to me. "Raven..."

"For the love of God, let me finish." I snap back to my feet, pace the sidewalk. "I'm supposed to be on top of the fucking world, Jared. I beat cancer! And I fell in love! I try to watch the sunrise every morning, the sunset every evening. I stop to smell the roses, and I take every minute as it comes, appreciating it. At least that's what I'm supposed to be doing. And now, everything has changed again. I don't have to worry about my white blood cells killing me. Instead, I have a whole new threat for my life, this time from people I don't even know. Because of the man I love. Because of my brothers and what they did eight years ago."

"I don't think the two are related, Raven."

"Does it even matter? I kicked cancer!" I clench my hands into fists. "I don't want to be in danger anymore. I've had enough of it."

Jared doesn't say anything. He simply looks at me, his dark eyes full of...

"Pity?" I say to him. "Do not look at me with pity, Jared. I saw enough of that while I was lying in a hospital bed."

"Do you want to go to the burial?" he asks.

"Nice pivot," I say dryly.

"It's a valid question. You're not a family member, though I suppose you'll be an in-law once your brother is married. Usually only family members attend a burial."

"I suppose I should be there...for Falcon," I say softly.

What I mean to say is that I want to be there for Vinnie. But he's made it clear in no uncertain terms that he wants nothing to do with me.

So why does my heart still cling to him?

"All right," Jared says. "I can drive you to the cemetery. Or I can check if there's a funeral procession."

But then I think things through. Vinnie wouldn't want me there. Regardless of how I feel about him in this moment, I know one thing for sure. He wants me safe.

Would it be dangerous for me to go to the burial? Is that what the text is supposed to mean?

"I changed my mind," I say to Jared. "Let's just go home."

"All right. And I'll look into the text message. See if I can figure out where it came from."

I simply nod and let him lead me to our vehicle.

And I wonder...

I wonder why the universe allowed me to live, showed me this truly amazing love, only to take it away.

How is that fair?

When I was lying in bed, so sick I almost wished for death, I thought about life. About what is fair and what is foul. About how we don't really have a choice in the matter.

It's so true.

Caroline Gallo seemed perfectly healthy to me. Of course I don't know what her medical records showed.

But a heart attack?

I know they're more common in women than people tend to realize, but that doesn't make them normal. Especially for a woman in her fifties who is in otherwise good health.

Then again... I always took care of myself too. I have very few vices other than Orange Crush. It's full of sugar and preservatives and I should really give it up, but my illness taught me to enjoy the little things in life.

Yes, it all comes back to my illness. There are two periods in my life. Before cancer and after it.

And in the before-cancer days, I took care of myself. Exercised, ate well for the most part.

And still I got sick.

I have to give it to cancer. It doesn't discriminate.

It doesn't play fair.

Life doesn't play fair.

I had to accept that when I was sick. I had to accept that I got the raw end of some deal even though I didn't deserve it.

Hell, does anyone ever *deserve* cancer?

Of course not. No one does. I wouldn't wish what I experienced on my worst enemies.

A list of people that seems to grow with each passing day...

Now that I kicked cancer's ass, thanks to my brother's bone marrow, don't I have the right to live the rest of my life in peace? To enjoy every sunrise and sunset? Without being in danger?

I fucking deserve all of that.

I deserve a lot of things.

But I suppose fate will decide what I actually get.

And there's not a damn thing I can do about it.

2

VINNIE

Your life begins tonight, Vincent. You will see what awaits you.

My grandfather's—my father's—words race through my mind.

This whole thing makes me nauseated in a way I never knew possible. My mother. My poor mother. The deathbed confession she was trying to give me.

The man who raised me, who I love, isn't my biological father. He doesn't even know that.

My grandfather, my mother's father, is also *my* father.

How fucking twisted is this?

I should have stayed in Europe.

I can't call Mario Bianchi Grandfather anymore. And I'm sure as hell not calling him Father.

He'll just be Mario.

Mario. Mario, who's a rapist. Who committed incest. Who's taken countless lives.

At least my mother was eighteen.

God, did I truly just have that thought?

I'm actually grateful my grandfather isn't a pedophile? Just a man who raped his own daughter?

Thank God for small favors. But not fucking small enough.

Mario has something in common with his new business partner. I'm pretty sure Declan McAllister is an incestuous rapist and a pedophile.

How the hell am I going to protect Belinda when I have to go to Colombia tonight?

I have no one. My mother's dead, my father's in prison. Michael is dead, and I can't ask Savannah to step back into my world. Thanks to my father's—the man who I consider my father—machinations, she does not owe any more debt to the family.

There's no one to help me. Mario certainly won't.

There's no one to help me but me.

And I can't do anything from Colombia.

Damn.

Then of course there's Raven. My beautiful, sweet Raven. I love her so much it hurts. It literally twists my insides out.

I don't believe her father would ever harm her. I believe he loves his children.

But he's not the man she thinks he is. I don't know for sure, but he may have had a hand in sending Falcon to prison. I don't think it's what he wanted, but he may not have had a choice in the matter.

There's something so warped about all of this. Diego Vega's involvement with my family, with the Bellamy family.

Vega's dead, so I can't find anything out about him. I've scoured the dark web for information about him. He, or his people, scrubbed it clean.

The two minions with him that day, according to Falcon and his brothers, were never heard from again. They were most likely stopped at the border and either taken prisoner or killed.

And now I have to go to Colombia for a month.

Raven will be safer if I'm out of the country. That's reason enough to go.

What the hell did Mario mean when he said my life begins tonight?

Does anyone else know the true circumstances of my birth? Anyone besides Mario and my mother?

Because if any of our enemies do...

It puts a big red target on my back.

To take out Bianchi's son? That's a big fucking deal.

I was already his true heir. If they know that I'm a direct product of his loins, it's all over for me.

God... It's all making so much sense now.

No wonder he let me stay in Europe so long.

In his own distorted way, Mario loves me. Was protecting me.

Elmo, my bodyguard, is traveling with me to Colombia. He sits next to me at the gate, ready to board the chartered plane.

I buried my mother only hours ago, and Mario wants me on this plane.

A month.

So much can happen in a month.

I just have to make sure that Raven stays safe. She's my first priority. And unfortunately, Mario knows this.

She's my weakness.

But she's also my strength.

If I can bring down this family, then Raven and I can be together. Make a life of our own.

I'll do what I need to do in Colombia.

I fire up my iPad and read the notes about the people I'll be meeting—those involved in the piece of the trade that Giacomo Puzo was negotiating.

A lance strikes my heart. Not that I felt anything for Puzo, but he had a family. Two little girls. I may not have struck the blow that killed him, but I am ultimately responsible.

Sure, he was corrupt. The world is a better place without him. But who am I to play God?

Who is Mario to play God?

But putting a stop to him will save so many more lives in the long run. Puzo was a necessary casualty.

These thoughts plague me as I board the plane and take my seat. Elmo, next to me, is silent, his gaze cast outside the window.

The engines roar to life and I clutch the iPad tighter. The names and faces on its screen are the Colombia Cartel heads, local law enforcement, politicians—everyone has their slice in this pie. I'm about to jump headfirst into a viper's nest with nothing but my wits to protect me.

One thing is clear though. Being Mario Bianchi's heir gives me an advantage. A dangerous one, indeed. The fascination and fear that his name commands might be the only things keeping me alive in Colombia.

I lean back in my seat and let the outside world blur into nothingness. I am alone with my thoughts, an island amidst a sea of chaos. I imagine Raven's face, her soft smile and the way her eyes light up when she laughs. The thought of her gives me the strength to push through this ordeal.

As the plane ascends through clouds, though, I find myself thinking about the meetings awaiting me. Though I am armed with knowledge about these people, it's impossible to predict their intentions or anticipate their actions.

Will they respect me because I'm Mario Bianchi's heir? Or will they see me as a threat? A young buck trying to infringe upon their territory? Or worse, will they see me as an opportunity? A means of using my lineage against me?

I open my eyes as we hit cruising altitude. Outside the window is pure darkness. It almost looks serene and peaceful, a stark contrast to the war brewing inside me.

I have to stay focused. I can't afford to let my mind wander too much. I have a part to play, a role that I can't jeopardize with emotions or distractions. Which means...I've got to truly leave Raven behind me.

I start going through the files on my iPad again. Faces and names swirl before me, each attached to an extensive list of sins. Extortion, human trafficking, drug smuggling—just another day in the life of these people. My job is to convince these terrible people that I'm one of them, that their secrets are safe with me.

The plane jolts slightly and Elmo looks at me. His eyes are dark and unreadable as they always are, but I note an edge of worry in them. I give him a nod, hoping to reassure him, before turning my attention back to the iPad.

I read the names again. There's Jacinto Agudelo, the cartel kingpin known for his ruthless business tactics and a penchant for torture. His eyes in the photo are cold, calculating. I'll be staying at his mansion in Bogotá, and my business will be mainly with him.

Next is Hernando Reyes, a corrupt politician whose greed

knows no bounds. And then there's Isabella Valentini, a fiery redhead who lives in New York and works with a trio known as "the Unholy Trinity," but who is apparently in Bogotá to negotiate for a Manhattan family.

The list goes on...

Until I see a face that makes me squint. A gaunt, very old woman, with whisps of snow-white hair. Deep wrinkles in her face, but still a shadow of beauty in her weathered features.

She's not nearly as well put-together as the people in the other photos here.

No name is attached to her photo.

Does this old woman have something to do with why I'm going to Colombia? I can't imagine they have much use for a woman of her advanced age. Hell, they don't have much use for women of any age.

Maybe she's a witness or something. Or the widow of a fallen don.

I shake my head to clear it. This woman is ancillary at best. The other names are well known in the cartel, the men Puzo was trying to recruit to his side.

Puzo's no longer an issue, thanks to me.

The purpose of this trip is to get these people to make a deal with Mario.

But why...?

How...?

Why is this woman's picture in here?

I stare at the document, blinking as if that might make her position in all this clearer.

My mind is a whirlwind of questions with no immediate answers. Even Elmo's usually reassuring presence does nothing to subdue my growing unease. There's a reason this woman's photo is in here, but I can't for the life of me figure out why. Maybe it'll be made clear once I arrive in Colombia.

My gut tells me there's more to the story.

There's always more to the story.

As I stare at this old woman, Raven's face flickers in my mind again. I'm not sure why. I mean, I'm constantly thinking about her, but why should this old woman trigger the thought?

Something in her eyes, maybe?

Raven has beautiful eyes. So beautiful that you can get lost in them. I swear to God, the first time I saw her, her eyes took me in so much that I barely noticed she had no hair. And her smile is a beacon in the storm that is brewing around me.

I must protect her at all costs.

Which means leaving her in my past.

3

RAVEN

V innie's face.

His handsome face, olive complexion, perfect jawline, rugged black stubble...

He comes toward me.

Kisses me.

But then...

His face morphs into nothingness as I'm lying in a hospital bed, tethered to machines that beep in a steady rhythm.

Beep. Beep. Beep.

The sound chases away the image of his face, and I'm left staring at sterile hospital walls. My skin is cold, pale—too pale. I shiver. The thin blanket covering me does nothing to ward off the chill that seems to seep into my very bones.

Someone knocks at the door but I can't answer it, can't muster the strength to do anything but keep my eyes fixed on the muted television screen across the room. The door creaks open, casting a shadow over my bed.

It's him again. Vinnie.

I want to reach out, to call out to him, but just as suddenly as he appeared, he vanishes into thin air.

Across from me, the heart monitor flatlines.

My heart drops.

Another face emerges.

A child's face.

Belinda.

And the flatline.

Always the flatline.

"No," I manage to croak out with what little energy I have left. "No...not yet."

But then another sound blends in with the unwelcome silence—a shrill ringing that slices through the dull hum of the machines like a knife through butter. It's my phone, tucked away in the pocket of my robe hanging off the chair next to my bed.

The ringing doesn't stop. It continues relentlessly, each chime reverberating in my head like a resounding echo in an empty cavern. I summon all my strength to sit up and retrieve the phone, every muscle screaming with effort as I extend an arm and grasp it.

I press, press, press the button. Bring it to my ear.

But the ringing...

It doesn't stop.

Doesn't stop.

It continues, a sharp, jarring contrast to the now silent heart monitor. I try to say something, but no words come out, as if the cold of the room has frozen my vocal cords. My head swims as I fight against a rising tide of nausea and inexplicable fear.

"Hello?" It's more of a croak than a word, barely audible over the relentless chiming.

No response on the other end.

Silence.

Silence so sudden it's jarring.

The ringing stops. For a moment, all I can hear are my own ragged breaths echoing in the sterile silence of the hospital room.

Just as I am about to hang up, I hear it. A whisper on the other end of the line—so soft, so faint that I almost miss it.

"Raven..."

I grip the phone tighter. "Who's there?"

Again, the soft whisper.

"Raven..."

It sounds familiar, somewhere deep within my memory, a voice long forgotten. A female voice, shrouded in the mists of time and pain.

"Who are you?" I demand, trying to find strength in my voice.

The room feels colder, more hostile.

The silence stretches on, leaving me hanging by a thread. My heart pounds like a drum, each beat echoing the ticking clock on the wall above me.

Finally, the voice speaks again. "Remember..."

Then nothing.

Only silence.

I keep the phone pressed against my ear for what feels like forever, straining to catch any other whisper that might come through. But it's useless.

All I hear is the silence and my own labored breathing.

Remember...

The word echoes in my head like a silent scream. Remember what? What does the voice want from me? My mind races through several possibilities, but nothing seems to fit. The past is a muddle of fragmented memories, treatment sessions, and painful goodbyes. Sifting through it feels like walking through a maze with no exit in sight.

My head throbs as if my brain is trying to physically push out the memories lodged deep within me. I wince, pressing my free hand to my forehead as if that may somehow alleviate the pain.

Flashes of faces flicker before my eyes—my parents, my siblings, friends, doctors, Vinnie—but none of them match up with the voice on the phone. I squint at each image, trying to force a connection, a semblance of recognition, but I come up empty each time.

The room darkens around me, shadows creeping over the stark hospital walls as night falls. The cold seeps in deeper.

I'm alone.

Utterly alone.

I open my mouth to call for a nurse...

But my voice. It's gone.

The machines make no more sound.

I look around the sterile room.

Everything is in black and white.

I'm not here.

I'm not here.

I'm not here...

I JOLT UPWARD IN BED, the dream still fresh in my mind.

My heart is pounding like it wants to escape my chest, each beat a thunderous echo in the still darkness of the room. Beads of cold sweat trickle down my forehead and drop onto the sheets. I am alone, and for a moment, I struggle to remember where I am.

Reality slowly sinks into me.

I am not in a hospital. I am home, safe and warm under piles of blankets in my own bed. The rhythmic ticking of the clock on my bedside table lulls me back, bringing with it a sort of comfort.

"The dream..." I murmur to myself as I rub my hand over my fuzzy head.

I shake off the remnants of fear that gripped me so tightly just moments ago.

That voice.

That haunting whisper telling me to remember.

To remember what?

I reach out blindly in the dark for a glass of water sitting on the bedside table. The condensation makes it slippery. I bring it to my lips, the water cool and refreshing as it trickles down my parched throat.

It's not the first time I've had this dream. I had versions of it a lot during my cancer treatment. I always assumed it was a side-effect of the chemo.

The dream is always so vivid.

Too vivid.

The sterile walls of a hospital room, the relentless ringing of a phone, the lack of color at the end...

And Vinnie.

Vinnie's face that disappeared in front of me and sent me hurtling back into that hospital bed.

That's new. Of course, I didn't know him when I had the dream during my treatment.

And that familiar feminine voice... The voice that told me to remember. That's new, too.

I close my eyes tightly to dispel the images, but they refuse to be erased. The ticking of my clock grows louder in my ears, each tick-tock a reminder of the dream's dreadful heart monitor.

I draw in a shaky breath. Echoes of that soft whisper still linger in my mind, circling around like a mournful ghost.

"Remember..."

Frustration wells up inside me. I yearn for clarity, for closure, but all I am left with is an unquenchable thirst for answers.

With a sigh, I settle back against the pillows and stare at the ceiling. The pale moonlight streaming through the window paints eerie shadows on it, turning its smoothness into a canvas of my nightmare. The silhouette of my own face is reflected across the room, and for a moment, I am transported back to that hospital bed and surrounded by sterile walls, deafening silence, and suffocating loneliness.

Remember...

What the hell am I supposed to remember? What could those fragmented and horrific images mean?

"It's just a dream," I say out loud to myself. "Go back to sleep. You're safe here. Jared is in the next room."

It was just a fucking dream.

4

VINNIE

I've lost track of time. How long have we been in the air? Beside me, Elmo snoozes.

And I continue to read.

Nothing particularly interesting. Just that nameless old woman whose eyes pierce me through the old photograph.

I slip the iPad into my bag and lean back in my seat, my mind racing with potential scenarios. My thoughts keep coming back to Raven. Leaving her behind was one of the most difficult things I've ever done. But I can't risk her safety. She deserves so much more than to be dragged into this mess.

A jerk of turbulence rocks the plane, dragging me out of my thoughts. Elmo stirs beside me but doesn't wake up.

The next few hours pass in a blur of discomfort and tension. I plug my headphones in and try to watch a movie. I barely pay attention. I can't seem to get my mind off of that old woman...

As we descend into Bogotá, the lights of the city cast an eerie glow through the night air. The moment we touch down, everything becomes real. The danger I'm stepping into isn't just a series of names and faces on an iPad screen anymore. It's tangible.

I glance at Elmo, who now sits alert. He gives me a small nod.

That's his signal that he's ready.

For what, I still don't know.

We disembark into the humid night, the smell of jet exhaust mingling with the heavy tropical air. A black sedan waits for us at the edge of the runway, its tinted windows hiding the identities of whoever is inside.

Elmo walks toward the car first and greets the driver, who opens the door for him.

"Señor Gallo, welcome," the driver says as I approach.

I simply nod and slide into the back seat. Elmo gets in next to me.

We sit in silence as we ride through the city. About an hour later, we reach our destination right before sunrise.

Jacinto Agudelo's grand mansion looms large. The iron gates stand tall, dark, and imposing against the property, isolating and protecting it. There's an intricately carved crest on the gate—a shield, a calligraphic letter A at its center, divided into quadrants featuring a golden eagle, a blood-red rose, crossed daggers, and a gold coin, respectively. The crest is flanked by coffee and poppy branches and bears the Latin motto *Fortuna et Fatum* beneath a crown of emeralds. Above the crest are subtly-placed cameras.

The gates slide open, and the driveway stretches out, lit up vibrantly in the darkness. It's lined with towering palms and perfectly clipped hedges. The mansion is pale stone with tall arched windows. It looks less like a home and more like a fortress.

As we step out of the car, a man in a tailored suit emerges from the entrance. He is tall and lean with cold eyes and offers no greeting as he leads us through the ornate doors.

The man leads us into a grand hall with sweeping staircases on either side and a giant painting of an angry-looking man dominating the far wall.

A door opens behind us and we turn to see the man in the painting himself flanked by two burly guards. His graying hair is slicked back from his angular face, and he's dressed in a charcoal suit that probably cost more than most people make in a year.

"*Bienvenidos.*" He smiles, but it doesn't quite reach his eyes, which remain as cold as they are in his portrait.

"*Gracias*," I reply.

"Señor Gallo," he says. "I am Jacinto Agudelo."

Yes, Agudelo. From the documents.

"Señor," I say with a nod.

Already, we're getting off to an interesting start.

Agudelo.

The old woman.

Austin Bellamy. Mario. Puzo.

All connected in a web I don't fully understand.

I glance at Elmo for an instant before returning to Agudelo. His smile flickers at the corners of his mouth. My mind churns faster, the cogs slipping into place. He knows something.

"You must be exhausted after your long flight," he says. "Morehouse will show you and your bodyguard to your rooms. We will speak over lunch. Be prepared."

I nod. "I will be."

I'll study the documents the rest of the night if I have to.

"Puzo's dead," I blurt out.

Agudelo nods. "Yes. I've heard. I know why you're here, Vincent. I know what your grandfather wants."

He referred to Mario as my grandfather. Not my father. Probably a good thing.

"What exactly is your understanding of my...grandfather's wishes?"

Agudelo cocks his head. "It would appear he did not make you aware of the reason you were sent here."

"What are *you* aware of, Señor Agudelo?" I ask.

"I believe I said we'll talk over lunch."

With a polite nod, he turns to leave, his guards following. As I watch him go, a shiver runs down my spine. The man exudes power. I must tread carefully.

Morehouse—the man who greeted us at the door—appears from the side door. He guides us through a maze of hallways and stairs to reach our respective rooms.

My room is huge. The ceiling is lined with gold and the furniture is antique and polished. It screams opulence and wealth, way more so than Mario's or Declan McAllister's mansions.

I settle into the plush bed, pulling out my iPad to continue piecing together the puzzle that brought me here. I scroll through the reports on Puzo and Agudelo. The documents reveal a surge of unknown transactions between all parties involved, each structured meticulously to keep their tracks hidden. But nothing remains hidden forever.

The puzzle references meetings, deals, exchanged courtesies, all so vague, yet hinting at a web woven deeper than I originally anticipated. As I delve deeper into the documents, another picture of the old woman pops up—this time in Agudelo's account summary.

What the hell?

I focus back on the documents when a strange shuffling sound scrapes above me. I look up at the ceiling. Again, I hear the noise.

Then a tap. And another. Another still.

I stare at the light fixtures, waiting for them to flicker or something. Surely this mansion isn't haunted. But it *is* old. Probably just the house settling.

More taps. Slower this time.

Shuffling. And more taps.

I stare upward.

When the sound doesn't come again, I turn back to my work.

The hours blend into one another as I dissect each transaction.

I'm pulled out of my research as dawn breaks. A sliver of sunlight streams through the heavy velvet curtains. I stretch my stiff muscles and rub my weary eyes.

The information begins to coalesce into a clearer picture. A conspiracy of deep-rooted corruption. A sinister framework of greed and power.

But that's not why I'm here.

Sure, Mario wants what Puzo was after.

That's the official party line—the reason Agudelo believes I am here. To negotiate an agreement for the territory and money that Mario wants.

I'm well prepared for the task.

But as I continue to read what Mario has given me, I

realize there's a different purpose for my presence—one that Mario, at his advanced age, could not handle himself.

I cock my head at a soft knock on the door. It's Morehouse again, bringing me a tray of breakfast—cornmeal cake, scrambled eggs with tomatoes and green onions, guavas, and black coffee.

"Mr. Agudelo would like you to join him for lunch at one o'clock," he says.

"Yes, I know. *Gracias*."

Morehouse nods and exits.

I turn back to the documents, scanning through until my eyes catch on an encrypted message between Agudelo and an unnamed source, dated two weeks ago. It mentions an "Operation Falcon."

No.

No. It can't be.

Falcon can mean anything. A bird of prey can be a metaphor for an action, a plan, a person. As doctors say, when you hear hoofbeats think horses, not zebras.

But I can't shake the feeling.

Because in my world, Falcon has only one meaning—Raven's brother.

Falcon Bellamy.

5

RAVEN

I manage to get through the rest of the night without more nightmares—but only because I don't sleep.

I finally trudge out of bed at eight a.m., grab a quick shower, and head to the kitchen to make a pot of coffee.

Jared appears five minutes later.

"You're supposed to knock when you rise," he says.

I start the coffeemaker. "I thought I'd let you sleep."

"I'm not here to sleep." He rubs at his forehead. "You know the drill, Raven."

I sigh. "Yeah. I know. I'm going to try to set up a meeting with a new attorney today. I want to get right back to working on my nonprofit."

"Are you sure? After what happened with your last attorney?"

Like he needs to remind me.

"Yes," I say, pouring the steaming coffee into the mugs on the counter. "I can't afford to be passive anymore. Not after all that's happened."

Jared looks at me, his usually stern expression softening.

He reaches out and grabs a mug, sipping the liquid and wincing at its heat.

"You're a fighter, Raven," he says. "But remember, you're also a survivor. You don't always have to be on the offense."

His words are sincere, but they irritate me. How can I *not* fight? Vinnie is gone, and I may never see him again. God knows what he's doing in Colombia for his grandfather. My last attorney was murdered. My brothers have gotten in over their heads, and I'm getting texts warning that I'm in danger.

But damn it, I just beat cancer's ass, and I'm going to get this nonprofit up and running. Beginning with the big gala in a couple weeks.

"I appreciate the sentiment, Jared." I force a smile onto my face. "But I have to focus on something I believe in. If I don't, I'll be focusing on all the shit."

Jared nods, his gaze intense. "Just remember you have people who care about you. People who want to help."

I hear his words—I do—but they don't sink in. It's a familiar talk—the one where everyone subtly tries to convince me to step back, take a breather. But how can I? When there's so much at stake?

Before I can answer, the ring of my cell gives me a welcome interruption. With a sigh, I walk over and pick it up.

"Hello?"

"Raven?"

"Yes, who is this please?"

"My name is Emily Bennett. I'm an attorney with Fox and Levinson in Austin. I got your name from your father. He says you're looking for a nonprofit attorney."

"Yes, hello. My previous attorney..."

"I know what happened," she says. "I'm so sorry about his

premature passing and all that you and your family have been through because of it."

"We're...dealing," I say. "So my father called you?"

"Yes. I've worked closely with my colleagues on some of your father's dealings when a charity is involved. He tells me you're setting up a nonprofit for the benefit of blood cancer research?"

"Yes. All the initial paperwork has been filed, and I've got a gala scheduled next month to introduce the organization and help with funding."

"But otherwise you have funding in place?"

"Yes. I'll be handling the initial funding with my own assets and also with a donation from my sister, Robin."

"And your father?"

"Why would he be involved?"

"I suppose he doesn't have to be. I just assumed..."

I clear my throat. "You assumed because he's the beneficiary of my grandmother's estate, he'd be funding it."

She pauses before responding sheepishly, "I suppose I did, yes."

"I have a hefty trust fund that I've hardly touched. I don't need any grand infusion from my father."

"Good enough. The next step is to iron out the details of the organizational structure, finalize the board members, and draft all required policies and procedures. We also need to prepare for any potential legal issues that may arise in relation to your fundraising activities."

"Okay, what's our first step?"

"The first step is to review all the paperwork you've already filed. If you could email the copies to me by the end of the day, I can get on it immediately. Then we'll set up a meeting early next week to go over everything. Will that be all right?"

"Can we meet today?" I ask, glancing at the clock on the kitchen wall.

"Well...sure. I suppose so." Papers shuffle on the other end. "I have an opening at two this afternoon."

"That works," I say. "Should I come to your office?"

"Yes, that'd be best," she says. "And bring any documents related to the nonprofit."

"Sounds good. Thank you, Emily."

"It's my pleasure, Raven. I look forward to helping you with this noble cause."

I end the call.

"So we're traveling to Austin today?" Jared asks.

"How did you know?"

"I don't know of any major nonprofit law firms around Summer Creek," he says. "But are you sure you want to be out after that text you got?"

"Silly." I shake my head. "That's what *you're* here for, Jared. What good is a bodyguard if all we do is stay home?"

Jared grins, showing off his white teeth. "You got me there, Raven."

After I shower and dress, I gather all the paperwork Emily asked for while Jared makes some phone calls. Around noon, we hit the road in Jared's black SUV. He keeps his eyes on the rearview mirror more than necessary, making sure we aren't being followed.

"Should we be worried?" I ask, trying to sound casual.

"Better safe than sorry," he replies.

Can't argue with that.

We don't talk much during the long drive, and though I

normally don't mind silence, today it reminds me of the nightmare I had last night.

I erase the blurred images from my mind and pull up a novel on my iPad.

As much as I try, though, I can't get into it.

"Tell me about your life, Jared," I say, breaking the silence to get my mind off negativity. "You said you were a Navy SEAL, but you didn't work directly with Leif."

"No, we were in different units. I served for eight years, did a couple of tours in Afghanistan—which is where I met Phoenix—and a few other places I'm not at liberty to discuss."

I study him, wondering what stories those broad shoulders carry, what horrors those dark eyes have seen. He keeps his gaze on the road, but his jaw is clenched. Clearly, he doesn't share his past easily.

"That's impressive," I say.

"Maybe, but it takes its toll," he admits. "Lost a lot of good men out there."

The pain in his voice makes my heart ache. I reach out and lightly touch his arm. "I'm sorry, Jared. I didn't mean to pry."

He shakes his head, giving me a brief smile. "It's all right. It's been a while since I've spoken about it."

We fall into silence again as the distance dwindles between Summer Creek and Austin. Despite the heaviness of our conversation, I feel a strange sense of camaraderie with Jared. His guarded demeanor and repressed sorrow echo my own pain, my own struggles, and the losses of friends I made during chemotherapy. It's a bond born out of hardship that I never thought I'd experience with anyone else, let alone my bodyguard.

Upon reaching Austin, we arrive at Fox and Levinson. It's on the eighteenth floor of a giant skyscraper. We walk in together, I clutching my bag filled with important documents, Jared with his alert gaze sweeping over everything and everyone around us.

The receptionist greets us with a bright smile. "May I help you?"

I give her a small wave. "We're here to see Emily Bennett. I'm Raven Bellamy, and this is Jared. He's my...associate."

Minutes later, we are ushered into a spacious office over-looking the city. Emily Bennett is waiting for us, looking every bit as professional as I expected.

She stands a few feet from the floor-to-ceiling window. Her light blond hair is pulled back in a sleek bun, and she wears a white satiny blouse and sleek black pants.

She extends a hand to me. "Raven, it's great to meet you."

"You too," I reply.

"And this is?" Emily asks as she turns toward Jared.

"My bodyguard, Jared."

She nods and offers him a polite smile as they shake hands. She doesn't seem the least bit freaked out that I travel with muscle. Interesting.

"Please sit." Emily gestures toward the plush leather chairs across her desk.

Jared and I take a seat.

"So," Emily begins, "let's talk about your nonprofit."

I clear my throat. "As you know, it will be dedicated to the research and treatment of blood cancers, with the objective of clinical trials and helping individuals who can't afford treatment."

"Excellent." She nods. "I recommend a rigorous vetting process for prospective board members to ensure they share the same vision and dedication to the cause that you do."

"Absolutely," I agree.

"We need to delineate clear roles and responsibilities for everyone to minimize internal conflicts down the line." She pauses a moment. "We'll also need to determine our fundraising strategy. You said you have a gala planned, yes?"

"Yes," I say. "It's just an introductory event, really. We're hoping to get some initial pledges and establish connections with potential donors."

"Good start." She nods. "But one won't be enough. We need to think about long-term funding opportunities—corporate sponsorships, grants, recurring donations."

"Understood." I jot all this down in my iPad.

"And what about your mission statement? That's key to attracting both volunteers and donors."

I nod again. I already crafted a mission statement, but Emily's point made me reconsider. I had focused on the "what," but maybe it was just as important to clearly state the "why" and "how."

"Okay," I say. "I'll revise it."

"Great." Emily clears her throat. "And now, I have some excellent news for you."

"Oh?" I lift the beginnings of my new eyebrows.

She smiles. "I received word a few minutes before you arrived that there's a large cash donation waiting for you." She pushes a piece of folded paper in front of me.

I wrinkle my forehead as I take the paper.

Then I gasp.

6

VINNIE

My conversation with Austin Bellamy haunts me. He's a smart man, and he kept his answers to my questions succinct and sometimes evasive. I can't blame him for that. I'd do the same thing. Hell, I *do* the same thing.

My stomach is churning with nerves. I could be barking up the wrong tree, of course. "Operation Falcon" could mean anything.

But there's a reason I'm here. A reason Mario wants me here. Giacomo Puzo wasn't a family head. Mario could have sent one of his surrogates here to negotiate with Agudelo.

The clock strikes eleven. Two hours until the lunch with Agudelo. Two more hours to prepare, to analyze, to plan.

Agudelo is clearly a man who likes to keep his cards close to his chest.

As one o'clock draws nearer, I take a moment to freshen up, wash away the grime of sleepless research, exhaustion, and worry. Today will be a game of chess, and I need to be at my best. I dress in a crisp black suit and then make my way down the grand staircase into the hall where Morehouse is waiting for me. Exactly at one, he escorts me into a large dining room filled with light filtering in from the arched windows. The table is set with gleaming china and silverware.

Morehouse lifts his eyebrows as he shows me to my seat. Odd. What does he know? He's no doubt very faithful to his employer. I'll get nothing from him.

Agudelo enters the room, his presence immediately shifting the atmosphere. His smile doesn't seem to reach his eyes as he greets me.

As waitstaff fill our glasses with champagne and serve a delicate pâté, Agudelo begins to talk about the artwork in the room, but my thoughts wander back to the old woman. To Operation Falcon. If Agudelo is involved with the Bellamys, I need to tread lightly around him.

Agudelo is gesturing to a painting of two large-bodied people, a man and a woman, dressed in Edwardian fashion, with an equally heavyset cat in between them. "This of course is an authentic Botero, commissioned directly from the artist. I get calls at least once a week from museums all over the world begging me to donate it to them. But I wouldn't very well be able to enjoy it during dinner if I did that, would I?" He clears his throat, shifting his gaze to me. "But enough about my collection. How about we get down to business? Your grandfather has been very eager for our meeting."

I nod, careful to keep my expression neutral. "Yes, he has."

For the next half hour we discuss matters of trade, investments, and politics. Despite our talk, I can't shake the feeling that this isn't just about business. I've done my homework. I can answer every single one of Agudelo's questions with pretty extensive detail. But even as I spit out facts and figures, my mind keeps slipping away to that photo of the old woman. What does she have to do with all of this?

Agudelo's words are calculated, each sentence carefully structured. I'm beginning to understand the magnitude of his power and control in this world.

As we delve deeper into the conversation, I subtly steer it to the face that has been nagging at my mind.

"Señor Agudelo. My grandfather gave me a file full of names and faces, most of whom I'm familiar with. But there's one person I can't place."

Agudelo wrinkles his forehead. "And who is that?"

I grab my iPad, but he holds up a hand.

"Interesting that you would bring him up," Agudelo says. He rings for Morehouse.

Him? The picture is clearly of an old woman.

"Yes, señor?" Morehouse says when he enters.

Agudelo gestures to Morehouse, who bends down. Morehouse whispers something in his ear.

Then, "Yes, señor. Right away." Morehouse exits.

I lift my eyebrows in question.

"Another guest will join us momentarily," Agudelo says.

I take a drink of my wine. "I look forward to meeting another of your colleagues."

Agudelo chuckles. "Colleague?" He leans back in his seat. "Oh no, Señor Gallo. This is not just any colleague."

The tension is almost palpable as I wait for the mystery guest to arrive. My mind races with possibilities.

Morehouse enters, gesturing inside.

And my blood runs cold.

Suddenly, I'm back in Mario's office, in my teen years, being groomed to join the family business. Staring into the same ice-cold eyes I'm seeing now.

I jerk upward, squint to make sure I'm not seeing things.

It's been seventeen years, but I'd recognize him anywhere.

Same dark eyes, same slicked-back hair, though it's mostly gray now.

Same snakelike half smile.

"Señor Gallo," Agudelo says, "It would appear you two are already acquainted."

Again, I stay neutral, desperately trying to hide my shock.

"I... Yes," I manage to sputter out.

Diego Vega, the man I thought was dead and buried underneath the Bellamys' old barn, cracks a small grin.

"If it isn't the little cobra."

7

RAVEN

"Fifty million dollars?"

Next to me, Jared's brown eyes widen as well.

"I figured you'd be pleased," Emily says.

"Pleased? I'm flabbergasted." I rub my eyes just to make sure that I'm not hallucinating. "Where did this money come from?"

Emily smiles. "It came anonymously about an hour before you got here. It's already been wired into our client trust account."

"I can't accept it," I say. "Not if I don't know who it's from."

Jared turns to me. "Raven, I'm just an old military guy, but even I know you don't turn your back on that kind of cash."

My trust fund is worth ten times that. I figured I'd put about a hundred million of my own money into this, and Robbie was good for fifty million. Maybe one of my brothers kicked in to cover the rest.

"You have to tell me," I say.

"I would if I could," Emily says. "But like I said, the donation was anonymous."

"Why would they send it to you? The only person who knows—"

I close my eyes. "Of course. My father. Who else knew that you were meeting with me today?"

"You could ask him, I suppose," Emily says.

"Or you could just tell me."

Her face remains still. She's good. "I said I can't. It came in anonymously. It could've come from anywhere. But you're right. Someone knew to send it to me."

Who else could've known? Vinnie's family probably has that kind of money lying around, but he's in Colombia. And he's pretty much turned his back on me.

My mind races to the text I received on that burner phone.

Who was that Uber driver? And why would he be telling me I'm in danger?

"If it bothers you," Emily says, "you can always decline the donation."

It doesn't sit well with me. I feel like someone's poking me in the back of the neck. But Jared is right. I need to think of the people I can help with this money. The research that can be done on leukemia and other blood cancers.

"That won't be necessary," I say. "I just wish there were someone I could thank for their generosity."

"I understand," Emily says. "But anonymous donors stay anonymous for a reason. They're not looking for glory. They're not looking for gratitude. They simply want to help people."

I nod. "Okay. We should have plenty of money, especially after our gala, to get some grants set up and really start helping people."

"That's another thing we need to talk about," she says. "How do you want to set up distribution of resources? We have to have parameters or everyone in the country will be asking you for money."

"Anyone with a blood cancer who needs money should feel free to ask for it," I say. "Treatment is so expensive, and insurance eventually runs out. Not to mention those people who aren't insured at all."

"I understand how much you want to help everyone, Raven," she says. "But even resources as great as yours are going to be limited. Why don't I come up with some guidelines, and we can look them over at our first board meeting? Do you have any idea of who you'd like to ask to serve on your board?"

"Well, I guess I'll be on the board. Along with my sister."

"Anyone else in your family?"

"Normally I would ask my father, but he's so busy with everything else. Maybe my brother Falcon. He's the one who donated his bone marrow to save my life."

"Yes..." She looks down. "But isn't he an ex-convict?"

"He's innocent."

"He may well be. But in the eyes of society, he spent time on the inside and he's an ex-convict. I believe he pleaded guilty."

I stand. "He did, but he...had his reasons."

"I understand." Emily raises a hand, gestures me to sit back down. "And I understand how close you are to him. But I would advise against having him on your board."

I sigh. I hate it, but she's probably right. "All right. Maybe my brother Hawk then."

"Or someone not related to you," she says.

I sink back into the chair. "Who do you suggest?"

"I'd suggest maybe someone in the medical field. An oncologist, or perhaps a researcher."

"I could ask some of my doctors."

"That's certainly a good place to start. They'll be able to point you toward the people who are doing the cutting-edge research in the field."

I nod.

"Then you'll want an attorney, of course."

"Would you like to be on my board?"

She smiles. "I appreciate the request, but you and I don't know each other very well yet. Besides, it could be a conflict of interest. Because I'm representing you in getting the nonprofit together, I probably should not sit on the board."

I nod. I hadn't thought of that. Boy, am I in over my head.

She shifts through some paperwork. "You said your father was busy. You don't think he'd have the time?"

"I doubt it."

"I understand, but he's the Cooper Steel heir, and an excellent rancher in his own right here in the great state of Texas. He would be a perfect addition to your board."

"All right. I'll ask him then."

My father will never deny me anything, which is the reason I didn't want to ask. He'll do it even if he doesn't have the time.

"So, the gala," Emily says. "Tell me what you envision for it."

"I'm not sure entirely," I admit, tugging at the hem of my blouse. "I was hoping you might have a few ideas. I've got the venue locked in, but that's about it, and we're running short on time. I want it to be grand. Not just another dull charity ball where people stand around in their designer clothes and talk about how much they've donated."

Emily leans back in her chair. "Grand can be achieved," she assures me. "How do you feel about live entertainment? Perhaps a notable artist or band?"

I nod. "That sounds fantastic. Do you think we could manage that on such short notice?"

"There's no harm in trying," Emily replies. "We might even reel in some extra donations if we auction off a private performance or a meet and greet. I'll put out some feelers right away."

"Thank you."

"Think about your guest list," she instructs me as we prepare to part ways. "The right mix of people can help create the environment you're looking for at the gala. And it helps if they're well-connected."

"I've already sent out 'save the date' invitations," I tell her, "since it's coming up so quickly. The responses have been great. Of course, having my father's name attached doesn't hurt."

"That's a good move," she says. "Leveraging your family name will not only attract potential donors but reputable professionals as well. But try to think beyond the immediate, Raven. The gala is a launchpad for your foundation, and you want it to make waves."

"But why? Isn't the aim just to raise funds?"

She shakes her head. "Raising funds is certainly one of the goals. But more importantly, we need to raise awareness. People won't donate if they don't know about the cause or respect it. Your gala should show them that you're serious about making a difference."

A stab of apprehension hits my gut. "I hadn't really thought about it like that. I'm not sure how to get people to take me seriously."

"They will," she says. "You've got passion, and that's more than half the battle won. Now we just need to channel that passion into something tangible and compelling. Your story, your survival, and your dedication to helping others is already inspiring. Now it's about spreading that inspiration wider."

I nod, even as a nagging worry tugs at the back of my mind. I hope she's right, but the fear of failure is hard to shake off. It's one thing to dream big. It's another to bring those dreams to life.

"Remember," Emily says. "You're not alone in this. We're going to build a solid team around you, and I'll be there every step of the way."

"Thank you, Emily," I say. "This has been amazing. Is there anything else we need to take care of this afternoon?'"

"I think we're in good shape," she says. "Think about board members. We don't need to fill all the chairs in time for the gala. In fact, the gala itself will be a good place to gauge interest from people who may want to serve. But we need a skeleton board to get started. You, your sister and your father will be a good start, along with someone in the medical field."

"Got it." I rise. "Thanks so much."

"Of course, Raven." She rises as well, extending her hand to me. "It's a pleasure assisting you with such a noble cause."

I shake her hand, and then she escorts Jared and me through the office to the exit.

Once we step out into the humid Texas afternoon, my phone buzzes in my pocket.

My breath catches as I read it.

Even the raven can't fly forever. Sooner or later, it comes home to die.

8

VINNIE

I could take offense at the nickname. I could stand and meet his gaze, secure in my strength this time.

I could do any number of things.

But I don't.

I only stare.

Because if this is Diego Vega, then who the hell is buried underneath the Bellamys' old barn?

"Surprised to see me, Little Cobra?"

God, he still sounds like a snake. And he calls *me* a cobra?

I keep my expression impassive despite my racing heart. "Why would I be surprised?"

He smirks. "Let's just say that rumors of my death have been...greatly exaggerated."

"Your death?"

He smirks. "You know. A body was never recovered."

"You'll have to excuse me, Mr. Vega. But I've been out of the country—my own country—for over a decade. I only just returned. It was my impression that you no longer had any dealings with my grandfather."

"I don't." His eyes shine with contempt. "But you're here on your grandfather's business. And I have close ties to Mr. Agudelo here in Colombia."

"I see."

"I understand you're interested in the business of one of my colleagues, Giacomo Puzo."

Puzo was involved with Vega. Perfect. "That is why I'm here."

Agudelo nods. "Yes. We'll be talking about that later, but for now, why don't we just enjoy some dessert?"

Dessert turns out to be caramelized flan, but I can't taste it. I force it down into my stomach, which feels like it's cramping around every bite.

I stay expressionless.

But inside, my mind is racing. Not only about who the hell is buried under that barn. Who took Eagle Bellamy's bullet. But also about Raven's father, Austin Bellamy.

What is the connection?

I make it through the meal, hyperaware of Vega's eyes on me at all times.

I remember his words, long ago, at that meeting a few months before my eighteenth birthday.

Remember. Pride comes before a fall.

I thought nothing of it at the time. I was seventeen, and I thought I had the world by the balls. I hadn't yet seen what Mario was capable of doing to me. I was young and arrogant.

Full of pride.

Was Vega warning me about something? About what Mario would eventually do to me when I turned eighteen?

The conversation between Agudelo and Vega buzzes around me like flies I want to swat.

Until—

"How *is* Mario?" Vega asks me.

I swallow down a bite of flan. "His health is good. Thank you for asking."

"He's got to be in his eighties by now."

"He is." I nod.

"He must be part feline," Vega says. "That one has nine lives."

"The same could be said for you," I reply.

My words earn me another sly reptilian smile.

Once the dessert plates are clear, Agudelo rises. "That ends our lunch, gentlemen. As I have meetings tonight, I won't see any of you for dinner, but I'd like to continue this conversation tomorrow. Lunch again, I think."

"Of course."

I rise and leave the dining room, where Elmo waits outside.

"Will you be returning to your room, sir?" Morehouse asks.

I look at Elmo, who cocks his head at me. "No. My bodyguard and I would like to see some sites."

"Of course," Morehouse says. "I'll instruct the driver to take you around."

"That's kind of you," I say, "but we've already arranged for our own car and driver."

Morehouse raises his eyebrows slightly. "Oh?"

"Yes, I had Elmo arrange it. But thank you very much for the offer. Your generosity is noted."

I head back to my room and change out of my suit into jeans and a button-down. Then I knock on Elmo's door, which is adjoining to mine.

"Yes, sir?" he says, opening it.

"Let's go," I say.

Once Elmo and I are outside Agudelo's mansion, we wait.

"You sure you got a driver who isn't compromised?" I ask Elmo.

"Yes, he comes highly recommended."

I bite my lip. "Let's hope. We need to drive into the heart of the Chapinero district."

"The driver knows who we need to see."

I have no reason not to trust Elmo. He's had my back since I returned. I don't for a moment trust Mario.

"You can trust your grandfather," Elmo says as if reading my mind. "I've been with him for over ten years, and I'm the best on his staff of security. He wants you safe, Mr. Gallo. He told me as much."

I take a slow breath in. "Yes, well, I am his heir."

And his son, though Elmo doesn't know that. I don't think anyone knows that other than Mario and me. And my dead mother.

Our driver arrives in a long black Mercedes. He gets out of the car, and he and Elmo speak in Spanish.

If only I knew Spanish. I picked up a bit during my time in Europe, but not enough. I spent most of my time in Italy and in Eastern Europe.

Except for when I was in Tibet.

My Italian is pretty good, and that's close enough to Spanish for me to roughly translate what I see and hear, but I won't be able to speak clearly to anyone unless I have a translator present. Elmo's Spanish sounds pretty good, but I of course have no way of knowing.

The chauffeur opens the car door, and I slide into the back seat. Elmo gets in next to me.

"He's taking us where we need to go," Elmo says.

The streets of Bogotá blur past. The low hum of the engine feels like it's vibrating through my bones, a constant reminder that we're out of place here.

Once we're miles away from Agudelo's mansion, the road becomes uneven, cracked, and riddled with potholes that force the driver to swerve more than I'd like. Every turn feels like a gamble. Kids in tattered clothes dart between alleyways.

The buildings loom closer now, like they're closing in on me. Graffiti covers almost every surface—some of it crude, some of it warnings, and some just words I can't understand. A skinny dog limps across the street, ribs poking through its mangy fur. It pauses in the middle of the road, eyes wild and distant, as if it doesn't even care whether it lives or dies. My heart aches for it.

Elmo sits next to me, silent but alert. He doesn't say anything, but his eyes never stop scanning. He's got that look on his face—like we're driving straight into the devil's den. He's probably right. This is Agudelo's territory. Every crack in the pavement, every windowless building is a reminder of the people who disappear in places like this.

We hit another corner, and I see them—two men standing on a street corner, smoking. They look up as we pass, their eyes cold and calculating. One of them flicks his cigarette to the ground, and I catch the glint of metal tucked under his jacket. I don't need to look twice to know what it is.

The tension in the air thickens. We're getting closer to the meet, but it feels like the whole neighborhood is watching, waiting. I feel it in the pit of my stomach. The further in we go, the fewer options we have. There's no way out if this goes sideways.

I take a deep breath. We just have to make it through. Just a little farther.

The deeper we go into Agudelo's territory, the more the cityscape changes. The buildings grow taller and more foreboding, and the air grows dense with the stench of decayed trash and distant fires.

We drive past a group of children playing with a deflated soccer ball in a makeshift patch of dirt. Despite everything, despite their circumstances, they find joy. A sobering thought that hangs heavy in my mind.

A few minutes later, on the far south side of Chapinero, our driver comes to a sudden stop before a dilapidated warehouse that looks like it could crumble at any moment. The massive structure looms above us, casting shadows onto the cracked pavement.

Elmo exits the car and I follow suit, the door closing behind us with a hollow thud. The air is different here—thick and stale yet crackling with an unseen energy.

Our driver remains inside the vehicle, eyes straight ahead, his grip on the wheel unyielding. Around us, the distant laughter of children playing, dogs barking, and urban music fades into the background.

Elmo leads me towards the entrance of the warehouse. As we approach, two men step out, both tall and lean with hard eyes.

"Who are they?" I ask Elmo.

"I don't know. Don't ask. And don't tell them who we are. The driver says they have information."

"All right." I swallow, steeling myself. "Information about what?"

"I don't know. Your grandfather insisted on this meeting."

"And he didn't bother telling me about it?" I shake my head. "I'm supposed to be his right-hand man."

But of course, he doesn't fully trust me.

A smart man, my grandfather. Except he's not my grandfather, as I now know. He's my father. Biologically, at least. A degenerate who raped his own daughter.

I am the unfortunate result.

Elmo talks to the two men in Spanish for a moment. I recognize a few words.

"*Seguridad*," "*peligro*," and "Vega."

Security, danger, Vega.

And then...Bellamy.

With a Colombian accent, but it couldn't mean anything else.

Bellamy. As in Austin Bellamy. As in Bellamy Ranch.

With wide eyes, I turn my head to look at Elmo. He cuts his conversation short and turns to me. "They know of Bellamy."

"How?" I ask, the question barely above a whisper.

Elmo shrugs slightly. "News travels."

I shake my head. "Not like this. Not information like this."

Someone has been talking, someone who knows more than they should. And in this game, having unnecessary knowledge is dangerous.

Elmo looks at me, his dark eyes solemn. "Let's find out what they know."

"No names," I tell him as he walks back toward the men. "Not until we figure out how deep this goes."

He nods and begins speaking with them again, this time asking what they know about Bellamy.

The two men exchange a look and then answer in Spanish.

The wait is agonizing, but finally Elmo turns to me.

"Vega is building a new network. That's what Puzo was working on. Vega had a falling out with your grandfather years ago and was demoted within his organization. He disappeared, and now he's quietly rebuilding his network, which includes..."

"What? For God's sake, what, Elmo?"

"It includes a new smuggling route. Right through the Bellamy ranch."

9

RAVEN

"What is it?" Jared asks.

I gulp and show him my phone.

He wrinkles his forehead. "This is your actual phone. Not the burner."

I nod, swallowing—or attempting to swallow—the lump in my throat.

He strokes his chin. "So the text saying you were in danger came in on the burner. But this one..."

"Came to *my* phone." My heart is racing as I say the words. "From someone who knows my number."

"A cell phone number is easy enough to get," he says. "Which means..."

"Whoever is communicating with me on the burner is... not an enemy?"

He frowns. "I'm not ready to say that, but it appears they're trying to warn you."

"Warn me?" I echo, my mind whirling. "About what exactly?"

"I don't know. About Gallo, maybe."

"Vinnie?" I shake my head. "He's gone. He dumped me. He was very clear. He's probably somewhere in South America by now."

Jared takes a deep breath.

I wait for him to speak.

He doesn't.

"This isn't fair," I gulp. "Do they know what they're doing to me? I just survived cancer. I'm in the middle of doing some work of my heart to help others." I feel emotion coming up my throat, but I do my best to swallow it down. My voice cracks a little as I continue. "Do they have any idea what a death threat will do to a person who's already faced death once? I'm frightened, Jared."

"I know. I know." He lays his hands gently on my shoulders. "No harm will come to you as long as I'm here. I was hired to protect you."

My heart hammers and a shiver runs down my spine. "Should we report this? To the police or someone?"

Jared looks at me gravely and shakes his head. "Not yet. We don't know who we're dealing with or what their game is. If we go to the police now, we could scare them off."

I stare at the words on my phone's screen. "But we can't just ignore this."

"No," he agrees. "We definitely can't ignore it. I'll see if the number can be traced, but it probably can't be. My guess is it's coming from a burner phone."

I groan. "Of course it is."

"In the meantime, let's get you home. Your place is secure."

"Are you sure?"

He nods. "You've got the best system in place, but when

we get back, I'll call your brother and Phoenix. See if they want you to go somewhere else for the time being."

I bite my lip. "Where else would I go?"

"There is a place. We'll see if they think you should go there."

A place? What is he talking about?

I close my eyes and rub at my forehead. "I can't just disappear, Jared. I'm starting a nonprofit. I've got a gala to go to in a couple of weeks. I just can't..." I clench my hands into fists. "Damn it! Damn all of them! How dare they? I won't let this happen to me. I need to live my life. I can't let them force me into hiding."

"I understand. I really do. We don't know yet who we're dealing with. It could be related to Gallo and his family."

"Why would it be? He and I aren't together." I choke back a sob.

Jared opens the car door for me and I slip inside. He moves into the driver seat and starts the engine. It's a long drive home to Summer Creek.

I was so excited about the meeting with Emily. About getting a board together, about the new anonymous donation, about the gala.

Then one stupid text.

And my mood is shifted.

This kind of mood I never wanted to be in again.

So damn it, I won't be.

I have to face it all.

Jared gets on the phone quickly as he drives. He's talking to Leif. And after a while, it sounds like they've got Falcon on the line as well. All I hear is Jared's yeses and nos. I could tell him to put it on speaker, but frankly I don't want to deal with that.

I'll let them make the decisions. They know more about security than I do.

But they're not going to hole me up in some hideaway. They can't. I won't allow it.

The conversation seems to drone on forever. Again I try to read the book on my iPad. It doesn't work.

It's near seven p.m. by the time we get back to my house. Jared is probably starving. Normally I would be too.

"Don't you want to eat?" Jared asks once we're back in the house.

"I'm not hungry."

He narrows his eyes. "You have to eat, Raven. You're still—"

"Recovering." I cross my arms. "Yes, don't I know it. I kicked cancer's ass, and now someone wants to kick mine in return. What the hell do they think they're doing?"

Even the raven can't fly forever. Sooner or later, it comes home to die.

Then I gasp.

I'm *home*.

This is my home.

Maybe I *should* leave.

But no. I clench my fists again. They are not going to kick me out of my home. I don't even know who "they" are.

"So are you going to tell me?" I ask Jared.

"About what?"

"Your talk with Leif. And my brother. It sounded like you got him on the line."

"Yes, we did. Falcon wants you at the safe house."

"A safe house?" I put my hands on my hips. "I'm not going."

"Raven..."

"Look, I have a state-of-the-art system here, as you know. I have *you* here. I also have a trust fund, so if you want, hire five of your biggest, toughest friends. All armed. You can stay in my fucking living room." I plunk myself down on the living room couch. "But I will not leave my home. I won't stop working on the nonprofit."

"You can still work on the nonprofit from the safe house."

"Not hands-on. I can't meet with people, and I can't—"

"Listen," he says, interrupting me. "My job is to keep you safe. And until we know who sent this text and what exactly it means, you'll be the safest locked away in a location that no one knows about."

I cock my head. "What are you even talking about?"

"I'll let your brother explain."

"Fine. I'll give him a call."

"You don't have to. He should be here any minute now."

I sigh.

Just then, the doorbell rings.

I start to walk toward it but Jared gestures me to stop. "You don't answer the door anymore, Raven."

I look back at him, raising an eyebrow. "It's my brother."

"Yes, it is." He quickly walks ahead of me, holding a hand to keep me in place. "But you need to get used to not answering the door. I'm here, and I'll answer it."

He walks to the door, opens it, and my brother walks in.

Falcon's dark hair is mussed as usual, and he's wearing jeans and a T-shirt.

I run into his arms. "Falcon, what's going on?"

He strokes my peach-fuzz head. "We're trying to figure it out, Ray."

I look up at him, wiping a tear from my cheek. "It can't have anything to do with Vinnie. He's gone."

"He is, but it's no secret how he feels about you or how you feel about him."

"So you think someone's using me."

"That's my best guess. Someone is using you to get to him."

I break from my brother's embrace and walk a few steps away from him. "But he's out of the country. They can't lure me somewhere and then expect him to come rescue me. He's not here."

"They may not know that, Ray."

"Oh for the love of God, Falcon." I turn around and face my brother. "These are mobsters. They know everything."

Falcon doesn't respond.

No doubt because he knows I'm right.

"Listen," he says. "When I went to prison, I had Hawk build a safe house. Savannah and I stayed there for a while after I rescued her from Miles McAllister. Vinnie's been there too."

"He has?"

"Yes. We brought him there when he first came back into this country." He grabs my hand, squeezes it. "I know you love him, Raven. And I know he loves you too. I believe he's a good man, but he had to make a choice. I believe his choice was a good one. If he's going to bring down his family, his hands are going to get very dirty. Neither he nor I want you anywhere near that."

"Yes, I know. You both think you can make my decisions

for me." I roll my eyes. "Poor little Raven with her bald head. Poor little Raven who needed her big brother's bone marrow. Poor little Raven who can't take care of herself."

"Christ, Raven," Falcon says. "You know that isn't what we think."

I poke him in the chest. "I'm not so sure about that anymore."

He closes his eyes and takes a deep breath. "Let me see the text."

"No."

He opens his eyes and glares at me. "Let me see it, Ray."

"Jared already told you what it says."

"I know that. And he already gave me the number, and we're working on tracing it. But I need to see it. I need to see the words."

"Why?"

He clenches his hands into fists. "Because I'm already mad as a rabid dog, and I need to use my anger. Seeing that text might just give me the extra anger I need to see this motherfucker taken down."

I walk up to him, run my hands up and down his arms. "Falcon, you're happy now. You're out of prison, and you're with the woman you love. You're going to be married. Don't you want to live your life? Just live your life?"

"Of course I do."

"So do I. Can't we just—"

"No, we can't," he says. "You're my sister and I love you. I will protect you no matter what."

I sigh, take my phone out of my purse, pull up the text, and hand it to Falcon.

His neck and cheeks turn red as he reads it.

Yes, there's the anger. This is the Falcon who got through prison. The one who ruled his cell block.

He did what he had to do. He got more years tacked onto his sentence because he attacked a man with a shiv. He did it to save his own life, of course. But the shiv was contraband. He shouldn't have had it in the first place.

He hands my phone back. "You can continue to use this phone, but not to talk about any of this. Use the burner for that."

"I don't even know who gave me the burner."

He frowns. "That's true. We'll get you another one."

"How many phones am I supposed to keep track of?"

He lets out a deep breath. "As many as it takes, Ray."

I sigh, shove my phone back in my purse. "I suppose Jared already told you about *this* text." I hand him the burner.

"He did."

"So who is texting this burner, anyway? That guy who hijacked my Uber?"

"We're still looking into that," Falcon says. "But whoever is doing that doesn't seem to mean you any harm."

"They told me I was in danger, and then a couple hours later I got that horrible text."

"Yeah." Falcon rakes his fingers through his hair. "Leif, Jared, and I are going to figure this out, Raven."

"I can help."

"No. You stay safe. I'm going to get you to the safe house."

I stomp my foot on the ground. "Damn it, Falcon. How can I get this nonprofit off the ground if I'm not around?"

"Savannah's going to help. And Robin. I've already talked to both of them."

I blink. "You dragged your fiancée and our sister into this?"

"They're not the ones in danger. You are, Raven. And they don't want any harm to come to you any more than I do."

I let out an exasperated huff. "So that's it then. I can't stay in my own home, which, by the way, has the best security system in the world."

"No, Raven. You can't."

"What if I refuse to go?"

"Then I'll pick you up, toss you over my shoulder, and take you there myself."

"Oh, yeah, Falcon Bellamy." I cross my arms. "Big man. Likes to push women around."

I regret the words as soon as I say them. My brother's not like that. He's never been like that. But he does take his big-brother responsibilities a little far sometimes. Not so much with Robin and me, but definitely with Hawk and Eagle.

"Fine," I relent. "But I just met with an awesome attorney. She really understands my vision."

"Savannah and Robin understand your vision. They'll take care of all of this, get the gala ready."

"You are *not* keeping me from the gala," I say.

"I don't want to," he says.

"You're not *going* to." I grab Falcon's hands. "I will go to your safe house. I will lie low. I will do what I can from there, and let Savannah and Robin do the legwork. But I *will* be at that gala, Falcon. I will be there. And you will be there. Our parents will be there. Robin and the rest of our family will be there. I want everyone there. I don't care how much security we have to have. But I *will be at that gala*."

10

VINNIE

"You're kidding," I say.

Though I already know he's not. Austin Bellamy may be the Cooper Steel heir and a successful rancher, but there's something crooked about him.

Something crooked about how his oldest son went to prison for a crime he didn't commit.

And something very crooked about whoever is buried on his property.

Plus, I already know he had Brick Latham killed because he thought he was a threat to Raven.

But it makes me wonder...

Was Latham *truly* a threat to Raven? Or was he a threat to Bellamy himself?

"Does he know anything else?" I ask.

"No," Elmo says. "I've got all the information we need to take back to Agudelo."

I raise an eyebrow. "But we won't be taking *all* of it back to Agudelo, right?"

"Right."

Elmo speaks again to the informants in Spanish. Then we all shake hands. The informants slink away.

"Now what?" I ask.

"We get the hell out of here," Elmo says.

Sounds good to me. This place makes my skin crawl. I'm on high alert the entire time, hyper aware of anything and everything that is a threat. I don't trust these men as far as I can throw them. Especially since I can't understand what they're saying. I suppose I should take some Spanish lessons.

But who the hell has time for that? I took Spanish back in high school, and of course spent some time traveling through Spain when I was in the EU, but not enough apparently. Most of my time in Spain was spent in Barcelona, and they speak Catalan there. Similar to Spanish, but just different enough for my ears to have a hard time understanding.

My knowledge of Italian has helped a little. I can pick out words and phrases from what they're saying. But damn, they speak so quickly.

I hurry out of the warehouse to the car that's waiting.

"I wish we weren't staying at the Agudelo house," I say.

"Yeah, I agree. We can't speak freely there."

I press my lips together. "On the other hand, keep your friends close and your enemies closer. He needs to think I'm a friend. I need to make this deal happen so my grandfather will trust me enough to take over."

I say no more.

Though I do believe our driver is trustworthy, and I doubt he can hear us, I don't know for sure. For all I know, he could be an enemy. He could have surveillance equipment in the backseat.

Mario could be having us watched at this moment.

So could Agudelo.

It's doubtful, as we put a lot of our own surveillance in place, but I still can't be a hundred percent sure that we haven't been followed.

I can't be a hundred percent sure of anything at this point.

Damn. Bellamy.

What the hell is his role in all of this?

That Texas rancher who wears jeans and cowboy boots and bolo ties. Blond and blue-eyed, with his all-American good looks. Married to a Mexican beauty queen, Starling Esparza.

Father to five beautiful children... One of whom is an ex-con.

Fuck.

It all must come together in some way.

Mario thought I would be here for a month. After reading through all of the documents, and my meeting with Agudelo —which included Vega as well—I think I can be out of here in two weeks. I can get this deal made. The sooner I get out of here, the sooner I can get back on my home turf where I have the advantage.

Another big lunch tomorrow at the Agudelo home.

I need to find out what I can about Bellamy before then. Though I doubt there's a way to access the dark web from the Agudelo home. Everything probably goes through a huge network that he keeps track of.

My only chance is to get this deal settled as quickly as I can and get back home where I can research Bellamy more thoroughly.

So many pieces to this puzzle. Not one of them seems to fit together.

Mario Bianchi.

Diego Vega.

Giacomo Puzo.

Jacinto Agudelo.

Brick Latham.

The old woman in the photo.

And Austin Bellamy.

And whoever the hell is buried under the Bellamy barn.

Then my jaw drops.

The EPA. My contact there. How when I called her, she was already working on keeping the Bellamys from excavating that particular parcel of property.

Oh my God.

Bellamy never had any intention of excavating that property. Because he knows. He *knows* what's under there.

What if *he* is the one who started the process at the EPA?

But if that's the case... Why would he tell his boys that he was getting ready to excavate that area of his land?

If he knows what's there, he knows that would freak them out.

Is that what he wants? His sons in a state of panic?

His sons having no choice but to come to me for help?

None of this makes any sense at all.

I'd like to talk to Elmo, but he's my bodyguard and my translator. He's not my friend. Not even my colleague.

But he knows everything that I know for this trip at least. He has to, in order to interpret.

When we return to the Agudelo mansion, our driver hands us each a pamphlet on points of interest in Bogotá.

"For when Agudelo asks you what we did on our sightseeing tour," Elmo says.

I nod. "Of course."

When we get into the mansion, Morehouse greets us. "Mr. Agudelo had to make a quick overnight trip," he says, "but he'll be back for your lunch meeting tomorrow."

An overnight trip? Where? And why?

I know better than to pose these questions to Morehouse. He won't betray his employer.

"Good enough," I say.

"Dinner will be served for you at eight p.m.," Morehouse says. "In the dining room."

I nod. "That will be fine. Thank you."

"We will have another dinner guest as well," he says. "Señor Agudelo's daughter, Daniela."

"All right."

Daniela. Right, Agudelo has a daughter. I learned that when I researched him in preparation for this trip. She's eleven. The same age as Belinda McAllister.

Fuck. Belinda.

She reached out to Raven and to me. Her nanny is trying to help her, but she has limited resources. And she probably needs her job.

The thought of what Declan McAllister is doing to his daughter...

I can't go there.

I will rescue Belinda, somehow. At least I know her life isn't in danger. McAllister may hurt her, but he would never take her life. She's a pawn. Chattel. And she's already been promised to me.

I hate the fact that she has to live for another couple of weeks in those horrid circumstances, but I can't help her right now. I have to finish this current project.

I check my watch. It's four thirty. A little over three hours until dinner is served and I meet Agudelo's young daughter.

I sigh and walk up to my suite.

The room has been fully serviced.

All new towels, and a box of chocolates on my pillow.

I didn't sleep last night, and I'm exhausted.

Without changing my clothes, I lie down.

And blackness falls.

11

RAVEN

I have to hand it to my brother.

This safe house is invisible. Hidden in plain sight.

It's on a property adjacent to a ranch, made to look like an abandoned dwelling for ranch hands. Seven other houses encompass the small neighborhood, all abandoned. It's slightly set apart from the other residences, but not so much so that anyone would take notice.

"Access is completely restricted and protected by multiple layers of security," Falcon says, showing me the front door. "This entrance is reinforced, the locks are electronic, and"—he points to a subtly-placed camera overhead—"video surveillance shows every point of entry to the home. Entry requires a thumbprint."

"So can you add my thumbprint so I can—"

Falcon holds up a hand. "No, Ray. You need to stay here. We'll add Jared's thumbprint."

He's got to be kidding.

But I'm too tired to argue about it.

When we arrive, instead of a foyer, there's a security room

where someone can monitor every surveillance camera and control access to the house.

"Jared will be able to communicate with anyone outside the house through satellite technology. The room is equipped with a secure landline and encrypted communication," Falcon says.

Impressive. I'll be totally imprisoned.

We leave the security room and we enter a comfortable-looking living area.

"Hawk and I wanted this place to feel like as much of a home as possible. There's a living room, dining room and kitchen. The living room is furnished with leather recliners and a leather sectional." He gestures to a huge flatscreen TV. "If you're bored, there's this. And a bookshelf."

"Great," I say. "I can catch up on all my soaps while under lock and key."

Falcon doesn't react to my sarcasm, and leads me into the kitchen. "I took the liberty of stocking the fridge for you. Bread, fruits, vegetables, lots of meat. Use those up first. If you end up staying here longer, there's plenty of nonperishable cans in the pantry."

"Falcon, you *said* I would only be here until the gala."

"Right," Falcon says. "Just in case, though."

"There is no *just in case*."

Falcon closes his eyes and takes a deep breath before continuing. He points to a door off the side of the kitchen. "That leads you to the garage. It's built for two cars." He opens the door to the garage and points to the rear. "It's hard to see from here, but there's actually a tunnel that connects to the main part of garage. If you follow it down, there are two electric vehicles and one gasoline-powered car stored underground, in the event you have to make a quick getaway."

"Let me guess, Jared will have the keys?"

"Yes, Raven, he will. That's his job." Falcon rubs at his forehead. "I've added a stockpile of gasoline underground."

Falcon continues showing me around. The house has three bedrooms. He demonstrates how to properly shut the blackout curtains in each room.

"Don't allow any light in, Ray," he says.

"Guess I'll have to get a spray tan before the gala."

"For Christ's sake, I know you don't want to be here, but would you take this seriously?" Falcon sighs. "Each bedroom is equipped with a wall safe as well, for storing important documents or sensitive materials. I'll leave a couple grand in cash in each one."

He then shows me a large closet that houses medical supplies, and the security room, which has access to telemedicine. Attached to each room is its own en suite own bathroom facility with a shower, toilet, and basic toiletries.

And of course, the most important thing—

"The house possesses a massive backup generator in case of interrupted powers or power outage," Falcon says. "We're in Texas, after all, and keeping the house cool is necessary."

"What about candles, matches, everything else?"

"It's all here," Falcon says. "Hawk and I put a lot of thought into this house. You have to remember, Ray. I was in prison. I didn't have a whole hell of a lot to do."

I gesture to a door off the kitchen. "Where does that lead?"

"Basement," he says. "It mostly serves as an underground bunker, but there's also a home gym and a shooting range."

I raise an eyebrow. "Shooting range? Really? Won't that alert people around that someone is here?"

"The house has been fully soundproofed and has extraordinary measures to prevent any kind of eavesdropping."

So no one will be able to hear me if I scream. Lovely.

"Escape routes and safe exits are built in, allowing you to leave discreetly in case of emergency." Falcon hands me a notebook. "They're all outlined in here."

I flip through a few pages of the notebook. The details are extensive, to say the least.

"Is the house staffed with any security personnel?"

Falcon shakes his head. "The fewer people who know we're here, the better."

Already I feel isolated.

Goosebumps pop up and down my arms. "Falcon, I don't think I can do this. After all those years I spent going from one hospital to the next, and then when I was home, isolated in my room. Not able to go out, unable to see the sun."

Falcon wraps his massive arm around my shoulders. "I know, Ray. I'm sorry. But we can't take the chance. Not with these threats you've been getting."

"But why would I be getting threats?" I pace the area. "Vinnie and I aren't together anymore. He left me. He's in Colombia doing some deal."

"Vinnie may have left you," Falcon says, "but that doesn't mean his feelings for you went away. Right now, the Gallo enemies see you as a way to control Vinnie. It's not fair, and I hate it with every cell in my body. But it's the way it is, Raven. I almost lost you once, and I won't do it again."

"Fine." I sit down on the loveseat. "I'll do what you think

is best. But I *will* be out of here in time for my gala. You say Savannah and Robbie will do the footwork. My attorney Emily can help. CJ can help as well."

"Christ, Raven, you told CJ you were here?"

"No." I sneer at him. "I didn't tell anyone. I'll just tell them all that I'm not feeling great, and my doctors told me I need to rest. And that I need some people to help with the footwork."

Falcon nods. "That's smart, Raven."

"It's awful." I cross my arms. "Robbie will freak out about it, I'm sure. She'll be afraid I'm getting sick again. I'll have to tell her some bullshit story about trying to do too much too soon."

"That could easily be true," Falcon says. "You *have* been overexerting yourself, Ray."

I shake my head. "It's not true. And I haven't done anything that I wasn't fully capable of handling. I made a promise to myself when I got well, Falcon. I promised I'd watch the sunrise and the sunset every day. Smell every flower I came across." I look around the windowless room. "How can I do that in here?"

"You can't," he says flatly.

"I know. That's the point."

He sighs. "Raven—"

I throw my hand in his face. "Don't even say it. Don't even say that if I had stayed away from Vinnie Gallo, none of this would be happening."

"I wasn't going to say that. Christ." He sits down on the sofa, running his hands through his hair. "You think I want to keep you from someone you love? None of us wants to do that. The thought of not being able to be with Savannah..."

He closes his eyes, wincing slightly. "It hurts just to think about."

"You said Savannah and Vinnie stayed here."

"They did. I was with Savannah. She had to be hidden from the McAllisters. That's how I ended up violating my parole. I had to go to that hearing."

"Yeah. I know. And I understand why you did it."

"I know you do. I'm so sorry you have to be separated from someone you love."

I sigh. "He left me, Falcon. But I don't for one minute believe that he doesn't love me."

"I don't believe that either," Falcon says. "That's why you're in danger, Ray."

12

VINNIE

Daniela Agudelo is *not* eleven years old. She's a beautiful young woman with gorgeous olive skin, hair that's black as night, and dark chocolate eyes. Her lips are painted ruby red, her lashes long and lush.

Not eleven by a long shot. Probably early twenties. The documents said eleven. How did Mario get the age wrong?

"You must be Mr. Gallo," she says to me in only slightly accented English. "I'm Daniela." She holds out her hand.

I shake it lightly. "It's a pleasure. I was told you were eleven."

She chuckles. "I'm not sure where you got your information. I'm seventeen. Eighteen in a few months." She pouts her lips. "It's very nice to meet you, Mr. Gallo."

"Yes, the feeling is mutual," I say.

She gestures toward the dining room. "I hope you enjoy the meal. Our chef has prepared *ceviche de camarón con mango* for an appetizer."

"Sounds great."

She narrows her gaze. "Would you do me the honor of sitting by me?"

"Of course, Señorita Agudelo." I hold the chair for her as she sits down.

I take my own chair and read the printed list of courses at my seat.

Ceviche de camarón con mango.

Ajiaco Santafereño.

Lomo al Trapo con Chimichurri.

Ensalada.

"*Ensalada* means 'salad,' I know that." I point at the remaining entries on the list of courses. "What are all the rest of these?"

Daniela smiles. "The ajiaco is a traditional Colombian soup with three types of potatoes, shredded chicken, corn, and a touch of guasca leaves. It's garnished with heavy cream and capers, served alongside avocado slices and white rice."

"Sounds very tasty," I say.

Daniela smiles. "It is, Señor."

"And this next thing. With chimichurri?"

She nods. "Lomo al Trapo, the main entrée. It is our chef's specialty. Beef tenderloin cooked directly over hot coals while wrapped in a salt-covered cloth and served with a fresh chimichurri."

"Which is...?"

"A sauce made from cilantro, parsley, garlic, and olive oil. The beef will be accompanied by golden baby potatoes roasted with herbs and coconut rice."

"Which brings us to the salad. What does your chef usually serve with his?"

"I believe tonight's salad will be made with hearts of palm, ripe avocados, and cherry tomatoes in a lime vinaigrette."

"It all sounds wonderful," I say. "You speak as if you have more than just run-of-the-mill culinary knowledge."

Her face brightens. "I've always been interested in the culinary arts." She then casts her gaze to the floor. "Unfortunately, my father doesn't value higher education for women."

I frown. "Yes, that sounds familiar. My grandfather doesn't either. I, however, don't share that philosophy."

Her big eyes widen. "You don't?"

"No, I don't."

She takes my hand delicately. "I understand you're promised to a young lady back in Texas."

"I am."

Just the thought of Belinda being promised to me makes me nauseated. Not because I'm engaged to an eleven-year-old. That marriage will never happen. But because of what she's going through—possibly this very moment—at the hands of her father.

"I am promised as well," she says. "To Señor Vega."

I stop my jaw from dropping. Vega must be in his sixties.

"I guess I just assumed he was already married."

"He was. His first wife passed away eight years ago."

"I'm sorry to hear that."

A staff member brings in the first course. "Wine, señor?" he asks me. "It's Argentinian Malbec."

"Yes, please."

The staff member nods and fills my wine goblet.

I take a drink, letting the fruity wine glide over my tastebuds.

Daniela takes a second glass, clinking it to mine. "So tell me, Señor Gallo, what are your interests?"

She's asking about my interests? That's odd.

"My only interest here is making a deal work with your father and, apparently, your fiancé."

She narrows her eyes. "I'd like to offer you my services."

I nearly spit out the splash of wine in my mouth. "What do you mean your *services?*"

She bats her eyes. "My father asked me to...take care of you this evening since he's not here to see to your entertainment."

I blink a few times. "I don't require any entertainment."

"What about a night out on the town?"

I bite my lip. "I'm afraid I'm exhausted."

"Then a night in," she says demurely, leaning in.

"I'm afraid I have too much work to do this evening."

"You do understand what I'm offering you," she says, her tone flirtatious.

Yes, I'd be an idiot not to pick up on her innuendo. I find it all disgusting. She is beautiful, but I'm not even slightly interested in someone underage. Hell, I'm not interested in anyone overage either. I'm interested only in one woman—a woman who I can't have.

"I do," I say. "And I'm not interested in an evening with a child."

She widens her eyes. "Do I look like a child to you?"

I can't answer that truthfully because indeed I mistook her for a twenty-something when I first saw her.

"What you look like is irrelevant," I say. "You are a child in my eyes. I'm afraid I must decline."

She wrinkles her forehead. "No one declines, Señor Gallo."

"Then let me be the first, Señorita Agudelo."

"Please, Daniela. Or Dani, if you prefer." She lays her hand over mine. "And it may interest you, Señor Gallo, that here in Colombia the age of consent is fourteen years. It is not a crime to take a woman of my age for the evening."

She *is* beautiful. Just by the way she speaks I can tell how intelligent she is. And that's in what I assume is her second language. Frankly, I don't give a damn whether she's legal or not. A man my age has no business sleeping with a woman under eighteen. Hell, I don't have any business sleeping with a woman under twenty-five.

Daniela should be following her interests, her passions. Studying cooking if that's what she desires. Or something else. She can make a life for herself, I can tell that much just from a short conversation with her.

Damn. She has a lot in common with Belinda.

I hate when my mind goes to her. And what her father's undoubtedly doing to her this evening. I wipe the thought from my head. But still… That child should be preparing for life as a virtuoso pianist. She has a gift. She's a prodigy.

Perhaps Daniela is too. Perhaps she has the capacity to become a master chef.

"Daniela," I begin, "I'm not interested in any *entertainment* this evening."

She twists a strand of hair around her finger. "I know what I look like, Mr. Gallo. I know how beautiful I am. People have been telling me I'm beautiful since I was twelve." She sticks her chest out, nearly knocking me out of my seat. "I was an early bloomer, you see. And don't feel like you have to be some kind of hero. You don't. I've been entertaining my father's colleagues for the last two years."

Two years? She's been doing this since she was fifteen?

Apparently, this particular family doesn't require their females to remain virgins until they're married.

Of course, my own family is a crock on that front anyway. My mother was no virgin when she married my father. She had been raped by her own father and left pregnant with me.

"Don't you have anything to say to that?" Daniela asks.

I put my wine glass down and look deep into her eyes. "To be honest, Daniela, I find that very sad. You should never have to do that. You should never have to give yourself to men as entertainment. Certainly not at your father's orders." I feel another pang of nausea in my gut. "You're seventeen years old. I'm thirty-four. I'm twice as old as you are."

She scoffs. "Thirty-four is young. Most of the men I entertain here are in their forties or fifties."

"Then I feel even worse for you."

She wrinkles her nose. "I'm not asking for your pity, Señor. I'm asking you to let me entertain you this evening."

"Thank you," I say, "but again, I must decline."

She bites on her firm lower lip. The expression in her eyes has turned from flirty to...frightened?

"Is everything all right?" I ask.

"It's just... If I *don't* entertain you, my father will be angry."

I lean in, lower my voice. "Why would he be angry?"

"He'll think you didn't find me attractive enough. That I didn't do my job."

"You're perfectly attractive, Daniela. You and I both know that. But you're way too young. Tell him I'm an old prude or something."

She looks down. "Men don't turn me down, Señor."

"I'm afraid this man *is* turning you down."

"He'll punish me." She grabs my hand, squeezing tight. "Please... Let me come to your room."

"No. I can't do that."

"Please..." She looks around nervously.

"May we not speak freely?" I ask in a whisper.

"I don't know."

The staff comes in to clear the dishes from the first course.

I rise. "If you'll excuse me, Ms. Agudelo, I'm going to go out on the front veranda and have a smoke before dinner."

I don't smoke, of course, but I did bring a few cigarillos. I nod to Elmo, who's in the next room. He rises and follows me out.

"Everything okay, Mr. Gallo?" Elmo asks.

I look around. "May we speak freely here?"

He frowns. "There are cameras here. But if we walk away from the house, they shouldn't be able to capture any sound."

I nod, and we move away as I light my cigarillo. I inhale, letting the smoke float over my tongue.

"She thinks I want to bed her."

Elmo doesn't look overly surprised.

Why would he be? He's been working for Mario for years. He knows the drill.

"I don't understand it," I say. "If Agudelo wants to give me the gift of a woman, why not hire a professional? He's pimping out his own daughter?"

Elmo presses his lips together. "In his defense, she's gorgeous. Probably way better-looking than most professionals."

Seriously? My opinion of Elmo just went down several notches. "I'm sure he could find the most beautiful women in Colombia to be of service," I say. "No, Elmo. There's something else at work here. Something much more sinister."

"You think so?"

I nod, taking another drag on my cigarillo.

"She seems fearful. That if I don't let her entertain me, she'll get in trouble. Be punished."

Elmo chuckles darkly. "She probably didn't even entertain the idea that you might turn her down. I mean, look at her."

"She's not eighteen yet, Elmo. She's a child."

"Oh? I would have put her at twenty-one or twenty-two. Either way, age of consent here is only fourteen."

Christ, does everyone check the rules to see if they can fuck a teenager before heading to a foreign country? My opinion of Elmo slides down another few notches.

"My information said she was eleven. Can you believe that?"

"Hmm," he says, "I see what you mean. Something else is going on."

"Yes. She spoke freely about offering herself to me. I'm pretty sure the whole place is bugged."

"It is." Elmo says. "I've been subtly casing things. Every room is bugged with video and audio."

I nod. "That's no less than I expected."

I look around, and a moment later, Daniela is outside, joining us. She's still beautiful, but she looks a little deflated compared to before. There's an uneasiness in her eyes, and I catch the slightest trembling in her lower lip.

"Great," I mutter to Elmo. "Here she comes."

My bodyguard looks at her. "She *is* a beauty."

"Unfortunately, I'm only interested in one beauty. And it's not her."

Elmo subtly nods. Then he turns to her. "Is there something you need, Señorita Agudelo?"

"Yes," she says. "I need to speak to Señor Gallo. In private."

13

RAVEN

I don't reply to my brother. What is there to say?

He's most likely right.

"Everything that you need is here," Falcon continues. "Plenty of food. Like I told you, I brought in a couple weeks' worth of fresh food. If you're here for longer than that, you can get into the nonperishable items."

I let out a huff of air. "And like I told *you*, I'm not going to be gone any longer than that. I *will* be at that gala."

He doesn't reply.

"That's nonnegotiable," I say. "Jared can be there. Plus you and Leif…. Figure it all out. Figure out how to get me safely to that gala, because I will be going. If you're not here to take me, someone else will be."

Falcon lifts his eyebrows at me.

"What about our father? How do you think *he'll* feel that you've got his daughter imprisoned here?"

"He's all for it, of course," Falcon says. "Nothing is more important to Dad than your safety. All of his children's safety."

"Does he know I'm here?"

"If he asks, which he probably won't, I will tell him that you're safe."

I bite my lip. "Oh my God. Dad doesn't know about this place?"

"Only Hawk and I know about this place. And Leif. And of course Savannah and Vinnie. And now you and Jared."

"Eagle doesn't know?"

"You know I love our littlest brother as much as you do," Falcon says, "but he hasn't been the most trustworthy person."

I bite my lower lip. Eagle's my baby. He's always been my baby. But Falcon is right. He's made some stupid-ass decisions, and now, something else is going on with him. Something that apparently involves Leif's sister, Scarlett Ramsey. No one is forthcoming about it.

"I see you're not disagreeing with me," Falcon says.

"No, no."

"Is there anything else you need before I go?"

"Are you kidding?" I look around. "This place is self-explanatory."

"I'll have eyes on you at all times."

"No." I nervously eye a security camera in the corner. "I don't want someone surveilling me while I'm sleeping or in the shower."

"No, of course not. But I'll have eyes on the place. I'll know if anyone comes or goes. Jared has been briefed on everything about the house. No one will know you're here."

"What if someone saw us drive up?"

"Trust me. No one did."

I cross my arms. "If you say so."

I want to trust my brother. I want to believe him. Then I think of that drone that flew over my house while Vinnie and I were there.

How can I be sure I'm still not being watched? How can I be sure there aren't drones flying above the safe house even as we speak?

"I need to go now," Falcon says. "No one knows you're here. I haven't told Savannah. Only you and Jared know."

I frown. "You haven't told Hawk?"

"I haven't. The fewer who know, the better."

I bite my lip again. "I truly am in danger, aren't I?"

Falcon nods solemnly. "I could lie to you, Ray. Try not to worry you. But you've already faced death. You been through the worst thing a body can go through. I won't belittle you by lying to you."

"Do you know who's been texting me on the burner?"

Falcon shakes his head. "I don't know. I've got Leif looking into it, and he's the best. But burners are notoriously hard to track. Impossible in most cases. At least whoever it is seems to have your best interests at heart."

"I wish I could remember more about that Uber driver. The one who gave me the burner. It's just... That day is such a blur."

"I understand. We'll get to the bottom of this, Raven. Our family just got you back in one piece. We're not going to lose you."

"I'd prefer that too," I say, letting out a nervous chuckle.

"Then stay here. Lie low. Work on your nonprofit, but let others do the legwork."

I kick at the floor. "It's not like you're giving me a choice."

"You always have a choice, Raven." He looks into my eyes.

"You're not a prisoner. But I'm asking you, as your brother. Please stay here."

"You're not going to play the bone marrow card?" Another nervous chuckle.

He grins. "I can't play that card with you. That wouldn't be fair. I'm simply playing the brother card. I need you to be safe."

I nod, relenting. "I'll stay. But only until the gala."

He sighs. "All right, Raven. You'll be at that gala. Because I'll make sure I eliminate any threat to you before then." He starts to head toward the exit.

"No, Falcon." I grab his hand. "You have Savannah to think of. Don't you get yourself involved in this. The last thing I want is for you to go back to prison."

His gaze darkens. "Oh, I'm not going back to prison, Raven. Not ever."

"Good."

I've heard my brother say on more than one occasion that he would do it all over again to protect Eagle. But I don't know that he would.

He must've lived through hell.

Just as I did.

And I sure as hell don't want to go through everything I went through again.

"Listen," Falcon says. "I know this sucks. I know you don't want to be here. I wish it were different, Ray. When I went to prison and asked Hawk to build this place, it was for exactly this reason. In case one of us needed it. I'm damned glad it's here. I'm going to try to figure out who's been texting you from this burner and who sent that threatening text to your regular phone. I've left a burner here for you. I want you to use it to get in contact with me. If you can't get me or Leif, call Hawk."

"What about Eagle? Dad?"

Falcon frowns. "I don't want to drag Eagle into this right now. Part of me feels like he's a loaded gun. And as for Dad?" He shifts his gaze back and forth. "Like I said, I don't want him worrying about you. He and Mom have been through enough."

I simply nod once more.

Falcon finally departs, and I take stock in the kitchen.

I suppose I'm going to have to be the one who cooks for Jared and me.

But he gets there before I do. "I'll be cooking, Raven."

"You don't have to do that."

"This place is a fortress," he says. "I won't have a lot to do here to keep you safe. The least I can do is keep you fed."

I sigh. "Fine."

"I'm thinking steak and potatoes for dinner. Sound good?"

"Sure. Whatever."

One thing I will do is eat. Whether I'm hungry or not. Because I've got to keep my body strong.

Because I *will* be at that gala. Whatever else is going on must end.

And if my brother can't figure it out?

I'll figure it out myself.

14

VINNIE

"Please," Daniela says. "You have to help me."

I look around. "Are we being spied on?"

She shakes her head. "He can probably see us. I don't know. Sometimes he has drones flying around that I swear to God are invisible to the naked eye. But no one can hear us out here. I'm sure of that."

I turn to Elmo. "Do you believe her?"

"Hell, I don't know. His setup is every bit as good as your grandfather's."

I hold back a wince at his use of the word *grandfather*.

Elmo doesn't know. No one knows.

"What is it that you need?" I ask Daniela.

"I don't want to marry that old man."

I nod slowly. "I hear you. I don't want to marry the person I'm supposed to marry either."

"My father..." She bites her lip. "He said he'd give me to you."

I nearly fall off my feet. "You just told me you were

promised to Vega. Your father knows damned well that *I'm* already promised too."

"He said he'd make it part of the deal. Part of the deal with your grandfather. He would marry me to you if I could get you to ask for my hand."

"I'm twice your age, Daniela." And I'm desperately in love with someone else, though I have a feeling her father already knows that. He'd be a fool not to know everything there is to know about me.

"I want to go to the States," she says.

"There are plenty of ways to go to the States," I say. "Get a student visa. You seem very intelligent. I'm sure you could get into one of the many schools that have openings for international students."

She shakes her head with a huff. "You think he'd let me go to school?"

"You're not in school now?"

She frowns. "I have private tutors. This is my last year. If this doesn't work, I'm going to be forced to marry that old man. Vega." She tugs on my arm. "Please. It's my only chance to get out of here. We could get an annulment once I'm in the US. You don't even have to sleep with me if you don't want to. I don't care about any of that. I just want to get out of here. I want to go to the US and pursue my dream. I can't marry Señor Vega. I just can't."

"You'd rather marry me?" I shake my head. "I'm not available. And I'll never love you."

"At least you're handsome. Tall. I only see a few gray hairs at your temple."

"And what will he offer me," I ask, "if I take you off his hands?"

"I doubt it will change any deal you're making with him," she says. "This is for me. To get me out of marrying Vega."

"And you think this man loves you?" I scoff. "I'm disgusted by what fathers do to their daughters in this world."

"In his way." She looks down. "He doesn't touch me."

"But he lets other men touch you."

She nods, biting her lip. "Yes. But no one has ever been abusive."

I lift my eyebrows.

"All right. Not horribly abusive." She swallows. "Maybe I've been slapped around a little here and there."

"Is the slapping consensual?"

She shakes her head slowly.

"Then that's abusive, Daniela." I pace around her, shaking my head. "It makes me sick how people like you have been raised to not even recognize abuse when it's happening to you. Just him letting other men have you is abuse. It's sure not love."

"Do you? Do you know what real love is, Señor Gallo?"

I don't answer.

She can probably see it written all over my face anyway. Because I do know what real love is. I know what it feels like to love a person so much that it hurts, to love a person so much that you'll leave her to keep her safe.

To love a person so much that you'll kill for her.

I sigh.

Fuck.

Am I actually considering this? A marriage in name only, just to get her out of here. Away from her father. Away from the men he forces her to service.

I don't know what the marriage laws are in Colombia, but

with her father's permission, we could probably tie the knot here. I could take her home, get the marriage annulled, and once she's eighteen, she can apply for legal status.

I don't want to marry her. There's only one woman I want to marry, and I can't have her.

But if we can strike a deal with Agudelo, get Mario involved, break my engagement to Belinda...

Will Raven understand?

Then I nearly laugh at the absurdity of the thought.

I left Raven. I left her for her own good. I can't be with her, so it really doesn't matter who I marry.

All that matters is that I take down my family. Put an end to this legacy built on blood and money.

If I can help Daniela in the process, I should do so.

Just as I'll help Belinda if I can. Get her removed from her father's home.

But would that be a disservice? That little girl has everything. What if she got stuck in some foster home where she's mistreated, perhaps hurt in a more horrific way? Or worse, stuck in a group home where she gets no attention at all?

She needs to study music. Pursue her gift.

I draw in a breath. I make a choice. Because really, what other choice is there? I'm not some knight in shining armor. Far from it. Hell, I've taken two lives, and I'll take more before I'm done.

The voice of the old Tibetan monk haunts me.

Go now, with the strength of your spirit. Embrace the unknown. Continue your journey, and live your life to its fullest potential.

What good am I if I don't help those who need helping?

How could I live with myself? This must be part of my journey. Part of why I'm here in Colombia.

The deal with Agudelo is not the main reason. I can get that wrapped up in the next couple weeks, and Mario, Agudelo, and Vega will all be content.

I've learned that Vega—or at least someone claiming to be him—is not dead and buried, and I've learned that Austin Bellamy is involved in some dirty dealings. I've learned that the old woman in that photo factors into all of this somehow.

And I've learned that I can't resist a damsel in distress.

All part of the journey. All part of living up to my potential.

I'll save Daniela.

I'll save Belinda.

And somehow I'm going to get back to Raven and save her too.

15

RAVEN

For the first few moments when I woke up this morning, I forgot where I was.

I was in my bed, in my home. Maybe Vinnie was snoozing next to me, or maybe he had gotten up to make a fresh pot of coffee.

Then reality came down on me like a ton of bricks.

No. I'm in the safe house.

Vinnie is in Colombia and wants nothing to do with me.

Jared had breakfast ready by the time I padded into the kitchen, wearing a robe I found in the closet of the bedroom. Yeah, somehow Falcon figured out my clothes sizes and filled the closets with several weeks' worth of clothing. Mostly T-shirts and sweatpants.

The kind of clothes I wore when I was getting treated for cancer.

These will do for now, but I'm going to have to find a stunning dress for the gala. I guess I'll find someone online and send them my measurements.

Breakfast is scrambled eggs, sausage patties, and hash

browns. I take a bite. It's actually pretty good. Jared put something spicy—paprika maybe—in the eggs.

"I didn't realize you were so adept in the kitchen, Jared," I say.

He shrugs. "I've been single a while. A man has to learn to fend for himself if he doesn't want to live off TV dinners and take out for the rest of his life."

I look him up and down. There's certainly a lot more to this man than meets the eye.

After breakfast, I take a quick shower and then get down to business. First I have to call Robin. I take out my phone and dial her number.

"Hey Ray, what's up?"

I draw in a deep breath and attempt a feigned sick voice. "Hey, sis. I'm afraid I've got some bad news."

"Oh, gosh, are you okay?"

"Yes, I'm fine, but..." I swallow. I hate lying to my twin sister. "I think I've overexerted myself a bit in the planning of this gala. I hate to ask for your help, I know you're busy, but I've got to take it easy for the next few weeks. Want to make sure I'm in prime health for the big day."

"Falcon already alerted me that I'd need to take a more active role. Consider it done. What do you need? I know you got the venue booked already."

"Yes." I put the phone on speaker and open an email with a list of things to take care of from Emily. "I can still make a lot of calls and emails, but I need you to be the in-person contact if necessary. First there's the caterer."

"I know just the place. A friend of mine, Lorraine, owns this fabulous gastropub. Lots of high-end appetizers, and steaks that are to die for."

"I'd rather use Bellamy beef, if possible."

"I'm pretty sure they already use our beef, but I can make arrangements to get it to them wholesale. Then you'll just be paying for the food prep and the waitstaff."

"Sounds good. And you know the menu? You know what's good?"

"I go there at least once a week. Lorraine is good at what she does."

"Perfect. I'll leave you with that. I also want to hire a string quartet and a DJ."

She pauses. "I don't know much about that. But I'm sure there are sources to find those online. The venue probably has some contacts, certainly for the DJ. For the string quartet, maybe you could contact a local university? I bet UT Austin has a lot of great strings players who are champing at the bit for gigs."

I make a note. "Okay, I'll take care of that." I scan through my email from Emily. "And then there's décor. I definitely want floral arrangements, but the venue is pretty fancy already."

"I've got it. There's a florist right next to Lorraine's. Easy trip for me to make." She pauses. "What about audio-visual and lighting?"

"The venue takes care of that part. I'll give their stage manager your contact information, though, in case they need you to go in before the day of."

"Good."

I take a deep breath. Robbie really is a great sister. She's taking on all of this without question. It's nothing overly complicated, but it's a lot of busywork, and she already has her hands full on the ranch as one of our veterinarians.

"Anything else, Ray?"

"I think that's it for now. Just shoot me a text if you have any questions. Thanks so much, Robbie. You're really saving my ass here."

"*You're* the one who's going to be saving asses, Ray. I'm just doing what I can to help. I'll head over to Lorraine's right now. Love you, bye."

"Love you too." I end the call.

Okay. Next is Emily herself. I dial her number.

"This is Emily."

"Hey Emily. It's Raven Bellamy."

"Raven, yes! I was about to call you and check in on your plans for the gala."

I sigh. "That's what I'm calling about. I've been ordered by the doctors to go on bed rest for the next few weeks before the gala. I already have my sister helping take care of some of the arrangements, but I'm afraid I'm going to need a little extra help from you. I'll be compensating you for your time, of course."

She laughs. "Raven, I'm happy to do the work *pro bono*. This is a great cause. I'm so sorry to hear you're not feeling well, though."

"I'll live."

At least, I hope I will.

"What can I help you with?"

"The guest list, mainly. Most of the people I've invited will be coming, but I have a few empty seats I'd like filled. Do you have any...philanthropic contacts?"

"I know quite a few. Including some whose lives have been touched by cancer. I'm happy to make some calls."

"Good, thank you. I'd also like to arrange a silent auction."

"Wonderful idea. My firm has contacts with plenty of local businesses who would be willing to donate items or packages. In fact..." Her keyboard clicks in the background. "An old mentor of mine in Colorado has some pull with Steel Vinyards on the Western Slope. I bet we could get them to donate something."

"Wonderful. If you don't mind making those calls on behalf of the foundation, I'd really appreciate it."

"It would be my pleasure, Raven. And while I have you, have you managed to find a doctor who would be interested in joining the board?"

I smile. "That's my next call."

"Perfect. Take care, Raven. Again, I'm so sorry to hear you're under the weather."

My stomach twists. All the lies.

"Like I said, I'll live."

"I'm sure you'll be fine. I'll start making calls right now. Talk to you later."

"Sounds good. Bye."

The call ends.

My next call is to Landon Michaels, an oncologist who works at the hospital I was treated in. He and I never worked together, which means he would have less of a conflict of interest. I call his office.

"Dr. Michaels's office. This is Sherri speaking."

"Hi, Sherri. Is Dr. Michaels available? I'd like to speak with him."

"One sec." Typing and shuffling paper for a second. "Actually, he's in his office right now. May I tell him who's calling?"

"Raven Bellamy."

"Of course. I'll transfer your call."

"Thanks."

A few seconds pass.

"Dr. Michaels speaking."

"Yes, thank you for taking my call, doctor. My name is Raven—"

"Raven Bellamy, yes. Sherri told me. You're the daughter of Austin Bellamy."

"Yes, I am. Perhaps you have heard that I am organizing a nonprofit for the treatment and research of blood cancers. We have a gala coming up in a couple of weeks."

"Let me stop you right there. How much would you like?"

"I'm not asking for a donation, though of course if you're interested in making one, we won't turn you down." I let out a nervous laugh. "But actually, I wanted to know if you'd be interested in sitting on our board. Your expertise would be invaluable to our cause."

"I'm flattered, Ms. Bellamy." He pauses. "When did you say your gala will be?"

"In a few weeks. You would be invited, as well as Mrs. Michaels."

"There isn't a Mrs. Michaels."

I slap my palm to my forehead. "Sorry, I shouldn't have assumed."

"Not a problem. I'm divorced." He chuckles. "Perhaps I'll see if I can scare up a date."

"You would both be welcome. We won't be starting board meetings until after the gala, so you wouldn't have to do anything until then but show up."

"Sounds good."

"So you'll join the board?"

"I would be delighted to."

"Wonderful. I'm actually resting up a bit before the gala, so my sister and my attorney will be the main contacts. But this number is my personal number, so please feel free to call me if you have any questions."

"Glad to, Ms. Bellamy. I'll see you in a few weeks."

"Yes, you will."

"Ciao."

The call ends.

Ciao? That wasn't how I would expect a doctor to end a call. Dr. Michaels seems like an interesting fellow. But I did my research on him before calling. He graduated top of his class at the Northwestern Feinberg School of Medicine, did several stints of service with Doctors Without Borders, and has glowing reviews from his patients online.

I don't have much time to think about it, because my phone then starts ringing. A number I don't recognize.

Probably a telemarketer, but the area code is local. It could be someone calling about the gala. I bring the phone to my ear.

"Hello?"

"Yes, hello. Is this Raven Bellamy?"

"Speaking. Who, may I ask, is this?"

"Smith. Jack Smith, Ms. Bellamy. I'm calling you about your foundation."

His voice is deep, but it has a bit of a squeak to it. He sounds almost nervous on the other line. But if this is a potential donor, I'll keep talking to him.

"Yes, did you have any questions? Perhaps you're interested in making a donation?"

He chuckles lightly. "I already made a donation, Ms. Bellamy. I submitted it through your attorney."

Oh, my God. The money didn't come from my father?

"Are you the anonymous donor? The fifty million?"

He pauses. "Yes, I am."

"Wow, sir. I wish there was a proper way to express my gratitude. Money like that is going to really get the foundation started off right."

"That was my hope. And there *is* a way you can express your gratitude."

"Yes, sir. Anything."

He pauses. "I would like for the donation to remain anonymous. I don't want any glory. But I understand that there is a gala coming up. I would love a seat at the table. I'm willing, of course, to pay for my plate."

"That won't be necessary, sir. Your donation more than makes up for it." I pull up the guest list on my laptop. "There are a few empty seats available. I'm having my attorney work on filling them, but I'll absolutely make sure one of them stays open for you. Jack Smith, you said?"

"Yes, ma'am."

"I'll mark you down. You will be *most* welcome, Mr. Smith."

"Please, call me Jack."

"Of course. Jack."

I'll call him Your Majesty if he wants, for that kind of money.

"I'll send you an official invitation if you'd like. That has all the information you'll need."

"I actually got the information already. A friend of mine is one of your board members. That's why I called. I'll be there with bells on, as they say."

Interesting. Maybe he's a friend of Robin's. Or more likely my father's.

"Then it sounds like you're all squared away. We will see you at the gala, Mr. Smith. And thank you once again, from the bottom of my heart. This kind of money is going to do an immeasurable amount of good."

"I'm sure it will, Ms. Bellamy. Take care."

Three weeks later...

I'm finally back at my own home.

The weeks at the safe house passed uneventfully, thank God.

I chose the evening gown myself from an online catalog. I sent my measurements to a dressmaker, and the gown is waiting for me when I'm finally allowed to return to my home.

The gala is tonight.

A hairstylist—I have hair now, though it's only an inch or so long—and makeup artist arrive to help me get ready.

The gown is a deep emerald green, a color that complements my dark hair. The fabric is a rich, flowing silk velvet. The gown is tailored with a strapless sweetheart neckline and a delicate bodice with intricate beading and tiny emerald crystals.

I've managed to put on some weight, so the gown fits me beautifully.

I've been practicing what I'll say. I asked my father to say a few words to introduce me.

Hawk will escort me, as Falcon will be escorting Savannah.

How I wish I could arrive on Vinnie's arm.

But it's not to be.

Jared, of course, will also be accompanying Hawk and me. But he's promised to be discreet. Most of the guests don't know that I've hired a bodyguard as personal security, and I don't want them to feel as if something bad might happen during the event.

"Your hair is coming in beautifully," the stylist says.

I frown. "I suppose I don't really need a stylist."

"Don't be silly. You're going to look elegant. Have you thought about earrings?"

"Some emeralds, I think. My mother has some she's lending me."

"Perfect. Where are they?"

"In that box over there on the dresser."

The stylist returns, holding the earrings. "These are beautiful. And I see there's a necklace to go with them. May I?"

"Yes, please."

She places the necklace around my neck and puts the earrings through the pierced holes in my ears. "Lissette did a beautiful job with your makeup. You look lovely."

"I definitely needed some blush," I say. "I haven't seen the sun in a while."

"Busy making arrangements for the gala?"

I bite my lip. "In a way. Either way, I'm looking pretty pale."

"Don't be silly. You have a lovely tone to your skin."

"That comes from my mother. She's Mexican. But none of my brothers and sisters are as dark as she is."

The stylist smiles. "She must be a beauty."

"Yes, she is."

I'm looking forward to seeing my mother and my father tonight. I haven't seen anyone besides Jared for the last several weeks.

"All right," the stylist says. "Stand up now and take a look at yourself in the full-length mirror."

I do so, and I can't help a gasp as I look at myself.

My dark, short hair is styled sleek, and though I never imagined myself with short hair, I have to admit it looks a lot better than no hair at all. In fact, it looks pretty smart and sophisticated. Maybe I'll keep it.

"What do you think?" the stylist asks.

I turn to her, beaming. "I can't thank you enough. You came highly recommended, and I see why."

She smiles. "Lissette and I are a team. We have our own salon in Austin if you'd ever like to visit us there."

"I absolutely will."

"Perfect. If you're done, I'll pack up, and you can be on your way."

"Yes, the gala is in San Antonio. Not quite as far away as Austin."

"I'm sure it will be a lovely affair."

I can't help myself. I walk swiftly toward her and give her a hug. "Thank you. Thank you for helping me to remember that I'm beautiful."

"You're radiant," she says. "You have lovely thick dark hair, and fine features. But even if you didn't have that, your radiance comes from inside, Raven. Anyone can see it. And no one can cover it up."

Once the stylists are gone, I take another look at myself.

I'm glad she thinks I'm radiant. All I think and think about is that I haven't seen the sun for so long. When I got to leave that bunker this morning, I just wanted to stand in the daylight and do nothing.

That's what I'll do tomorrow. After the festivities.

No way am I going back to that safe house. I'm going to lie in the sun all day.

Someone knocks on my door. It's Jared, of course. No one else is here. I open it.

His dark eyes widen. "You look amazing."

"You're not so bad yourself." He fills out his tuxedo perfectly with his muscled body.

"Your brother has arrived."

"All right. I'm ready."

Hawk is maybe the most handsome of all my brothers. The tallest of the three at six foot five, he's the only one to inherit our father's eyes. With his tanned skin tone and black hair, they stand out in a brilliant sky blue.

His tux is jet black, of course, with silver button covers, and around his neck is an emerald-green bow tie.

"No bolo?" I tease him.

"God, no. I hate those things. I can't believe Dad still wears them."

I giggle. "Well, he's a Texan through and through."

He smiles at me. "You look gorgeous, sis."

"Thank you. I wasn't sure the stylist would be able to do much with my hair, but I'm amazed."

He squints. "And your eyebrows, they're all grown back."

"Pretty much." I take out a compact and admire them. "Just a little help from an eyebrow pencil."

"And are those your lashes?"

"Falsies," I say. "But mine are coming back in strong."

We leave my house, and a black limo stands out front.

I turn to my bodyguard, raising a penciled-in eyebrow. "You're not driving us, Jared?"

"Nope," he says. "Your brothers insisted that you go in style tonight."

"That's wonderful," I say. "You can come with us. That way you don't have to drive."

He smirks. "I know what my job is, Raven. You won't be out of my sight all night, and that includes the drive. I'll be right across from you."

The driver gets out of the limo, opens the door, and Hawk helps me in. He slides next to me, and Jared slides in after him, taking the seat facing us.

"Champagne?" Hawk asks.

An open bottle sits in the center console, and three flutes sit in secure holders.

"Oh no, I couldn't," I say. "I'm still not drinking much with my meds and all. Besides, I'm way too nervous and excited."

"You don't mind if I have a glass, do you?" Hawk asks.

"Of course not."

"Jared?" he asks.

"As much as I'd love it, I need my full faculties tonight."

Hawk nods. "Of course." He expertly pours himself a glass of the sparkling wine and takes a sip. "Good stuff."

The drive is about an hour, and though I'm used to wearing sweats and loose T-shirts, I'm not uncomfortable in the elegant dress. I've missed this. I've missed dressing up, going out.

Growing up, I was always the girly girl while Robbie was the tomboy. She grew out of a lot of it, and I'm sure she'll look beautiful tonight at the gala. But this is me in my element. I love beautiful clothes. I love looking pretty. I love being noticed.

I got my fair share of being noticed during my treatment. On the occasions when I wasn't in the hospital, people would stare at my bald head. I got used to it. But now I'm going to be noticed because I look pretty.

I feel like myself again.

When we arrive at the gala, the driver gets out and opens the door for us. Hawk exits first and helps me to my feet. Jared follows.

Photographers are flashing, and reporters are there.

"Ms. Bellamy," a reporter asks me. "Would you like to say a few words before you enter your gala?"

"Good evening," I say. "Thank you for being here. I'm very excited to get my new foundation off the ground."

Photos are snapped, and Hawk waves away the rest of the reporters as we enter the grand lobby of the hotel where the gala is being held.

Then the ballroom. It's early yet, and only the organizers are here, along with Robin, Emily, CJ, and my parents. Falcon and Savannah enter soon after. The silent auction is set up on one side of the wall. The bar is open, and my father is already drinking a bourbon.

"Let's get you a sparkling water or something," Hawk says.

"That sounds great." I swallow. "My throat is drying up."

"I'll be right back."

Jared stays a few feet away from me, unobtrusive.

Hawk returns from the bar and hands me my drink with a huge smile.

I drop my jaw as I notice the vivid color of the liquid in the glass. "Oh my God, is that Orange Crush?"

His grin widens. "Do you think your sister would set up a gala for you and not be sure that the bar was stocked with your favorite?"

I take a sip and then notice a woman I haven't seen in weeks pass by.

"Oh my God, Robin!" I grab my sister as she walks by and give her a big bear hug.

"You'll muss my dress, Ray," she says.

Robin looks gorgeous, of course. She's wearing flaming red. She's always been able to get away with stuff like that. Her dress isn't quite as formal as mine. It's a sheath that goes midway down her calves. On her feet are strappy silver sandals with platform heels, the kind of shoes I would've worn before I got sick. I'm wearing simple black pumps tonight. I didn't want to take the chance of stumbling. It's been years since I've had actual heels on.

My attorney, Emily, is on the stage at the podium getting ready to make some announcements once more attendees get here. Already they're coming in droves, and soon the ballroom is buzzing with conversation.

The ballroom is softly illuminated by chandeliers hanging high above, and the women's gowns shimmer in the light, while the men, impeccably dressed in tailored suits and tuxedos, exude sophistication.

Bartenders, dressed in crisp black-and-white uniforms, serve up a variety of cocktails and champagne, including the signature cocktail for the evening, a prickly pear margarita for a Texas touch. The faint sound of ice dropping into glasses accompanies the vibrant hum of the guests conversing.

Across the ballroom, the silent auction has begun, and clusters of attendees are mingling near the tables showcasing an array of luxury items up for bid. A soft ping from phones alerts guests as bids are placed, but other than that people are socializing quite nicely without staring at screens.

The string quartet—Robin was right about hiring college students from UT—plays softly in the background. The guests, who are a mix of socialites, philanthropists, and corporate leaders, move fluidly between the bar, the auction tables, and each other, exchanging greetings, smiles, and introductions.

Waiters glide through the room with trays of hors d'oeuvres—delicate smoked salmon canapés, mini truffle tarts, and brie bites—offering guests a taste before the formal dinner begins. Robin's friend Lorraine really outdid herself. I'll be having her cater all of my future donor events for sure.

The mini truffle tart is savory and delicious, and as I swallow it and take a bite of my brie, I look around.

Hawk is in conversation with Jared, and I look toward the entrance where people are still arriving.

And I swallow my brie bite nearly whole, taking a quick drink of my Orange Crush to avoid choking.

A man is here.

And he looks even better than I remember.

He's here.

Vinnie Gallo is here.

And he's not alone.

16

VINNIE

I returned several days ago, my new bride in tow.

Mario was pleased with the results of my trip, even though I wasn't able to complete the negotiations with Agudelo. One part I did complete was taking Daniela as my wife.

With her father's permission, we were married in Colombia the day before I left.

Daniela and I had already agreed that the marriage would not be consummated. She just wanted to get out of Colombia, and I was her ticket.

Declan McAllister won't be pleased, but that doesn't matter much to me. The marriage to Daniela is in name only, and once she has legal status in the US, I will be annulling it.

These are the terms she and I have agreed to. They're not the terms set by her father, but I don't care.

However, I've come across some information that has me on edge.

Raven's life is in danger. Not from Mario or from Declan McAllister. Not even from Jacinto Agudelo.

From someone else.

And as I think about it, I still can't believe it.

ONE WEEK EARLIER...

My negotiations on the territory for the cartel are nearly complete, and earlier today, with Agudelo's permission, I took Daniela as my wife.

The last couple of nights, though, the shuffling and banging that seems to be coming from my ceiling has become louder and more persistent.

It's got me on edge, and with this entire place surveilled all times, I can't exactly figure out where the sound is coming from or what it is.

Agudelo is gone a lot, overnight trips nearly every other day. But he's always back here for lunch, where we continue our negotiations.

He left again this afternoon for another overnight trip, and I've decided that surveillance be damned. I'm going to figure out what is going on above me.

And Daniela is going to help me.

I knock on the door to her room.

"Yes?" she says through the door.

"It's Vinnie. May I come in?"

"Of course."

I open the door. Daniela is in her sitting area, working on her laptop. Over the last few days, I've found out she's quite intelligent. Of course, I already knew that her love of cooking knows no bounds, and she really wants to study at the

Cordon Bleu in Paris. But her knowledge expands outside of her culinary interests. She's never left Colombia, but she knows so much about the culture and politics of Europe and the Americas. She and I have had many a late-night conversation about my overseas days, and her broad understanding of the way the world works is impressive, especially for someone of her young age.

A lot of that knowledge was gained from her shitty upbringing, which makes me sad. But I'm going to do my damnedest to help her make a better life.

I walk into her room and close the door. I look straight at her, deliberately avoiding the gaze of anywhere on the ceiling where a camera might be mounted.

"May I speak freely?" I whisper.

She takes my hand and mouths, "Let's go outside."

A few moments later, we're out on the back veranda, taking a walk down a stone path.

When she feels comfortable, she turns to me. "What is it?"

I lean in, keeping my voice low just in case. "Since I got here, I've heard some strange noises coming from above my room," I say. "Do you know what's above the second floor?"

She wrinkles her forehead. "Just the old attic. It's probably just the house settling."

"That's what I thought at first as well." I stroke my chin. "but the noise almost has a rhythm to it. It comes and goes."

She frowns. "What are you asking me, Señor Gallo?"

"Call me Vinnie." I can't help a small smile. "We're married. I think we're on a first-name basis at this point."

"Sure." She returns my smile. "Vinnie."

"How would I get to the attic?"

"There are stairs at the end of the hallway. But the door is always locked. No one's been up there in… I'm not sure how long." She purses her lips. "When I was a little girl, I always wanted to go up there and explore, but my father forbade it. He told me stories of ghosts that haunted the old attic."

"And you believed him?"

"I was only a little girl, Vinnie. Of course I believed him. If you ask me if I believe him now, obviously I don't." Her gaze darkens. "But now that I know more about what my father and his colleagues do for a living, I figure there are things up there that I'm not meant to see. Things I don't *want* to see."

I grab her hands. "I want to know what's up there, Daniela. Can you help me?"

She takes a deep breath, looking into my eyes. "If you're asking me if I can unlock the door, the answer is no. I can't. Only my father has those keys."

"What about Morehouse?"

"Morehouse has keys to everything. But he would never betray my father."

"Do you know where Morehouse keeps the keys?"

She bites her lip. "How would I know that?"

Apparently she's not going to be any help at all. I let go of her hands and turn away from her. "Thank you for your candor, Daniela."

"Wait." She runs around me and plants herself in my path. "Just because I can't help you with this doesn't mean you're not going to help me, does it?"

I shake my head. "Men like me don't go back on their word, Daniela."

"Oh, thank God." She sighs in relief. "I really do want to leave. I just know there's a much better chance of a good life for me in the United States."

"I'll see that you get that chance." I look toward the horizon. "You're not the first young woman I've come across who is intelligent and talented but is being placed in a box."

She takes my hand. "Yes, the girl you're betrothed to."

"Not only her. My own mother." I inhale deeply and let it out on a whoosh. "She could've made so much more out of her life."

"I'm sorry for your loss." Daniela pats my hands gently.

"Thank you. I appreciate that. At least I know my mother is at peace now." I grit my teeth. "Meanwhile, my father's rotting away in a prison cell."

Technically not my father, but still the man who I think of as my true father.

"There's nothing you can do for him?"

I sigh, shaking my head slightly. "Not at the moment, anyway."

"Listen," she says. "You've been so kind to me. Let me try to help you." She looks up toward the roof of the house. "I have to admit I've always been curious about the attic myself. I'll see what I can do."

I lean forward and give her a kiss on the cheek. She really is a lovely girl. "Thank you. Please let me know what you find out."

"I will. Do you want to go back to the house now?"

"Yes, I suppose that would be best."

She places a hand on my shoulder. "Don't worry about these walks we have, the talks we have outside the house.

When my father asked me about them, I told him you were courting me."

I raise an eyebrow. "And he bought it?"

"Yes, but not in the way you think." She looks down. "He knows you're in love with another woman, Vinnie."

I jerk backward. "Oh?"

"Yes. He told me so. He asked me if that mattered to me."

"And what did you say?"

"I told him that it didn't matter. That this was a business deal, an alliance, and nothing more."

"Good. Thank you."

She presses her lips together. "There is one thing you should know, though."

"What's that?"

She swallows. "Alliances are forged through marriage, but they're maintained through children. My father will expect grandchildren, Vinnie."

"You're still very young."

"That doesn't matter to him."

"I'll get you back to the United States. After that, we'll figure things out from there."

"Sounds good to me."

We walk in silence back to the house.

An hour later, there's a knock at my door.

I open it, and Daniela stands there. She grabs me into a hug and presses her lips to mine.

It feels all wrong, and I'm about to push her away when I see her eyeing a camera in the corner. She's putting on a show, of course. I feel her slip something in my pocket as she pulls away.

She then smiles at me and leaves without a word.

Back in my room, I look at what she shoved into my pocket.

It's a key, along with a note.

Midnight. You have two hours. All surveillance will be off.

I nearly drop my jaw. How did she manage that? I shudder to think of what—or, God help her, *who*—she had to do. I never wanted her to help me that way. But I have the key now, and I have the cover I need.

I must take this opportunity.

At midnight, in the darkness of the hallway, I pad lightly toward the end of the hallway where the door to the attic stairs is. I unlock it and open it, stealing quietly up the creaky stairs.

I inhale the smell of a musty attic. Mothballs, cobwebs, dust.

I don't dare make a sound. Are there cameras up here as well? Microphones? Are they part of the main system? I have no idea. If I'm caught, it will be the end of my time here and of the deal with Agudelo.

But my curiosity is piqued, and I need to know what he's hiding up here.

He must be hiding something. Why else would he lock the door?

I've been here for over a week now, and I've never seen anyone go near this door.

I don't have a flashlight on me or my phone. I didn't want to take the chance of anything alerting any possible cameras.

No lights have come on, so there are no motion detectors.

Good.

I keep walking, and every time a wood board creaks

beneath me, I stop, my body going rigid. Did anyone hear that? Did anyone see that?

Agudelo isn't home, but Morehouse is, as well as the housekeepers and other staff.

I keep walking, walking, walking...

Until I finally hit a wall, nearly stumbling.

I put my ear up to the wall.

No sound, until—

Tap. Tap. Tap.

The rhythm.

The same rhythm. And then more slowly.

Tap... Tap... Tap...

And then quickly again.

Tap. Tap. Tap.

Oh my God. Why didn't I notice this before?

It's Morse code. SOS. Three shorts, three longs, and then another three shorts. Someone is in this room.

Do I knock on the wall? Do I dare make any noise?

I fumble around in the dark, moving against the wall, looking for a doorknob.

There isn't one.

"Who's there?" I whisper as harshly as I can.

But no way are they going to be able to hear me.

So I knock on the wall. Lightly at first.

Nothing.

Then I knock again, this time louder. *Knock. Knock. Knock.*

And then...

"Is...someone there?"

The tone is weak, and the voice is scratchy. It's female, and it sounds like an older woman. An elderly woman, even.

Perhaps the old woman whose photograph has haunted me since the plane ride to Colombia?

How do I respond?

"Yes. I'm a friend. Here to help you out."

She doesn't respond. Maybe she didn't hear me.

I walk along the wall until I get to the back of the house. And—

"Yes!" I whisper.

It's a door. A slider, and it's locked, of course, but at least I know how I can get in.

On a whim, I try the key Daniela gave me. It doesn't work.

"Hello," I say. "Can you hear me?"

"Are you really here to help me?"

"Yes, I am. Can you open the door?"

"It's locked," she says.

I sigh. Of course it is.

I look around with something to unlock the door with. My eyes have adjusted to the darkness, and I spy a rusted toolbox. I approach it and crack open the lid. The tools are as rusty as the old metal box. Pliers, a hammer, lots of screws and nuts...and a long screwdriver. I can use it to jimmy the lock.

I return to the door and kneel to start working the lock. The faint sound of metal grating on metal fills the air as I gently maneuver the screwdriver, attempting to unlatch the bolt that seals the door shut.

"Are you still there?" the woman's voice pierces through my concentration.

"Yes," I whisper back. "I'm trying to open the door."

I return my attention to the stubborn lock. Just as my

patience begins to wane...a soft click. Tension eases in the door as relief washes over me.

"I've got it," I whisper to myself. I slide the door open and look into the dim room. Only a bed and a chair, and on the bed lies a frail woman, her hair white as snow and her eyes shimmering.

It's her. The old woman from the photos.

Her eyes widen as she looks me up and down.

"Mario?"

17

RAVEN

I gulp back the sadness that attempts to overtake me.

Vinnie is back.

And he's with a woman.

Not just any woman, but a young and beautiful woman with flowing black hair and big dark eyes. Her skin is a shade darker than mine, and her lips are full and ruby red.

And her dress...

Black. Black velvet and slimming. Showing off an amazing body. Not to mention her ass.

My heart sinks. Has he truly forgotten me so quickly?

I gulp.

Hawk walks toward me. "Ray? You need to hold it together."

"Who is that with him?" I demand.

"I don't know, sis. And it doesn't matter." He wraps his arm around my shoulders, giving them a squeeze, but I see in his eyes that he finds Vinnie's companion quite attractive. "Tonight is *your* night. Tonight is the night you've worked your ass off for. And you look beautiful."

I let my hand wander up to my short hair. I hate the fact that I'm envious of her long, gorgeous locks.

Was I seriously just thinking I might keep my hair short?

No, I want my long flowing hair back. I want my long thick eyelashes back.

I want my long and lean body back.

I'm still too thin. I haven't regained all of my muscle mass. That will take a while.

But the woman with Vinnie? Her body is perfection. Perfect hourglass.

He never loved me.

He was lying.

As much as I adore Savannah, her brother turned out to be just another jerk.

Not that she would know. He was gone for seventeen years. Savannah was only ten when he left for Europe. She may remember him as a loving older brother, but he's no longer that person.

How did this happen?

"Don't let it get to you," Hawk says again. "Emily's about to make an announcement that we need to get to our tables for dinner. After dinner, you're going to have to make your speech. Are you up for it?"

I steel my resolve. I stand straight.

Push my shoulders back.

The superhero pose.

I had to imagine myself in that pose when I was in the hospital, but it's something my mother taught Robbie and me when we were little girls. That we could be Wonder Woman if we wanted to. All we needed was confidence, and the first step was to look confident.

I take that pose now, and then I take Hawk's arm and walk to our table at the front of the ballroom. I catch him taking a few extra glances at the woman on Vinnie's arm, but I decide not to say anything. I'd rather not think of her right now.

Falcon and Savannah, Robin, Emily, Mom and Dad, Hawk and I, and Eagle are seated here.

My skin is tingling with nerves. With anger. The meal, chosen by my sister off of Lorraine's menu, is elegant. We begin with Texas Gulf crab cake garnished with avocado and mango salsa, and then on to roasted poblano corn soup with smoked paprika oil. Good old Texas staples and some of my favorites. Too bad they all taste like cardboard on my tongue.

The main course is seared filet mignon—with beef from Bellamy Ranch, of course—with chipotle bearnaise sauce and herb-infused butter served with garlic mashed potatoes and grilled asparagus spears.

I converse with my tablemates, answering their questions in a haze as I force the tender steak down. Again, normally a favorite of mine, but I can't enjoy it. I do my best to keep a happy face on.

The waitstaff clears the dinner plates, and dessert is laid out—tres leches cake with a bourbon caramel sauce. Once coffee and after-dinner drinks are served, my father wipes his lips with his napkin.

"You ready, sweetheart?" he says to me.

I glance around, looking for Vinnie. His table is near the back. I didn't even know he was on the guest list. Hell, I didn't even know he was back in the country.

"Give me a moment," I say, rising. "I need to...gather my thoughts."

"Of course."

People begin talking again, visiting the silent auction tables. I make my rounds, breathing deeply, shaking hands and forcing smiles.

Until I see Vinnie walking toward me.

Alone.

18

VINNIE

A *week earlier...*

The old woman squints at me. "Is that really you, Mario?" She reaches a trembling hand toward me. "My God, you haven't changed a bit."

Mario. I do look a lot like him. When he was young, he looked remarkably like me, only he was a couple inches shorter.

"I knew you'd come, Mario." Her eyes fill with tears. "I never stopped believing."

She wipes at her eyes with the sleeve of her worn dress, her gaze never leaving my face. For a moment, I can only stand there in shock, my mind racing to catch up with what I am hearing. What should have been a simple mission is now turning into something far more complex.

Oh my God. *This* is why Mario sent me here. This is why he wanted Puzo out of the way. This is why he wanted to work with Agudelo. The territory is nothing.

This woman is why I'm here.

"Serena?" I say.

She nods, tears forming in her sunken eyes.

"I never stopped loving you, Mario. I always knew you'd come back for me."

Serena Deville. The one woman Mario loved. The woman his father wouldn't let him have.

The woman who was taken from him but not murdered.

No.

He said what they did to her was far worse.

How long has she been here? She's older than Agudelo. Did his father bring her here? Has she been kept prisoner all this time? What did they do to her?

Torture her? Rape her? Starve her? Beat her?

My guess is all four and then some.

The thought sends a wave of shocking anger coursing through me, but I stifle it.

I need to focus. She needs help. Now.

"Serena," I whisper again, stepping further into the room. "I'm not Mario. I'm his... He's my..." I fumble for words, my mind spinning. The truth would be complicated and hard to believe, especially for someone in such a fragile state. "I need to get you out of here, Serena."

"Get me out?" she repeats my words, her voice barely a whisper. Her eyes, so full of hope a moment ago, seem to flicker with fear. "But how? The door is always locked."

"I have a key," I reply. "We will leave this place together."

"But the guards. And Señor..."

"I'll deal with them," I say before she can finish her sentence. I don't know exactly how yet, but one thing is certain. I won't leave her here.

Perhaps Daniela can help me again. I'll get Serena out of here somehow. I have a two-hour window to get her out of the room and to someplace safe without anyone knowing. Agudelo isn't here, but his staff is. Morehouse is.

I glance around the room and spot an old blanket. I drape it over Serena's frail form and help her sit up on the bed. She's weak but manages to hold onto me.

"We need to be quiet and swift," I tell her.

She nods, clutching onto my hand.

I help her stand and then lift her into my arms. She's light as a feather. I take her out of the room and into the dimly lit attic. We move as silently as possible towards the concealed staircase leading down.

The house is eerily quiet. The silence seems to stretch out around us, amplifying the softest of sounds—Serena's strained breaths, my pounding heart. As we creep down the stairs, I can't help but glance back over my shoulder every now and then.

Just when we reach the landing at the bottom of the stairs, a soft creak echoes from somewhere down the corridor.

I pull Serena behind an aged wooden armoire that's pressed against the wall. The scuffling of steps grows louder before gradually fading away.

"Who was that?" Serena whispers.

"A guard, maybe. Or one of Agudelo's men," I say, trying to keep the fear out of my voice. "We can't wait around to find out."

Gently, I carry her through the corridor to my room, where I pound on Elmo's adjoining door. My heart beats in my chest like a drum, each thud echoing loudly in my ears.

Elmo opens the door, his eyes widening when he sees

Serena. But then he regains his composure. "Daniela came to me. I've got a car ready to go. How much time is left?"

I look at my watch. "Only fifteen minutes."

"We should be able to make it. Are you packed?"

"I never unpacked." I pat my pocket. "I keep my passport on me at all times."

"Good. Let's go. Daniela's already in the car."

"Did she know...?"

He shakes his head. "No. I had a suspicion about why we were really here, but I wasn't sure."

"And you didn't tell me?" I grit out.

"I was under orders from your grandfather. But you've done it. He'll be pleased." He looks over his shoulder. "Let's go before the security comes back on. We have to be careful of the night guards. Morehouse and the other staff are all in bed."

I nod.

Agudelo is gone for the night, and I'll be gone by morning.

With both Serena and Daniela.

So the deal won't be finalized.

Mario won't care.

Because I have what he ultimately wanted me to get for him.

The drive to the airport is long, and the air in the car is tense. Serena is, of course, out of it, and Daniela is gripping the armrest for dear life, her nails digging into the leather.

It's clear that a lively conversation isn't going to help pass the time on the drive to the airport, so I get out my laptop. It's connected to the Internet through my phone.

Agudelo will try to come after me. Vega as well. And then

there's McAllister to deal with too. I have to figure out a way to make sure all three of them are taken care of.

First there's Vega. I have a feeling he'll be the slipperiest of them all. After all, he convinced my entire family that he was dead for years. And Mario Bianchi is a difficult man to deceive.

In my observations of Vega the last two weeks, I've noted only one consistency—he attends a local soccer match every Sunday in some sort of devotion to his roots. He invited me along to the game last weekend and bought me an empanada from a local street vendor, who recognized him immediately. Perhaps there's a way to poison him through there.

Then there's McAllister. I haven't gotten the chance to know him too well, besides our interactions at his home and then at the hospital. In both instances, I was otherwise occupied. First with Belinda, and then with my dying mother. I'll have to hire a private investigator to figure out his routine and then work from there. He will not be happy about my marriage to Daniela, so I'll have to make a strike on him pretty quickly as well.

I'll also have to figure out a way to make sure that Belinda is taken care of in the wake of her father's demise. I make a mental note to get in contact with some trusted sources with social services.

Which brings me to Agudelo. He will be the easiest. I've been able to observe him in pretty close quarters the past three weeks. His routine isn't terribly predictable, but his propensity for lavish parties is. Every weekend he hosts several of his friends at his mansion along with an assemblage of female escorts. Daniela, thank God, was no longer required to attend these parties after we announced our engagement, but I was still expected to make an appearance. Agudelo, even after the engagement, encouraged me to take one of the women to my bedroom, but of course I never did. His friends did, though. One by one they would disappear into one of the mansion's many bedrooms.

Agudelo himself would wait until the last of his friends had taken a woman and then retire to his study for a cigar, usually around midnight. That will be when he's at his most vulnerable. I send a few messages to some Bianchi allies on the ground here to see if they can't get in to one of those parties and take him out after he retires.

I bet there's an in through the waitstaff. He always hires a bunch to hand out booze and hors d'oeuvres. Maybe if I can hack into his finances, I can figure out which caterers he hires and go from there.

Luckily, this is something I'm quite good at. Every so often while I was in Europe, I had to scrape a few bucks off of some demented millionaire's bank account to keep my own funds safe. I make sure that my VPN is still secure and then open a custom hacking tool on my laptop—a program I coded myself while overseas, designed to exploit common vulnerabilities in financial databases. I know Agudelo keeps most of his money in the Banco de Bogotá, as I've seen his checkbook a few times whenever he's made payments. I access the bank's website and then launch a phishing attack, planting malware that allows me to bypass the security layers. Within minutes, I've gained access to Agudelo's encrypted financial records.

I skim through the information, looking for any information on who Agudelo has hired to cater his raucous parties. Looks like he's engaged the services of a place called "Sabor Ajiaco" for his last several events. That's my in.

I'm about to log off and wipe my digital trail clean when I notice a few big transfers of money from Agudelo's account. They've both been made in American dollars, which seems odd. The first is a $100,000 transfer to someone named J. Smith. I can't help a laugh. That's a fake name if I ever saw one.

But the next transfer makes my blood run cold.

Fifty million dollars. Dated the same day I flew to Colombia.

Made payable to the Raven's Wings Foundation.

Present Day...

The ballroom is buzzing with chatter, laughter, and the clinking of champagne glasses. Crystal chandeliers hang from the ceiling, casting sparkles over the elegantly dressed attendees. I stand near the entrance, greeting guests and keeping a watchful eye on the room. This event is crucial for the Bellamys' public image—and for my own plans.

I scan the crowd, pausing here and there on familiar faces. Politicians, businessmen, socialites—all here to support a good cause. The Raven's Wings Foundation is a noble effort, dedicated to funding blood cancer research and treatment. It's a legitimate cause, which makes my presence here all the more important.

Then I see her.

Raven.

She's standing near the stage, talking to a small group of admirers. Her short dark hair, barely grown out, catches the light and frames her face in a way that's both striking and delicate.

Her dark eyes shine with a light that's hard to ignore, her smile genuine as she speaks to her supporters. There's something about her, something raw and real, that pulls me in.

Has pulled me in since the first time I laid eyes on her, when her head was covered in dark peach fuzz. My heart beats faster in her presence, and my groin tightens. I can hardly breathe as images of devouring those full pink lips invade my mind.

They were the softest and sweetest lips I've ever kissed...

I draw in a breath and walk toward her, the need to be close to her nearly overwhelming me.

I should stay away. I promised to stay away.

But damn...

I weave through the crowd and nod at people I mostly don't recognize. After all, I've only been back in this country a couple months, not counting my time in Colombia. When I reach her, she's just finished her conversation and turns to face me.

"Vinnie," she says, her voice warm and inviting, as if what transpired between us never happened. "I'm glad you could make it."

"Raven." God, her lips. They glisten with a silvery effervescence. "I wouldn't miss it for the world. Congratulations on the event."

"Thank you," she says, her gaze locking onto mine. "It... means a lot to have your support."

For a moment, we stand there, the noise of the ballroom fading into the background. I'm struck by the depth in her eyes. She's been through hell and back—part of it due to me—yet she stands here, a pillar of strength.

Does she remember what we shared?

What we said to each other?

Of course she does. And she probably wants me to get the hell out of here. But for the sake of looking good for the board of her new foundation, she's remaining cordial.

What I really want to know is if, under her warm façade, her heart is breaking like mine is in this moment—this moment when we must pretend to be mere acquaintances.

"I have to admit," I say, leaning in slightly, "I'm impressed by what you've accomplished. The foundation, your journey... It's inspiring."

Her smile widens, a faint blush coloring her cheeks. "That means a lot...coming from you."

Does it?

Or is this part of the show?

Before I can respond, an amplified voice interrupts us.

"May I have your attention please."

I look toward the front of the ballroom where a man stands at the podium. Austin Bellamy, dressed like the Texas rancher he is. At first glance, his black tuxedo and crisp white shirt seem like normal cocktail attire, but the bolo tie with the turquoise gemstone slide shows his roots.

What *doesn't* show is the grisly side of him I've recently discovered.

"Thank you all for coming this evening to our gala in support of my daughter's new foundation, Raven's Wings. We won't take up a lot of your time, but it's only proper that the founder herself say a few words. Come up here, sweetheart."

Raven waves me off and makes her way through the crowd to step up to the microphone. The room falls silent, all eyes on her.

"Good evening, everyone," she begins, her voice clear and strong. "Thank you all for being here tonight and for supporting the Raven's Wings Foundation for the research and treatment of blood cancers. This foundation is incredibly personal to me, and I'd like to share a bit of my story with you." She pauses and scans the room. "A few years ago, I was diagnosed with leukemia. It was the most terrifying moment of my life. The uncertainty, the pain, the endless treatments—it was a battle I wasn't sure I could win. At first, I was overwhelmed by fear and despair. The thought of losing my life, of leaving my loved ones behind, haunted me day and night."

The audience is silent, hanging on her every word.

"I remember the nights spent in the hospital, staring at the ceiling, wondering if I would ever see another sunrise. Each day was a struggle, not just physically but emotionally and mentally. The treatments were brutal. There were days I couldn't get out of bed, days I wanted to give up. But through it all, I found strength in the love and support of my family. They were my rock, my reason to keep fighting."

She takes a deep breath, her eyes glistening with emotion.

"My brother Falcon was my greatest support. When the doctors said the traditional treatments for my type of leukemia had failed and that I needed a bone marrow transplant, he was the only match out of three brothers and a twin sister. Without a second thought, he stepped up and gave me the ultimate gift."

Without a second thought? Raven's need got him an early

release from prison, though I understand why Raven isn't mentioning that fact. Everyone here knows anyway.

"His bone marrow saved my life. His selfless act cured me, and I stand here today, cancer-free, because of him. Falcon, thank you from the bottom of my heart."

Across the room, I see Falcon Bellamy stand up and nod at his sister. He looks good in a tux, but it's so odd seeing him in anything other than ranch wear. Savannah is beaming next to him in a midnight-blue gown. Neither of them looks at me. They might not even have realized I'm here.

The audience applauds, some wiping away tears.

"But our journey didn't end there," she continues, her voice gaining strength. "Surviving cancer gave me a new purpose. I knew I had to give back, to help others facing the same battle. That's why I founded the Raven's Wings Foundation. Our mission is to fund research and provide treatment for blood cancers, to give hope to those who need it most."

She pauses, looking around the room, her gaze firm and determined.

"I want to share a moment that changed my perspective during my treatment. The night after the transplant, I should have been ecstatic, but I was feeling particularly low. I was tired of the pain, the uncertainty. I felt like I was losing myself. My brother Falcon sat beside me, held my hand, and told me that it was okay to be scared, that it was okay to feel weak. He reminded me that being strong doesn't mean never feeling fear or pain—it means pushing through despite those feelings. It was in that moment that I realized strength isn't about never falling. It's about getting back up every time you do."

I can almost hear the words in Falcon's voice. He was

speaking about his time behind bars. Savannah has told me
that he learned that survival on the inside depended on
internal as well as external strength.

The room is silent. I look around at the awed faces.
Everyone seems captivated by Raven's words.

"This foundation is not just about finding a cure. It's
about supporting patients and their families, about providing
hope and strength to those in the darkest moments of their
lives. Tonight, your generosity will help us continue this vital
work. Together, we can make a difference. Together, we can
give hope to those who need it most."

She steps back from the microphone and the room erupts
in applause. As she makes her way down from the stage, she
catches my eye and smiles.

As the applause dies down, I know two things for certain.

One—I've given up Raven Bellamy for her own good, but
I'll never love another. Not even the gorgeous woman, my
blushing bride, who I brought to this event as my plus-one.

And two—

I will kill a man tonight to protect her.

19

***

RAVEN

It's not difficult to smile at Vinnie.

He's Vinnie, after all. He may have left me, but I don't for one minute believe he doesn't love me. He may have a beautiful young woman on his arm—more beautiful than I could ever be—but I still believe he has feelings for me.

Why else would he be here tonight?

He certainly didn't have to shell out the three thousand dollars per plate to get a last-minute ticket to the gala.

But he did.

He did it for me. To support my endeavor.

That's what I choose to think, anyway.

When we talked, his date wasn't with him. He didn't mention her, and I didn't mention her either.

None of my business, after all.

I did my best to paste on a smile and treat him like any other potential donor. I'm a better actress than I thought.

I make my way through the crowds, stopping to chat to

individual donors and other guests. With warm gratitude, I take many large checks that are given to me.

Raven's Wings is doing well tonight. My heart bursts when I think about the many people we'll be able to help. The research we'll be able to fund.

At some point, I have to figure out which one of these guests is Mr. Smith, the person who gave me the fifty million dollars. I want to pull him aside discreetly and thank him, but I haven't been able to locate him yet.

"Ms. Bellamy," a voice says.

I turn to face Dr. Landon Michaels, the oncologist who agreed to sit on our board. I recognize him from the photo on his website.

"Dr. Michaels"—I take his hand—"it's such a thrill to finally meet you in person. Once again, I can't thank you enough for being willing to serve on the board to lend your expertise."

He smiles warmly. "When you called me, I couldn't say no. I believe in what you're doing here." He scans the crowd. "Your sister and your attorney have been wonderful to work with, but"—he looks back at me—"I know working with you will be even more of a pleasure."

I nod. "I appreciate your confidence in me."

He looks me up and down. "If you don't mind my asking, which physicians treated you?"

"I don't mind at all. I was privileged to be treated by several amazing physicians, Dr. Leonard Smith and Dr. Victoria Jensen among them."

"Both excellent in their field," Dr. Michaels says. "I'm so glad they were able to get you into remission."

"Yes, so am I." I chuckle nervously. "But unfortunately

standard treatment didn't work for me. I actually owe my life to my brother Falcon. He donated the blood marrow that saved me."

"You mentioned that in your speech." He clears his throat. "Would you care to dance?"

My hands become clammy. Dr. Michaels is a nice-looking man—light-brown hair with a little bit of silver around his temples. Lovely green eyes. And tall. I like tall men.

His shoulders aren't as broad as Vinnie's. And his facial features aren't as sharp, as rugged.

But screw Vinnie. He has his own date. The dance floor is beginning to fill up, and the string quartet is playing a waltz. Later, a DJ will come out to play more contemporary tunes.

I hate myself for it, but I do a quick scan of the room to see if Vinnie is within eyeshot. He's not on the dance floor. In fact, I don't see him or his date. I turn back to Dr. Michaels. "I would love to dance with you, Doctor."

I let him lead me to the dance floor. I put my right hand into his left and place my left hand on his shoulder, while he slides his right hand around my waist and pulls me closer than I'm comfortable with.

I step back just a touch.

He seems to get the message.

I know how to waltz, but my goodness, it's been a long time.

It comes back to me quickly, and Dr. Michaels is a fluid dancer and an excellent leader. I'm proud that I don't step on his feet at all.

I catch a glimpse of Jared standing on the edge of the wall, watching me like a hawk.

And then my brother, Hawk, also watching me like his namesake.

Falcon and Savannah are dancing, as are my mother and father.

Robin is dancing with a man I don't recognize. She didn't come with a date, so good for her.

Eagle is still sitting at the table, his hands folded together. He looks uneasy. I'll never stop worrying about him.

Leif Ramsey is on the dance floor with his beautiful wife, Kelly, a fiery redhead.

Dr. Michaels and I don't speak much, and when the dance ends, I give him a smile. "Thank you."

"May I get you a drink?" he asks.

I shake my head. "I'm keeping my alcohol consumption to a minimum. Although I have to admit those prickly pear margaritas look amazing."

"I'm not much for sweet drinks," he says, "but since it was the specialty cocktail of the evening, I tried it. It's actually on the tart side. Quite delicious. Are you sure you can't try at least one? Doctor's orders?"

I sigh. "You know? I will try one. Thank you."

He leads me to one of the bars where the line is only two deep at this point. Once we get to the bar, the bartender smiles at me. "Ms. Bellamy, what is your pleasure?"

I open my mouth, but Dr. Michaels speaks first.

"A prickly pear margarita for the lady, please. And I'll have a Macallan, neat."

"Of course, sir."

I'm a little taken aback. I don't particularly like men speaking for me. Dr. Michaels is probably trying to impress me.

The bartender prepares my margarita and hands it to me. I take a tiny sip.

Dr. Michaels is right. It is tart. A good tart, with just a touch of sweetness, and then of course the smokiness of the tequila.

"Delicious," I say.

"Thank you," the bartender says as he slides Dr. Michaels his glass of scotch.

"Obliged." Dr. Michaels hands the bartender a fifty-dollar bill.

The gala has an open bar. Tips aren't exactly discouraged, but they're not required. The foundation will be tipping the bar staff at the end of the night based on the final totals.

But Dr. Michaels is trying to impress me again.

I wish it were working.

"And thank *you* very much, sir." the bartender says with bright eyes.

Dr. Michaels looks back at me with a cheeky smile. Yeah. The fifty-dollar tip was a flex.

Then again, Dr. Michaels is a successful oncologist. Perhaps he's a legitimately generous man, wanting to pay it forward to someone who likely makes a tenth of what he does.

But I'm not buying it. Maybe it's because my gut is right about Dr. Michaels, or maybe I'm just comparing him to the version of Vinnie I thought existed until a few weeks ago.

He leads me to one of the bar tables and sets our drinks down. He takes a seat.

I'm not comfortable spending any more time with him when I have an entire gala of people I need to talk to.

I pop down in the seat across from him and paste a smile

on. "Thank you so much for the dance and for the drink, Dr. Michaels. If you'll excuse me, I need to mingle."

"Oh?" He lays his hand over mine. "I was hoping we could spend more time together."

"You can call my office anytime." I slide my hand out from under his and stand.

"Better than that." He gets to his feet. "How about dinner next weekend?"

Way to be put on the spot. I grab my handbag and fidget with it to give me a second to come up with some sort of gentle rejection.

But then I reconsider. Vinnie has moved on. Why the hell shouldn't I?

"Sure." I give Dr. Michaels another smile. "That sounds lovely. Give me a call and we'll set it up."

"Wonderful. There's a new Spanish-Asian fusion restaurant I've been dying to try."

I smile and whisk away, only to be stopped again soon by another attendee.

"Wonderful job, Ms. Bellamy. I wish you the best of luck." The speaker is a man I don't recognize.

"Thank you so much, sir, and thank you for coming."

Next, two women stop me. "Lovely time. Please accept this donation."

I know better than to look at the amount. I simply take the check. "Thank you so much for your generosity. Thank you for being here and for your support."

Onto the next, as I glance across the room to see Jared with his eyes on me.

And then, a hand clamps on my shoulder.

I turn to see Vinnie.

"Vinnie," I gasp.

"I need you to come with me, Raven," he says.

"I'm in the middle of my gala."

"Please. It's urgent."

"The silent auction will be ending soon. I have to announce that—"

He pulls me away toward the nearest exit.

Across the room I see Jared running after us.

A moment later, we're inside a small conference room, no lights on.

Vinnie clicks the door shut.

"I couldn't stay away from you," he says.

And then his mouth comes down on mine.

20

VINNIE

I push my tongue between Raven's lips. God, she tastes so sweet. A bit of smoke from tequila, sweetness from the tres leches cake.

And just her.

Yes, the sweetest lips I've ever tasted.

They're even sweeter now after a month away from her.

Her bodyguard will come soon.

All I can do is kiss her.

But a moment later, she pushes at my shoulders, breaking the kiss with a loud smack.

"Vinnie..."

I caress her cheek. "My God, I've missed you."

She wraps her hand around my wrist. "You have a date. I have—"

"A bodyguard. I know."

"He's been watching me with eagle eyes all night." She cranes her neck over her left shoulder. "He'll know you dragged me in here."

"I know." I narrow my eyes at her. "I've locked the door, Raven."

She raises her eyebrows—she has eyebrows now, and she's so damned beautiful. "He'll consider you a threat."

I bore my gaze into her. "And you, Raven? Do *you* consider me a threat?"

I crush my lips to hers once more.

Her eyes flicker with a mixture of fear, surprise, and desire as she pushes me away again. "Vinnie..." she whispers against my mouth, but this time her voice trails off into silence, uncertainty clouding her usually fiery eyes.

"Do you?" I press again, my voice husky, but I don't give her the chance to respond. Instead, I seize her in my arms once more and press my lips against hers.

This time, she doesn't pull away.

My heart pounds as she clutches at the sleeves of my jacket. I'm lost in her, drowning in the taste of tequila on her tongue and the feeling of her body pressed against mine.

But then reality intrudes. The sound of heavy footsteps outside the door brings us back to earth.

"He's coming," Raven breathes against my mouth.

"Let him," I growl. I have her in my arms, and I'll be damned if anyone takes her from me now.

She shakes her head, pulling away from me with visible regret. "Vinnie, we can't. Not here, and not now."

I drop my hands to her waist, anchoring her to me as the footsteps draw closer. "Then when, Raven? I need you."

Before she can answer, a loud knock sounds on the door. Raven flinches at the noise, her eyes fluttering shut as if she's bracing for a blow.

One final glance into those dark eyes and I pull her back to me again, stealing one last kiss like a thief in the night. The taste of tequila and cream lingers on my lips as I pull away.

She trembles slightly as she entwines her fingers with mine, a silent plea shimmering within her gaze.

The knock on the door grows more insistent, a gruff voice following it. "Raven? Everything all right in there?"

"Stay," I whisper against her lips, my eyes locked onto hers.

She gives me a small nod before stepping away and straightening her dress as she moves toward the door. Her glance back at me is full of promises and unspoken words.

She opens the door, revealing her burly bodyguard. "I'm fine. Please. Let me be." Before he can protest, she closes the door and locks it again.

"I'm yours, Vinnie," she says. "Please. I need you too."

I pull her back into my embrace, pressing my lips onto hers. This time there's no fear in her eyes, only a burning desire that matches my own. Our bodies meld together as if they were two pieces of a puzzle that have finally clicked together.

The world outside the door doesn't exist for us right now. It's just us, breathing each other's air.

But then she pulls away again and looks at me with those dark eyes that speak volumes. "Vinnie," she whispers, her voice shaky. "Promise me this isn't just tonight."

I cup her face in my hands and gaze into her eyes, wishing I could grant her wish.

I want nothing more than to be with this woman forever.

But not until I can guarantee her safety.

So I don't reply. I simply reach under her gorgeous green gown. "I can smell you," I say. "I can smell how wet you are for me."

A blush creeps up her neck as she bites her lower lip, her eyes filled with equal parts embarrassment and anticipation. She grips my shoulders. "Vinnie..."

"I want to taste you, Raven. I want to make you moan my name over and over again."

She shivers at that, a small groan escaping her lips. It's the most delectable sound I've ever heard.

I kneel, shove her dress up around her waist, and inhale the sweet nectar between her legs.

It's dark in the room, but I remember the beauty of her pussy, how red, sweet, and succulent it is.

I trace my fingers over the lace of her panties, eliciting another gasp from her.

I push the fabric to the side and run a finger over her slick folds. She moans out loud at the touch and clutches at my hair.

The taste takes me by surprise. It's even sweeter than I remember. I bury my face between her and explore every inch of her with my tongue.

Her moans fill the room, each one louder than the last as I work my magic on her. She weaves her fingers through my hair, tugging in rhythm with the strokes of my tongue.

Her breathing grows heavy, her chest heaving with every gasp as I continue to pleasure her. She digs her nails into my scalp.

I take my time with her, savoring the taste and feel of her under my touch. I grip her hips to hold her steady as she writhes against me. Each moan and gasp drives me on further.

Without warning, she climaxes, her body convulsing as I continue my assault. She cries out my name, the sound echoing in the small room and sending shivers through me.

And then she sinks to the floor next to me, panting. Her eyes are closed, but a satisfied smile plays on her lips. Slowly, she reaches out to me, pulling me into an embrace. We stay there for a while, just holding each other.

But my hard cock needs more. I need to be inside her. Inside Raven just once more.

This dark conference room is hardly a lush bedroom, and she deserves better.

But I need her.

And I believe she needs me just as much.

She opens her eyes and casts her gaze to the bulge beneath my pants. She swallows, a rush of pink flooding her cheeks, yet she doesn't shy away from my need for her.

"Vinnie." She traces the hardness straining against the fabric of my pants.

The touch sends bolts of pleasure shooting through me.

Without another word, I quickly release my aching cock. Her breath hitches in her throat as she takes in the sight of me.

"Raven…" It's barely a whisper, but it carries all the depth of my need for her.

She nods, licking her lips. I guide one of her hands to stroke me. I'm being gentle with her, but I don't want to be.

I want to thrust inside her, make her scream in pleasure and pain.

I want to claim her as mine, in every sense of the word.

"Look at me," I command, my voice hoarse with anticipation.

Raven does as she is told, her eyes meeting mine, the lust in them mirroring my own.

My heart pounds as I push her back onto the floor and thrust inside her.

21

RAVEN

He's inside me.

I'm so full, so complete.

Still so sensitive from my climax.

"You like that?" he says, his teeth clenched. "You like how I feel inside you, baby?"

"Please," I whimper. "Don't stop."

His response is a guttural growl, his body moving in rhythm with mine. His muscles are taut, powerful, and each movement sends a pulsing wave of pleasure through me. He's relentless, his desire matching mine. He pushes deeper. I gasp, clutching onto him as I take in the overwhelming sensation.

"Take it, Raven," he grits out. "Take me. Take all of me."

I'm only too happy to take all of him.

I wish he'd never stop.

I wish I could capture this moment in time. This moment where there's only Vinnie.

Only me.

Only us.

"I need you," I whisper into his ear, my voice shaking.

"And I you," he growls back.

He quickens his pace and there's no more room for words, our gasps and moans the only language we share.

Each thrust pushes me closer and closer to the edge, a crescendo of pleasure building up within me. It's intoxicating, overpowering. It's almost too much to bear.

Above me, Vinnie is a vision of raw masculinity. His chest rises and falls with each labored breath. His face is a mask of concentration, of pure, unadulterated lust.

"Don't stop...." I beg again.

Then lightning.

Thunder.

The all-consuming wave hits me out of nowhere and surges through my body like an electric current, stealing my breath away.

Vinnie throws his head back and roars.

I feel every pulse of his release. Every. Single. One.

We lie there, bodies intertwined, our breath mingling in the quiet space between our parted lips. The pulsing rhythm of our hearts begins to slow, returning to a calm beat that echoes through the silence.

"Raven," he murmurs, his voice husky. "You're incredible."

I look into his eyes and see a universe of emotions swirling within them—desire, satisfaction, gratitude.

Love.

And...regret.

"I feel the same about you," I whisper, snuggling closer to him.

"Fuck." He pulls out of me and shoves his cock back into his pants. "How the fuck am I supposed to live without you?"

"You chose to leave me," I say.

He doesn't respond.

He knows the truth as well as I do.

Finally, "You know I had to do that."

I sigh. "I know you *said* you had to do it."

"Do you think I would have you in danger?" He shakes his head. "You're in danger right now. More than you know."

"You and I are the only two people in here." I raise an eyebrow. "Unless you're a danger to me?"

"I am." He pounds a fist against his chest. "Because of the name I carry. The genes I carry. The business I—"

I rub my forehead "For the love of God, Vinnie, shut up. This isn't anything I haven't heard a million times before. You can't be with me. I'm in danger when I'm with you. Let me tell you something. I faced death. I faced my own mortality. And I've decided that I would rather live one second of wonderful than a lifetime without the man I love."

Even in the dim light, I see the hard lines of his face soften.

"Do you find that surprising?" I ask.

"To the contrary," he says. "I understand more than you know. But let me tell *you* something, Raven. I don't want to live in a world without you in it. I would rather you be alive and safe and healthy, even if it means not being with me."

I scoff. "Well, despite what just happened between us, it appears you got over me pretty quickly."

He furrows his brow. "What's that supposed to mean?"

I look down. "You came here tonight with a woman on your arm, Vinnie. A very beautiful woman. A very young woman. Seems I was pretty easily replaced after all." I sigh. "I used to have hair like that, you know. Hair like my sister. Like my brothers."

He moves my dress back around my waist and over my legs. Then he reaches out to my hair, touches the short locks that don't yet cover my ears. "Your hair is beautiful, Raven. Even without hair, you are the most beautiful woman I've ever laid eyes on."

Words he's said before. Words that made me tremble all over the first time he said them.

But now? Even though they still make me shiver? I hear them for what they truly are.

Simply words.

I cross my arms. "So you're not going to explain to me why you're here with that woman?"

"Do you truly want to know, Raven?"

"Yes. I do."

"Then understand this. What I'm about to tell you is going to sound shocking, but I need you to promise me that you'll allow me to explain. I have a reason for everything I've done."

"Fine. Go on."

"Her name is Daniela. Daniela Agudelo. And she's my wife."

22

VINNIE

Raven's beautiful face goes still, like she's frozen mid-breath. For a second, she doesn't say anything, just blinks, and I can see her processing the words. The light in her eyes dims.

I see shock, hurt, betrayal.

Her lips part slightly, like she's about to say something, but nothing comes out. She just stares at me, her jaw tightening as if she's trying to hold back a wave of emotions. A flicker of anger, too, a flash that she tries to hide, but it's there, raw and sharp.

And then, just like that, she pulls back, as if I'm a stranger she's never met, her face becoming a mask—closed off and unreadable. The silence between us is heavy, suffocating.

"It means nothing, Raven," I tell her.

She shakes her head. "I thought you were supposed to marry Belinda."

"Plans have changed. And not everyone is happy about them."

"Myself included," she says.

I grab her hands. "Raven, I love only you. I'll never love anyone but you."

"Yet how easy it was for you to marry another." She snaps her hands out of mine and smooths them down her dress. "I should really get back to the gala. God knows what I must look like. I'm going to go to the ladies' room."

"You look beautiful."

She grabs her clutch and takes out a compact mirror, examining her reflection. "I'm sure you kissed all of my lipstick off."

"You don't need lipstick, Raven. You're perfect just as God made you."

She throws the compact onto the floor, scattering tiny shards of glass around her. "God made me with hair, Vinnie! Then He saw fit to take it away." She shakes her head vehemently. "No! I won't let you make me go there. I made it through the storm, Vinnie. I won't go back there. Not for anything. Not even for you."

"Don't you see?" I say. "You and I want the same thing then. I want you to live your life. Have a long happy healthy life that you deserve. I'd rather you have that, even if it's not with me."

"Well, you've made your point. It's not with you. You've married someone else."

"I told you it means nothing," I say for the third time. "It's business. Simply a business arrangement. Just like it was supposed to be with Belinda."

She pushes my shoulders with more strength than I knew she had. "You've made your choice, Vinnie."

"Yes. I've chosen you, Raven. I've chosen your life. You're in danger if you're anywhere near me. I shouldn't have come in here with you. I should've been able to control myself."

She sears her gaze into me with so much fire that I actually take a step back. "Why didn't you? You've got a beautiful wife—younger and with more hair—who you could've satiated yourself with. You don't need me."

Christ. If only I *didn't* need her.

Both of our lives would be so much easier. Less dangerous.

She has no idea what her father is up to. And I don't know enough about it yet either, since I left Colombia in secret in the dark.

Perhaps Bellamy is being blackmailed. Forced into doing the cartel's bidding.

His land is right on the border, a perfect place for mules.

Then again, he's the heir to the Cooper Steel fortune. He has billions. He could stop the cartel if he wanted to.

Or maybe he couldn't.

There is one thing money *can't* buy.

It can't buy life.

It can't replace the person you love.

Which is the reason I've chosen to stay away from Raven.

And clearly I'm terrible at it.

"So how was she?" Raven asks.

"What?"

"Your hot little wife. What kind of a fuck is she, Vinnie? How does it feel to grab her long hair in your hands and yank on it as you sink yourself inside her?"

"I don't know," I say. "I told you it's business only. I haven't slept with her."

She rolls her eyes. "Right. Because I'm just *that* gullible."

"I don't believe you're gullible at all. I believe you have an incredible zest for life that most people don't." I run my hand up and down her arm. "You see things that most people don't. That's the opposite of gullible, Raven."

She slaps my hand away. "You really expect me to believe you didn't take that beautiful woman to bed?"

"I don't expect you to believe anything." I run my hands through my hair. "I can only tell you the truth. The truth is that I have not slept with Daniela, and I have no plans to. I've told you that it's a business arrangement. She understands it as well as I do."

She sighs. "I wish I could believe you."

I cup her cheeks, stare into her beautiful brown eyes. "You *can* believe me, Raven. I haven't slept with her, and I won't. But that changes nothing between us."

"Then what was this about then?" She gestures around the room. "You dragging me into this dark conference room? Fucking me? Kissing me?"

I let out a humorless chuckle. "I don't seem to have any self-control when you're around."

"I suppose I don't either." Her lips twitch.

I close in on her. "Do you regret it?"

She presses her lips together. "Of course not," she mutters. "I'll never regret any of it, Vinnie."

I want to tell her that I won't either. Because in most ways I won't, except for one.

I just hope this little tryst didn't put her in any further danger.

I grab her by the shoulders and lean in, my voice lowered. "I need you to listen to me, Raven. Listen good. There's a man at the gala tonight. A man who wants you dead."

She gasps, darting her gaze around the room. "My father is here. Jared is here. My three brothers are here. Do you really think anyone will get near me? He'd have to go through all of them."

"Those people can't protect you if they don't know who the threat is."

"Then tell me who it is," she says.

"I wish I could." I frown. "The truth of the matter is that I don't know for sure. I only know that a very bad man who I met in Colombia made a huge donation to your charity and a subsequent smaller payment to someone who I think might try to hurt you."

She widens her eyes. "How much was the donation? I've been taking checks all night."

"He didn't make the donation tonight. He made it the day I left for Colombia. Fifty million."

She slaps her hand over her mouth. "Oh, my God."

I narrow my eyes at her. "So you're aware."

"That fifty million was sent to my attorney, Emily," she says. "It was made anonymously, but then I got a call a week or so later from someone claiming to be the person who sent it. But I had no idea he might be in Colombia, or that he would have anything to do with you. He didn't have an accent or anything." She eyes me uneasily. "What was his name? The man who made the donation?"

"Daniela's father. Jacinto Agudelo."

She lets out a sigh of relief. "Oh, thank God. The call was from a Mr. Smith."

I grit my teeth. "A Mr. J. Smith?"

She bites her lip. "Jack Smith, yes."

"And he's here tonight?"

"He requested an invite. I couldn't turn down the guy who made a fifty-million-dollar donation, Vinnie."

I rub at my forehead. "And you just...*believed* him when he said he made the donation?"

"He knew about the donation. He knew it had been made directly to my attorney." She crosses her arms. "I'm not a dumbass, Vinnie."

"Has he checked in?" I ask.

"I have no idea. I haven't met him yet." She pulls out her phone and pulls up a file. "But I have the seating chart. I can tell you where he had dinner. I'll send it to you." She scrolls through her phone a second more. "Is he the one who's been sending me texts?"

I raise my eyebrows. "You've been getting texts?"

"Yes. On my regular phone. I got a threatening text. But on that burner phone—the one the fake Uber driver gave me —I've been getting texts warning me. Warning me that I'm in danger."

Damn. Austin Bellamy. He's the one who was behind the Uber driver hijacking Raven. But Raven doesn't know that.

Which means... Raven's own father knows she's in danger. He's trying to warn her.

But of course he can't let on how much he knows. Then she—and the rest of her family—will know of his involvement. Or at least suspect it.

I still have a lot of questions about Austin Bellamy. About his involvement with Diego Vega. About why Falcon went to prison. About who is buried underneath that old barn on their property. About his involvement with the cartels and "Operation Falcon."

"Do you know who's been sending the threatening texts, Vinnie? Because if you do, you have to tell me."

It could be anyone. It could be Smith. Or Vega himself. It could be Agudelo. It could be McAllister. Hell, it could be Mario.

After tomorrow, though, Mario will be in my debt.

I have what he wants more than anything. And the cost will be his empire.

23

RAVEN

If Vinnie knows, he's not responding.

"That's what I thought," I say. "I've got to get back to the gala."

I whisk past him this time, unlock the door to the conference room, and open the door.

Jared is waiting on the other side.

"Raven..."

I hold up a hand. "Please, you're not my father, Jared. You're my bodyguard. I don't need a good talking to right now. I don't need for you to tell me what a big mistake it was for me to go in there with Vinnie. What I do need is for you to escort me to the ladies' room."

"Of course," he says.

I don't know what to think about this situation with Mr. Smith, but I do know that I have a job to do tonight. Vinnie can figure out who Smith is and take him aside if necessary. Right now, I have to doll myself back up and keep playing hostess. Vinnie is here, Jared is here, and multiple generations of burly Bellamy men are here to protect me.

I get to the restroom door. "Keep guard here at the door and don't let anyone else in until I leave," I tell Jared. "I'll just be a moment."

Once I'm in the restroom, I smooth out my dress once more, check my face. My makeup looks good, though my lips are swollen and puffy from Vinnie's kisses, and my lipstick is nonexistent.

Still, my lips have a nice pink tone, so they'll do. I apply a little setting powder to keep my makeup from smudging, and I riffle through my clutch to find my lipstick.

I return to the ballroom, where the DJ has begun his set. Couples are on the dance floor, dancing to the hits of the seventies and eighties. The majority of my most likely donors are of that generation, so I curated the playlist specifically to get them in a good mood.

I head back to the table when Hawk waylays me. "Where the hell have you been?"

I blink a few times. "Just taking a break. Jared was with me the whole time."

Hawk gives Jared a stink eye. "Where has she been?"

"My brother seems to think he's my keeper," I say to Jared. "You don't need to answer that."

"She's fine," Jared says. "I take my position seriously."

Hawk simply nods.

I decide to change the subject.

"I'd say the gala is a success," I say nonchalantly.

Out of the corner of my eye, I see Vinnie. He's gathering his wife—God, his *wife*—and leaving.

Good. It's better that I don't see him.

"Who is that woman?" Hawk asks.

I roll my eyes. "Vinnie has apparently taken a new bride."

Hawk drops his jaw. "He's married to her?"

"Yes, he is," I snap. "And I would absolutely love it if we didn't discuss the matter further, Hawk."

I don't let him get a response in before I move away. I make small talk with a few more guests, and then I see Vinnie again, this time entering the ballroom without his new bride.

Where did she go?

Not my business, I suppose.

I work the room a bit, shaking hands and thanking people for their donations.

A moment later, the DJ takes a break and Emily mans the microphone.

"Good evening, ladies and gentlemen, and thank you for being here again. This is just a quick reminder that our silent auction will close in ten minutes, so get those last-minute bids in. Every dollar of each highest bid will go toward the Raven's Wings Foundation. With your help, we will continue our work of helping families dealing with blood cancers and helping research facilities find new ways to treat and cure them."

People head to the tables to make their bids, while I approach the bar to get something to drink. My mouth and throat are dry.

"Orange Crush, please," I say.

The bartender nods. "Of course, Ms. Bellamy. Coming right up."

He hands me my drink, and I take a sip of the sparkling orange soda, moving out of the way for the others in line. I sigh. Still tastes like sunshine.

Emily takes the mic once again after the bell rings to signal the end of the silent auction.

"Ladies and gentlemen, that bell signifies the end of our silent auction for this evening. We'll be announcing the winners one at a time. So let's get moving." She smiles. "First of all, the winner of our big-ticket item for the evening, the Caribbean cruise for two, is Brandon Brown."

I watch as the winner is congratulated by the people around him.

"Our cashiers are set up at the back of the room, so please make payment for your item before you leave tonight, and congratulations!"

She goes through the rest of the big-ticket items, including season tickets to the Texas Longhorns, a year's supply of prime beef from my father's ranch, a year's supply of fine wine from Steel Vinyards in Colorado, three nights in Las Vegas, and a motor scooter.

Then the smaller ticket items.

I simply stand and sip my Orange Crush while Jared watches me.

I'm thrilled at all the huge high bids we got. We've made a ton of money for—

"Raven Bellamy, congratulations!"

I jerk as Emily calls my name.

I didn't bid on anything.

"Congratulations, Raven," someone says to me, walking by.

"Yeah. Thank you."

We decided earlier not to prohibit our board members from bidding. If they wanted to bid and give extra to the organization, we were happy to have their support.

But I didn't bid on anything.

Someone must've bid in my name.

I walk through the crowd to find Robin, who is equipped with an iPad that shows all the bidders and winners.

"Robbie," I say. "I didn't bid on anything."

"Strange. It says here that you did. In fact, you're the only bid."

"That's so strange. I didn't even sign up to bid."

"It says right here, Ray. You won the gold pendant." She walks to the table and holds up a black velvet box. "Here it is."

The gold pendant? I don't remember that being on our list of items for the silent auction. Then again, I was organizing this whole event remotely. It could have easily slipped my mind.

But who could have bought this for me? Dad, probably. He's really proud of how all of this turned out.

I take the box from her and open it. I gasp. "It's gorgeous!" It's a pendant in the shape of a bird covered in black crystals with a small sapphire for its eye. It's large, about two inches in diameter, and suspended from a link chain. I turn the pendant over—

And I gulp, nearly losing my footing.

It's engraved on the back.

Even the raven can't fly forever. Sooner or later, it comes home to die.

24

VINNIE

He's here.

I feel his presence.

I just have to ferret him out.

Someone is here for Raven. Is her life in danger? I doubt it. But her freedom is.

If she's dead, she can't be used as a chip to bargain with. And someone here wants to bargain with me.

Or with Mario.

Perhaps even with McAllister.

And that person is here.

Evil is something that can be smelled. When you've been around it your whole life, you learn to recognize it, even if it's not physically present. It slinks like a shadow, weaving in and out of consciousness. You can smell its foul odor, like something rotting beneath the floorboards of an abandoned house.

I move through the crowd, scanning faces, studying body language, listening to whispered conversations. I catch a whiff of that stench. The scent isn't strong enough to pinpoint the source, but I know he's close.

Luckily, I have Raven's seating chart. I make my way to the table where Jack Smith is assigned. There are three middle-aged women dressed lavishly sitting at the table, but that's it.

"Pardon me, ladies," I say. "Was there a gentleman seated with you this evening? A Mr. Smith? I've found one half of a pair of monogrammed cufflinks that I believe belong to him, but I don't know what he looks like."

The lady in the center, wearing a mink stole over a light-green gown, shoots me a smile. "Goodness, we certainly are getting our fill of handsome gentlemen tonight, aren't we girls?"

The other two ladies giggle.

"You're very kind," I say, "but I am serious about the cuff-links. They look very expensive. I'm sure Mr. Smith would hate to be missing one of them."

The woman on the right, wearing purple and a diamond necklace, runs her hand through her platinum blond hair. "Are you talking about Jackie?"

I press my lips together. "Jack Smith? Possibly."

"Yes, he was here," the woman on the left—this one in crimson and wearing an enormous star-shaped sapphire brooch—responds. "Gladys, Henrietta, and I were so happy to have him at our table. Very handsome, very tall, very charming."

The woman in green—Gladys, possibly—takes a sip of champagne. "Prudence here might have just found her fourth husband."

All three of them erupt into laughter.

God, they're drunk.

"Was he wearing anything special?" I ask. "Most of the men here are in tuxes, but if he had a colorful bow tie or something..."

"No special bow tie." Henrietta wrinkles her nose. "And what a nice change of pace to see a man in traditional black tie. These days you have all these wacky fashions—"

"But he did have that lovely pocket square, Henny," Prudence retorts.

There's my in. "What did the pocket square look like?"

Gladys bites her lip. "Black and white. A... Oh, what do you call it? A dogleg pattern?"

"Houndstooth," Henrietta says.

"That's it," Gladys says. "Houndstooth."

"Thank you," I say. "That should help narrow him down. How long ago did he leave the table?"

"Not long ago." Prudence checks her slim Rolex. "Maybe ten minutes ago. He was headed to the dance floor, I believe."

"He invited us, of course." Gladys fans herself. "But these old knees have danced their last polka."

The three of them start cackling again.

"What about his hair? Was it dark, blond, gray?"

"Not a gray hair to be seen, darling," Prudence says. "Very dark hair. Couldn't be more than thirty-five."

"Thank you, ladies. Have a pleasant evening."

I give them a wink, and that of course sends them into another fit of laughter.

I head to the dance floor. People are moving and grooving to the beats of some disco song. I keep my eyes peeled. Finally I catch a fleeting glimpse of a man on the corner of the dance floor. He's tall, dark. Handsome in a dangerous sort of way. His eyes meet mine across the room.

Sure enough, his pocket square matches the ladies' description. I've found Jack Smith. My target for the evening.

A chill runs through me as a wicked grin spreads across his face. He knows that I know.

Is that him? Is he the threat to Raven?

He disappears into the crowd before I can get a better look at him. But I've seen enough. Something about him raises the hairs on the back of my neck. An animal instinct that warns me of imminent danger.

I push through the crowd, trying to follow his trail, but the sea of bodies surges around me and I lose him. I lean against a wall, scanning the room once more. Then I see him again, standing on the fringes of a group, watching me. He lifts his glass in a mocking toast and then turns away.

This time he doesn't vanish into the crowd. Instead, he leads me out of the ballroom and through the corridor that leads to the first-floor suites. He turns to face me, that same smug grin still pasted on his face.

"Gallo," he says, his voice smooth but laced with venom. "Or should I call you Little Cobra?"

Only Vega called me Little Cobra. So who the hell is this?

"Leave her alone," I say.

"I have my orders," he replies.

"I have new orders for you." I pull a pistol out of my ankle strap and point it at his head. "Stay away from Raven."

"You don't know who you're dealing with," he says.

"I don't particularly give a rat's ass. Anyone who threatens Raven—"

"You just don't get it, do you?" he says. "That necklace wasn't my idea. It was—"

I close the distance between us, pushing the nose of the gun to his temple. "What necklace?"

"The raven pendant." He grins. "The one she's holding now in her trembling fingers."

"Tell me everything you know, or be prepared to meet your maker."

He sniffs arrogantly. "You don't have it in you to kill."

I can't help a chuckle at that one. "Clearly you don't know anything about me. I don't know who sent you, but whoever it was hasn't done his homework."

He scoffs. "Are you kidding me? Of course he's done his homework. We know all about that Russian you killed in Eastern Europe. We know about Puzo. Self-defense and a peanut butter allergy? You've never killed a man in cold blood."

I push the gun into his temple. "Like I said, you didn't do your homework."

I'm bluffing, of course. Those were my only two kills. But I'm about to have a third, and it's going to be tonight.

I came here knowing I might have to kill a man to protect Raven. I came here prepared, and I came here knowing that I can do whatever I want. My grandfather will take care of everything.

Because I have what he wants.

I have *his* Achilles' heel.

"Who are you?" I demand again. "And who sent you?"

"You wouldn't believe me if I told you."

"Vega? McAllister? Agudelo?"

"Could be." He twists his lips. "But it seems to me, Little Cobra, you're not looking close enough to home."

Mario?

As evil as my biological father is, I don't believe he would kill someone who means so much to me.

Who else is close to home?

There's Austin Bellamy, of course. But no way would he allow his own daughter to be harmed.

What am I not seeing?

"Are you supposed to take her tonight?" I ask.

He doesn't reply.

I cock the trigger. "You'd better start talking."

He cocks his head in mock contemplation. "If I talk, you'll kill me anyway. If I don't talk, you'll never get the information you need. So not talking is my better option."

I move the nose of the gun away from his temple and pistol whip him across the head. He grunts and falls to the ground. I stand over him, kicking hard at his abdomen.

He curls into a fetal position, choking.

"Still don't want to talk?" I say.

He groans, gulping in air. His grin is gone now, replaced with a grimace of pain. He spits out a mouthful of blood and glares up at me with dark, feral eyes.

"No," he gasps.

I kneel beside him, pressing my knee into his chest. "Maybe this will change your mind." I place the nose of my gun against his forehead.

But he just laughs—a hollow, bitter sound. "Go ahead and shoot. It won't change anything. You can't stop what's coming."

The threat hidden behind his words sends a snake-like shiver down my spine. I pull back the hammer of my gun, but it's not fear that makes me pause—it's the warning in his voice. It awakens something deep within my gut.

"Last chance," I whisper into his ear. "Talk or die."

He laughs once more, a rasping sound that echoes down the corridor. I wait for a moment, looking for any hint of surrender in his eyes. But there's only defiance.

"Die then," I say calmly.

He doesn't flinch as I ready to squeeze the trigger, but the shot never comes. An iron grip wraps around my wrist, pulling the gun just as I fire. The silencer eases the noise, but the bullet ricochets off the marble floor, missing its mark by mere inches.

My heart hammers as I turn to face the new threat—a towering figure whose face is hidden by shadows. I strain to get a glimpse of him, but the dim corridor offers little light.

"Not yet," the man says, his voice a low rumble that barely registers above the ringing in my ears. He sounds familiar, yet oddly foreign. There's a casualness in his tone that contradicts his harsh action.

I try to break free from his grip, but it's strong, like iron.

"What the fuck?" I turn to see the face of the man who stopped me from shooting the asshole.

And I gasp.

25

RAVEN

"It's a beautiful piece," Robin says.

I read the engraving again.

Even the raven can't fly forever. Sooner or later, it comes home to die.

"Ray? You okay?"

Jared comes toward me. "Raven?"

I grab his arm. "I need to go home. Now."

"All right." He furrows his brow. "But I thought you wanted to—"

I shove the velvet box at him. "Read the back."

He fingers the pendant in his large hands, and his eyes widen. "Yeah. We're out of here."

"Ray?" Robin's eyebrows are arched.

"Everything's fine," I say. "Just... Tell Emily I wasn't feeling well. But I have to leave." I grab her hands. "I love you, Robbie. Thank you for everything for tonight."

"What am I supposed to tell Mom and Dad?"

I glance around the ballroom. It's after midnight now, and about half of the guests have already left. Those who haven't are either still on the dance floor, paying for their auction purchases, or still seated at their tables, my mother among them.

I don't see my father.

"The same thing. That I'm not feeling well. I'll be in touch."

Jared ushers me through the ballroom. I glance around, looking for Vinnie. He seems to have disappeared again.

Jared's hand on my back is steadying as we navigate through the maze of tables. A million questions whirl in my mind, none of them with any clear answers. The engraving on the pendant continues to throb in my thoughts.

Finally, we reach the hotel lobby and walk out the grand entrance, where the limo waits. Jared helps me into the car.

The ride home is quiet, punctuated by the rhythmic hum of the engine. I grip the velvet box that holds the pendant in my pocket, my mind exhausted and whirling at the same time. The limo stops, and Jared ushers me into an SUV, climbing in next to me and hissing directions at the driver. I don't have the energy to listen to what he says.

My mind is racing, and I don't realize how long we've been driving until Jared nudges me. "We're here."

I jerk back to reality, expecting to see my home on the Bellamy property.

But no.

"No!" I cry.

We're back at the safe house.

"I can't," I say. "I can't be here again."

Jared's eyes soften. "It's the only way we can be assured that you're safe."

"Safe?" I scoff. "I'm never safe, Jared. Not anymore."

"Raven…"

"Just drive," I snap. "Tell him to drive anywhere but here."

Jared closes his eyes and takes a deep breath in. "Fine." He nods to the driver.

I close my eyes again, and when the car stops, I open them.

And again.

We're not at my home.

We're at my parents' home. The same house where Brick Latham was killed a month ago.

This isn't where I want to be either.

"Damn it, Jared…" I begin.

"I have my orders, Raven."

"Your orders? You're *my* bodyguard, Jared. No one else's. I told you to take me home. To *my* home. Not my parents' home."

"Raven—"

"They probably aren't even here." I run my fingers through my short hair. "My mother was still at the gala when we left, Jared. Is this what you want? For me to be here alone?"

He shakes his head. "There are servants here. And I will be here."

"I don't want to be here. If you refuse to take me to my home, at least take me to Falcon and Savannah's."

"Those are my orders."

I throw my hands in the air. "Who the hell is giving you the orders? Falcon and Leif hired you. You don't work for my father. I don't have to stay here, you know. I can call a cab. Call an Uber. Hell, with my trust fund, I can call a fucking car dealership in the middle of the night and have a car delivered here. I'm not your prisoner."

"I'm doing what I can to protect you. That's my job, Raven. That's what I was hired for."

"Jared—"

"That's enough," he roars.

My eyes widen.

"I let you go into that conference room with Vincent Gallo against my better judgment," he says. "I allowed you that."

"You *allowed* it?"

"Yes. I allowed it because I knew it would be the last time you—"

I reach out quickly and slap him across the cheek.

For a moment, I see anger flicker behind his dark eyes.

In another moment, I'm almost convinced he's going to punch me.

His knuckles tense, and his hands are clenched into fists.

We stay still.

He does not attempt to touch me in any way.

"What do you mean it would be the last... What? What is happening to Vinnie? Where is he?"

Jared doesn't reply.

"You're fired," I say. "Your services are no longer needed. Get the hell out of here."

He stands his ground. "I'm not going anywhere."

"Help!" I yell. "Help me!"

I have no idea if any of the servants are within earshot.

I regard the large man before me. The man who could squeeze the life out of me in less than a second. Jared, who I've grown to trust, is now a stranger to me.

Clearly he's taking his orders from someone else. But who?

Falcon? My father?

Vinnie?

It could be any of them.

"Who are you working for?" I demand.

Again he says nothing.

"Answer me," I say, "or I swear to God I'll see that you never work again in the state of Texas. Hell, the whole country. The whole fucking globe."

He doesn't answer my question. "You're not going anywhere. You're going to stay right here in your father's home. I shouldn't have allowed you the indulgence with Gallo tonight. I'm going to catch hell for it."

All right. That means apparently he doesn't work for Vinnie.

He's going to tell me the truth, or I'll do the one thing he has to stop me from doing.

I'll put myself in harm's way.

26

VINNIE

"You," I grit out.

Raven's father stands over me, his grip tight around my wrist.

I wrangle free and then kick Jack Smith for good measure. He's still in a fetal position, and won't be getting to his feet anytime soon.

"Somehow I knew you had to be a part of this." I shake my head. "Who got to you? Mario? Diego Vega?"

He frowns. "Not everything is as it seems, Mr. Gallo."

"I'd say *nothing* is as it seems." I shake him by the shoulders. "Where is Raven? I happen to know this man was sent to kill her."

"She's safe. Jared has her."

"Why did you stop me from killing him?" I dig my nails into the shoulders of his blazer. "He wants to murder your daughter!"

He swats my right hand away. "Because as I said, not everything is as it seems."

I narrow my eyes at him. "You need to start talking,

Bellamy. You really need to start talking. Because you say you love that daughter of yours, but I can tell you I love her more. I would give my life for hers in an instant."

"And you think I wouldn't?"

I point to the assassin. "Who is this jerk?"

"A man who needs medical attention," Bellamy says.

"He needs to be six feet under."

Smith groans. "Help..." he rasps out.

"Yeah, I'll help you all right." I cross the room and leer over him. "Right into your fucking grave."

"I'm going to call 911." Bellamy meets my gaze. "They're going to come and take this man to the emergency room where he can get help."

"He's just had the wind knocked out of him. He doesn't need any help."

Bellamy cocks his head at me.

I slowly turn back to face him. "You're lying. You have no intention of calling 911. You know this guy. You stopped me from killing him." I take a slow step in his direction, keeping a second eye on the man on the floor. "What is your game, Bellamy? I know about the deal. About the drug smuggling. I uncovered all of it when I was in Colombia."

"I have nothing to do with that."

I roll my eyes. "For God's sake, would you just stop lying? Your cover is blown. You don't have to act like the high and mighty big man of Texas with me. I know better. If you're worried about me telling Raven any of this, don't be. I won't put her through that. But I will make sure she's safe. And let me ask you this, Bellamy? Is she safe from *you*?"

He rakes his hands through his graying blond hair. "Of course she's safe with me. Do you really think I would let anything happen to any of my children? Especially Raven, after what she's been through? I went to bed every night for years wondering if she would be alive the next morning."

"Then why did you stop me from shooting this fucking asshole when you and I both know why he's here?"

"Because, as I told you—"

"Things aren't always as they seem," I finish for him. "God, you're like a broken record, Bellamy."

I'm tempted to pistol whip the jerk. He's in his sixties. I could easily take him despite the fact that he's tall and muscled.

"Then tell me," I say. "Tell me how things truly are. Because right now it looks to me like you're saving the life of a man who wanted to do your daughter harm."

He closes his eyes, takes a deep breath in. "I've...made some mistakes in my life."

I scoff at that. "Who hasn't? Are you saying your mistakes led you to the dark side? Fuck you, Bellamy."

"Do you really want to play that card?" He shakes his head. "You stand there, judging me, when I know you're not a man of virtue either. You may indeed love my daughter—in fact, I believe you do—but that doesn't mean you're good for her."

Another scoff. "At the moment I'd say you're not much good for her either."

He sighs. "My children mean the world to me. Do you think it was easy for me to watch—"

He stops abruptly.

But I'm not going to let this slide. He just let his mask slip.

I point at him. "To watch your oldest child go to prison?

Tell me how easy it was for you, Bellamy. Because you and I both know there's more to that story."

He doesn't reply at first. He kneels next to the man still in the fetal position. "You okay, Dietrich?"

I knew Jack Smith was a fake name. And Austin Bellamy knows his real name. Point one for me.

"You hired someone to off your daughter?"

He looks up at me, his face stony. "Are you kidding me? You think I want to be involved in all of this?"

"Seems you *do* want to be involved in it. You've got a fortune. You could take your whole family, leave the country, live in luxury somewhere and not be bothered by any of this."

"Where would I go? Certainly not to South America."

"Who the hell said anything about South America? You could go to Europe. Hell, go to Monaco. It costs a mint to live there, but you've got the money."

He sighs. "You think I haven't thought about that?"

"Then why haven't you?"

He looks back down at the guy on the floor. "Because this is a fucking mess. A mess of my parents' making."

"Your father's been dead for decades, and your mother passed away over a year ago."

"Yes, I know. And I shielded my mother from what was going on within her company. Why do you think I had to let my son go to prison?"

"Because he confessed to shooting a cop," I say. "Quit making things up."

Bellamy helps Dietrich to his feet.

"You want to start explaining?" I say to him.

Dietrich is breathing hard and holding his stomach. "I was only following orders."

"Yeah, so were the Nazis. Sell it to someone else."

"I wasn't going to kill her," he says.

"You admitted it to me."

Bellamy steps between us. "His job was to make you *think* he was going to harm Raven, Gallo."

I scratch the side of my head. "But he received payment from Agudelo. Not from you."

Bellamy shrugs. "I hacked my daughter's Uber app. Do you think it's so difficult for me to falsify some financial records?"

I blink, unable to come up with a good response.

Bellamy shakes his head. "I knew who you were in contact with in Colombia, Vinnie. I knew you would be looking up everything you could about this guy. You really should work on being less predictable."

My mind races. "But why would you go to the trouble?"

Then it hits me. Bellamy did all of that so he could…

"You bastard."

Bellamy frowns. "I see you figured it out. I did it so I could get you put away. Attempted murder."

"Not *actual* murder?"

"He's wearing a bulletproof vest, of course."

"Yeah? I had my gun pointed at his brain. Wouldn't have helped."

"Which is why I had to intervene." Bellamy sighs. "You and I are on the same side, Gallo."

"Not from where I'm standing. You just admitted you wanted to send me to prison."

He clasps his hands together, not meeting my gaze. "We both want to protect Raven."

"Right. And you want to protect her from me."

He finally looks up, making eye contact with me. "Bingo."

"You think I don't want that? I love your daughter. No doubt about that. I'll probably never love again. But I will give her up a million times to keep her safe. She knows that."

"There are things you don't understand that are at play here," he says.

"I swear to God, if you try to tell me that one more time, you'll be able to get me on *two* charges of attempted murder." I pace the room. "I'm a member of the Bianchi family. You think I don't get how this works? If you think I don't understand something, then explain it. I've got a functioning brain, Bellamy."

"We need to speak in private."

I raise my hands to either side of my body, gesturing around the room. "What the hell do you call this?"

He shakes his head. "Dietrich doesn't know everything either."

I reach into my pocket. "I've had enough of your stalling. I'm calling the cops on this asshole."

"He hasn't done anything," Bellamy says. "I just told you that he wasn't going to harm Raven. His only job was to make you *think* he was going to do that."

"Forgive me if I don't take your word for it."

"You don't have to take my word for it. When it comes to my daughter, I speak only the truth." He turns to Dietrich. "You okay? I can have Paris take you to the ER."

Dietrich coughs. "I'm good."

"Then go. Get whatever medical attention you need, if any. Then lie low. I need to speak with Mr. Gallo alone."

27

RAVEN

I surge past Jared, pushing him out of my way, my dress rustling around my feet. I walk into our large country kitchen and head straight to the drawer where my mother keeps her sharpest knives—the ones she uses to slice through our beef as if it's butter.

I grab a big one, the fluorescent lights of the kitchen glinting off the steel blade.

I hold it up.

"Raven, if your intention is to try to harm me—"

"No, that's not my intention, Jared." I brandish the knife in front of him. "Why would I try to harm you? You're twice as big as I am. And of course I'm still recovering from my illness, as everyone is so quick to point out to me. Poor weak little Raven. Can't take care of herself."

"Then what are you doing?" he asks, his voice low.

"Going to do the one thing you won't let me do." I place the steel against my neck. "If you don't let me out of here, I'm going to slit my own throat."

He blinks. "You're bluffing."

"Am I though?" I stare him down. "I've faced death, Jared. Just as you have many times in the military. I love my life. Don't get me wrong. But I don't fear death. When my body was so weak and ill and everything hurt, I prayed for it."

He takes a step toward me. "I served overseas, Raven. Do you honestly think there weren't times when I prayed for death as well?"

"I'm sure there were. But what would my brother or my father or whoever is paying you do to you if they found me with a cut on my neck?"

He takes a step toward me.

"Stay back," I say, pressing the steel slightly farther into my neck. It's cool against my flesh, and in a warped way, it feels good. Almost freeing.

"You're not suicidal, Raven."

"Of course I'm not. If I were, I would've ended my life while I was lying in a hospital bed. But no, I fought. And I will fight you now with the only weapon I have. My safety."

"Your family only wants the best for you."

"What's best for me is to be in my own home, Jared. I can't spend my life running. I lost several years of my life already fighting that damned illness. I'm not going to lose the rest."

"You're in danger. You've been getting the texts."

"And I've also been getting texts from someone who's watching out for me. Are they coming from you?"

"No. You know they're not."

"Then they're coming from someone else who's watching out for me." I twitch my eyebrows up. "You have my back. My father and brothers have my back. In his way, Vinnie has my back. But you're forgetting one thing."

"What's that?"

"*I* have my back, Jared. I'm not helpless. For God's sake, you and I both know that I have the best security system on the planet in my home. I'm not going back to that safe house, and I'm not going to stay at my parents' house either."

He sighs. "Let me make a phone call."

I finally put down the knife. He heaves a sigh of relief.

"Don't make a phone call. It doesn't matter what anyone else tells you to do. You're *my* bodyguard, and I want to go back to my home."

"I'll see what I can do." He reaches into his pocket. "But it's going to take a phone call."

"Jesus Christ." I whisk past him out of the kitchen and head into the bathroom. My dress is a wrinkled mess, and my hair... Well, my hair is so short it can hardly be messed up.

My makeup still looks good.

I take care of business quickly, and then, while Jared's on the phone, I walk to my bedroom.

My bedroom where Brick Latham's body was found, his throat slit.

I wonder if his throat was slit using the knife I just had against my own throat.

Probably not.

Whoever did it didn't leave any evidence.

And that is odd in itself.

But my father and the police took care of it, and I trust them without question.

I walk back to the kitchen where Jared is finishing up his phone call.

"Yes, sir. I'll do that."

"You'll do what?" I ask.

"We have to wait here. For your father. And Mr. Gallo."

28

VINNIE

Bellamy's phone buzzes.

"I have to take this," he says. He walks away from me, back toward the ballroom.

I follow him. The hotel staff is cleaning up. The chandeliers have been dimmed and the silk tablecloths have been stripped away to reveal bare wooden surfaces.

Bellamy, still on his phone, paces. His dark eyes are distracted.

A waiter trudges by with an almost empty champagne tray and I take a flute. The bubbly liquid feels strange in my mouth, cold and flat. Kind of the way I'm feeling at the moment.

Bellamy ends his call and walks toward me. "We'll talk in the car. It's nearly an hour drive to my house."

"Why would I be going to your house?"

"Because," he says, clearing his throat, "Raven is there."

I cock my head. "Why is she at *your* house?"

"Her bodyguard had instructions to take her there. Either

there or to the safe house, and the only reason I'm mentioning that is because apparently you know all about it."

"*You* know about it?"

He exhales sharply. "Jared and I don't have any secrets. Though he came to us through Falcon's friend Leif Ramsey, I'm the one paying his bills. So when he found out about the safe house that Falcon and Hawk had constructed after Falcon went to prison, I found out as well."

I scratch the side of my head. "What the hell is your game, Bellamy?"

We walk out of the hotel, where Bellamy's car waits for us. His driver opens the back seat, and Bellamy gestures me to get in.

Though I don't trust this man as far as I can throw him, I don't feel that I'm in any imminent danger. The skin on the back of my neck isn't icy cold, and my heart isn't racing.

He slides in the seat next to me and grabs a bottle of amber liquid from the console. "Bourbon?"

I nod.

He pours me a finger as the car begins to roll.

He gestures to the partition dividing us from his chauffeur. "We can speak freely. This is soundproofed, though I trust my driver without question."

I take a sip of the bourbon. It's good, smooth stuff. Only the best for the Cooper Steel heir, of course.

Just like only the best for Mario Bianchi.

And his son.

"So where do I start?" he asks, more to himself than to me.

"At the beginning. Start at the beginning, Austin."

He raises his eyebrows at my use of his first name. "Good enough, Vinnie." He clicks his glass to mine. "Cheers."

I don't return his toast. Hardly seems like a *cheers* moment.

"You told me the last time we talked, at my office at home, that you had found information on me on the dark web. Records that were expunged when I turned eighteen."

"Yes. But I don't hold that against you."

"I didn't think you would. Just like I don't hold against you the fact that you've killed. Twice."

I let out a dull laugh. "So we both do our research. I wouldn't expect anything less from either of us."

Bellamy chuckles lightly. "It's a shame, Vinnie. If you weren't the grandson of Mario Bianchi, I'd really like you."

I glare at him. "I can't say the same, Austin. Anyone who does business with drugs—and God knows what else—isn't someone I respect."

This time he chuckles louder. "But isn't that what *you're* doing? You weren't down in Colombia for your health."

"No, I was down in Colombia to set a plan in motion."

He doesn't need to know that I didn't come up with the plan until I actually got there and found Serena and Daniela.

"So you think you can take out your grandfather?"

"It's not a matter of whether I think I can do it," I reply. "It's necessary. I can't let this go on. It cost me my brother, my father, and now my mother. It nearly cost me my sister. The woman your son loves."

"Savannah is a lovely young lady."

"She is." I look down. "I should've been here for her. I should've been here for my brother too. He'd be alive today if I had been. But I ran."

He lays a tentative hand on my shoulder. "You were a kid, Vinnie. You had your reasons."

I cock my head. Exactly how much does Bellamy know? Clearly he knows about my run-in with Misha. That I killed him. And he knows about Puzo.

"I was eighteen, Austin. A man in the eyes of the law. But I was a selfish little bastard."

"You returned. You returned to save your sister."

"Yeah." I scoff. "Seventeen short years later. That's hardly heroic."

"Hell, none of us are heroes, Vinnie." He gazes out the window of the car. "You think I haven't bent the rules in my day?"

This time I chuckle. "I know you have. I'd love to know why you allowed your son to go to prison. And, Austin, I'd love to know something else."

"Yes." He clasps his hands together. "Why I decided to excavate under the old barn near the Mexican border that's on my property. And why it was stopped."

"For what it's worth, I wasn't going to let that happen."

"Interesting. Why not?"

"I'm not going to tell you that. Besides, I think you probably already know why."

He rubs at his forehead. "My children are smart. Especially Falcon and Raven. All five of them are brilliant, but those two have an emotional intelligence as well. I know Falcon didn't kill that young cop." The muscles in his neck tighten. "I know damned well it was my youngest."

"Why didn't you tell Falcon that?"

"Because I love my children. And that's why I keep them on a need-to-know basis."

"Just how long has your family been involved with the cartels?" I ask.

"Not as long as you might think," he says. "But I had to make a choice when my father died. Our money comes from my mother's side of the family, as you know. She was the only child of Broderick Cooper of Cooper Steel."

I nod.

"But the ranch, that comes from my father, Brick Bellamy. The Bellamy family has owned this land for a century, and each one of us has added to it. When my father married Sandy, my mother, he built an empire."

"Yes."

"Let's just say this." He closes his eyes and takes a deep breath in before continuing. "There's not a lot of difference between a ranching empire and the organized crime empire your grandfather presides over."

"What exactly are you saying?"

"What I'm saying"—Bellamy takes a moment to drain his glass—"is that power is power. No matter how it is gained or how it is wielded. The cattle empire my father built and the...other operations he got involved in both served to consolidate power." He pours himself another drink. His hands are steadier than I expect, considering the topic and the hour.

He continues, "Power and influence are universal currencies. Money can be made and lost, but power and influence are constant. They exist in every society, every business, on every level. And where there is power and influence, people will do whatever it takes to protect it."

I shift uncomfortably in my seat as the words sink in.

"Ranching or manufacturing or shipping metal or

running an organized crime syndicate. It all boils down to the same thing."

I nod. "And that is?"

His dark eyes meet mine. "Control. You asked me why I allowed my son to go to prison. The answer is complex. It was something that had to happen at that time."

"But he's your son!"

"Yes, and he chose to confess to a crime he didn't commit." He slowly pours another splash of bourbon into his glass. "Someone had to pay. And yes, I could have prevented it, but it was to my advantage at the time not to."

I shake my head. "Sleight of hand. You got the focus on your son to cover something up you were involved in. You're a damned monster."

"A monster?" Bellamy chuckles, but without humor. "Vinnie, that's where you're wrong. I'm a businessman. I deal in power and influence, and sometimes the stakes are high."

"Don't you dare try to justify this!" I snap.

He takes another sip from his glass. "Justify? I don't need to justify *anything* to you, Vinnie. Not after everything you've done. You killed two men. You ran away from your family responsibilities for seventeen years. You played right into your grandfather's hands."

And there's nothing more I can say.

Because Austin Bellamy is exactly right.

So I go for it. I ask the question I'm dying to know the answer to.

"Tell me, Austin. Who the hell is buried under that old barn along the border?"

He looks away from me. "I'm sure I don't know what you're talking about."

It's a lie, of course. If it weren't, he wouldn't be so cavalier about it.

But I know instinctively that I won't get any more information out of him.

At least not tonight.

29

RAVEN

An hour later, a car pulls up. My father's driver gets out and opens the door as I watch from the front window. My father emerges, along with another dark figure.

It's Vinnie, just as Jared said.

I swing open the front door, but Jared waylays me. "Stay away from the door, Raven."

"But it's my father. And Vinnie. Neither of them will harm me."

"I have my orders."

I clench my hands into fists. I'm so tired of Jared and his orders. For a while, we were friends. Or I thought we were. Those three weeks we were holed up in the safe house together, we played a lot of chess, had a lot of good conversations.

He cooked some amazing dinners and so did I. He even served as a springboard for some of my ideas for the gala and the foundation as a whole, several of which I implemented this very evening.

I guess that's over now.

I stand back, wishing I had taken the time to primp a little.

Then again, I'm still in my emerald evening gown.

Though it's wrinkled, there's not much that looks better than this.

The door opens, and Vinnie walks through, followed by my father.

How I ache to run into his arms. Pull his lips to mine and kiss him urgently.

But he doesn't even look at me.

"Vinnie, do you know Jared, Raven's bodyguard?"

"Yes, we've met." Vinnie shakes Jared's hand.

"Daddy, Vinnie, what's going on?" I demand, placing my hands on my hips.

My heart is beating a mile a minute just being in Vinnie's presence again. I ache between my legs for him.

"Jared tells me you want to go back to your house," Dad says.

"Yes, and I don't appreciate being held here against my will." I cross my arms. "Falcon and Leif saw that I had the best security installed."

"Yes, but Raven, your safety is paramount," Dad says.

I look at Vinnie, pleading with my eyes.

"You don't really expect me to disagree with your father, do you?" Vinnie says.

I drop my jaw.

"Well, no... I just guess..."

"Vinnie and I need to talk," Dad says. "We have unfinished business to discuss. For now, Raven, I'd like you to stay here."

"Where's Mom?" I ask.

"She and Robin booked a suite at the hotel for the evening. She knew she'd be tired, and Robin and I thought that was best."

"Why?" I dart my gaze around the room. "Why can't my mother be in her home? What the hell is going on here, Daddy?"

"Let's just all go to bed," Dad says. "You and I will talk in the morning, Vinnie. It's been a long night, and Raven, you especially had a big evening."

"Stop coddling me!" I turn to Vinnie. "And before you say something, *you* stop coddling me too. You say you can't be with me for my own safety. Why don't *I* get a say in that, Vinnie? Why don't I get a say in anything? All three of you think you know what's better for me than I do." I raise my arms to either side of my body. "I've got news for you. I've faced down worse enemies than any that are out there. Cancer had a gun pointed at my heart for three years, and I beat it."

"Oh, sweetheart," Dad says. "If only it were that simple."

I scoff. "Do you think anything about living with cancer has been simple?"

"You're forgetting something, Raven," he says. "You lived with it. It ravaged your body. You were the one who was sick in bed. But your mother and I lived with it too. For those three years, your cancer ate away at *our* bodies, too. Either one of us would've taken your place in a minute."

"I fail to see what that has to—"

"Raven," Vinnie interrupts this time. "I understand what your father is saying. He's saying he would've died for you in an instant, and so would I. And so would Jared."

"Jared is paid well to protect me."

"Doesn't matter. He would still take a bullet for you. Cancer is anything but simple, but at least you had a chance against it. And you beat it." He crosses the room, takes my face in his hands. "You don't have a chance against a literal gun pointed at your heart, Raven. Or pointed at your head. Not with someone who's ready to shoot. Who's been paid to do a job."

I slap his hands away from my head. "I'm still standing. No one has shot me yet."

Vinnie sighs. "You know what? Your father's right. We all need a break. Please. Go to bed."

"I won't sleep in that room," I say.

"No," Vinnie says. "Sleep in a guestroom. With me."

My father steps forward then, his fists clenching. "You're not going to sleep with my daughter in this house."

"Fine." Vinnie rolls his eyes. "Your house, your rules. But I agree with you. No one's in any immediate danger here. Let's call it a night. We can all figure things out in the morning. But I have a phone call to make first."

"Vinnie..." I grab his arm.

He shakes his head. "It's your father's house, Raven. Please. Get some rest. Despite what's been going on for the past couple hours, your gala was a huge success. Revel in that. You did it."

"Robin and Emily did it," I say. "I was stuck in the safe house."

"We all know who did all the behind-the-scenes work, honey," Dad says. "Vinnie is right. You need to rest."

"Then I want Vinnie to stay with me," I say adamantly.

My father shakes his head. "You know what? I'm too

exhausted to fight you on it. You're both adults. I'm too tired to care at this point. There are so many other things on my mind." He looks toward Vinnie. "Do whatever you think is best. All I really care about right now is Raven's safety."

I absolutely *hate* that Dad is making this Vinnie's decision, not mine. Taking the advice of a mob boss's grandson over his own daughter's. But I'll take the win. And there are other concerns at hand.

"What about Mom and Robin? What about their safety?"

"They are safe. You don't think I have security on them?"

I bite my lip. Of course he does. My father would not leave anything to chance.

He seems different, though. He's always been an intelligent and self-assured man, but tonight he seems troubled. And not troubled in the way he was when I was sick.

No.

Something else is going on.

Vinnie has excused himself to make his phone call. He returns a few moments later.

"Come on." He takes my hand. "Let's get you to bed."

"I'll show you where you can both sleep," Dad says.

I furrow my brow at him. "Daddy, I grew up in this house. I know where we can sleep. I'll stay in the guestroom I used after Brick was killed."

He sighs. "Fine. Vinnie, will you be staying with her?"

Vinnie looks at me, at my father, and then back to me. "I think...I should stay somewhere separate tonight."

I grab his arm. "Vinnie!"

Dad nods. "You won't get any pushback from me on that one. Vinnie, you can stay in Raven's old room. Jared, I'll show you where you can bunk."

I shake my head. "I'm sleeping with Vinnie."

"Raven." This from Vinnie. "Let's not tempt fate. You know you're safer without me."

I scoff. "This place is a fortress. Falcon and Leif installed the best—"

He puts his fingers to my lips. "Things are going on that you don't know about, Raven. It's better that you remain in the dark."

"Better for whom?" I demand.

"Better for everyone." From my father.

But Vinnie doesn't disagree.

I open my mouth to balk at all of it, but a huge yawn splits my face.

I truly am exhausted.

So I won't fight it. They can have this battle. I'll be victorious in the end.

Without further argument, I make my way to the guestroom. I peel the dress from my body, hang it in the closet, and head to the bathroom to take a shower. I wash the product out of my short hair, scrub my face free from the makeup and false eyelashes, and then just stand under the shower, letting it pelt me. We're into the next day already. It's after two a.m.

And as much as I want to know what's going on, what I want more than anything at this moment is a soft pillow under my head.

30

VINNIE

Bellamy walks toward me but I hold up a hand. "You don't have to say anything. I'm not going near her tonight."

"That's not what I was going to say. I just want you to know that I mean it when I say that I love my daughter." He runs his hand through his hair, sighing. "I love all of my children."

"Did I say otherwise?"

"No, but I see it in your eyes. You wonder how I could let them be in danger like this. All I can tell you is that there are things at work that you don't know about."

I swear to God, this guy needs to learn a new tune. If I hear one more time that there are "things at work" with no further context, I may collapse in on myself.

"I know everything my grandfather knows."

"You don't, Vinnie." He places a hand on my shoulder. "But you will."

"Because you're going to tell me?"

"Because I won't have to."

"What the hell does *that* mean?"

But Bellamy says nothing more. He simply leaves, shows Jared where to bunk down, and then he returns.

Without continuing our conversation, he shows me to Raven's old bedroom.

I peel off my tux, lay the garments on a chair, strip myself of the rest of my clothing, and head into the en suite bathroom for a shower.

Once I'm clean and dry, I put my boxer briefs back on and slide between the sheets.

Will I sleep?

Doubtful.

But at least I know Raven is safe several doors down the hallway with both her father and Jared looking out for her.

It should be me, but it can't be me.

I have a wife. Sure, she's my wife in name only, but she is someone else I am responsible for. She's been great through all of this. She left the gala pretty early to go home and take care of Serena. I brought in a discrete staff when we got home, but Daniela has taken the role of caretaker seriously, and Serena seems to adore her.

Tomorrow.

Tomorrow I go to my grandfather.

I bring him to the house. And I give him Serena. His lost love.

In exchange for all his power—and the control I need to do what must be done.

I have no doubt that he will meet my demands.

And I—

The door cracks open, interrupting my thoughts.

"Who's there?" I whisper.

"Who do you think?"

Raven.

Sweet Raven.

"You need to go back to bed."

"I'm not asking you to fuck me, Vinnie. I'm not asking for anything. I just want to lie next to you, sleep with your arms around me. Because that's the only place I truly feel safe."

Her words haunt me. Slice into me like a dagger. Because though I want more than anything to be her safe place, I'm anything but.

"I'm glad I make you feel safe, Raven. But if that were truly the case, we would be together."

"That's what I want, Vinnie. And don't try to tell me it's not what you want."

"I'm married."

"And I never thought I'd say this," she says, "but I don't care. I don't care that you're married. Because I know you don't love her. I know you love me."

She speaks the truth, and she knows it.

I sigh, and I hold the sheet up, beckoning her to me.

We already made love, or rather a quick hard fuck, in the dark conference room at the hotel.

She's wearing nothing but a large T-shirt that probably belongs to one of her brothers.

Her hair is damp, and she smells like soap and almond shampoo.

Like Raven.

Like love and light and perfection.

She crawls into my arms, and I pull her against me, spooning her.

Of course my cock responds.

It hardens immediately, pressing against the curve of her soft backside. I grit my teeth and close my eyes, fighting off the primal urge to claim her right then and there.

I remind myself that this isn't about desire, at least not in that way.

Raven is more than a want. She's a need. An addiction. A love so powerful it hurts to breathe when she's around.

I feel every curve, every inch of her body against mine, and it's like fire coursing through my veins. The ache for her grows deeper with every beat of my heart.

She sighs contentedly as she nuzzles into my chest, tracing patterns on my bare skin.

She's so small compared to me. So fragile and delicate, yet incredibly resilient and strong. It's a contrast that never fails to mesmerize me.

"Vinnie," she says softly, breaking the silence, her voice a mere whisper in the dark. "Promise me you won't let go."

"I can't promise that, Raven," I reply, my voice choked with suppressed emotions. "I can't promise anything anymore."

She faces me, her brown eyes piercing in the dim light. They are filled with a sadness that matches mine, but there's also something else. Determination? Resolve?

"Then promise me this," she says as she places her small hand over my heart. "Even if you let me go physically, don't ever let go here."

Her words are like a punch to the gut. A crushing wave of love and loss and longing hits me all at once.

Tears prick at the corners of my eyes but I blink them back. "You have my word," I say quietly.

It's a promise I intend to keep. Even if it shatters my soul into a million shards.

Silence settles in between us once again, one that is comfortable and full of understanding. She sighs softly, wrapping her arms tighter around me.

"I wish we had met under different circumstances," she whispers after a while, her voice thick with unshed tears.

Her confession unravels something in me. A longing to step back in time and do things differently. To meet her when there were no complications, no promises made to other people. But that isn't the life I was born into.

"I wish for the same, Raven." I kiss the top of her head.

We lie there, tangled up in each other under the covers. The world outside our cocoon doesn't exist. The only thing that matters is the here and now. The rhythm of her heart-beat against my chest, the warmth coming from her body, the scent of her hair and skin.

"We can't keep doing this," I whisper, even though I know we both want nothing else.

"I know," she says, barely audible. She tightens her hold on me.

"But we have tonight." I bring my lips to hers.

"And tonight, I'm yours," she whispers.

The taste of her is enough to drown in. Enough to forget time, place, circumstance. Her breath hitting my face is like a reminder of everything I've ever wanted and everything I must let go.

Yet beneath the desire, there is a melancholy shadowing every stolen kiss, every gentle caress. The realization that each interaction might be our last. It's a sorrow that lingers heavily between us.

I slide my hand between her legs.

"Vinnie," she gasps, her breath hitching at my touch. She melts against me. The delicate lace of her panties is damp.

She reaches down to grasp me. I groan, shuddering at her touch.

The longing within me peaks, the need to connect with her on a deeper level overwhelms every sense in me.

Gently, I slide her underwear aside and dip my fingers into her. Her breath catches as I brush my thumb over her clit.

Even though we were intimate just hours before, the electrifying charge between us now is overwhelming. As if our bodies are recognizing each other for the first time.

I remove her panties and slide into her.

The room is filled with our heavy breathing and soft sighs as we move in sync with one another. This is slow and gentle, so unlike us, but it's what feels necessary in this moment.

She grips my shoulders as she arches her back. I feel the heat building within her, the clenching of her inner muscles compelling me to quicken my pace.

"Vinnie..." she sighs.

I bury my face in her neck, nibbling on the sensitive skin there as she trembles beneath me.

"I love you." I whisper it into her ear as my own climax approaches. The words come out desperate, raw—more of a prayer than a declaration of feelings we both know already exist.

"I love you too," she echoes.

And I thrust hard into her, releasing.

I grip her tighter, riding out the aftershocks of pleasure that ripple through me and into her.

Her body slackens beneath mine as she continues her own release. The rhythms of our breaths gradually slow to match each other's until we're left in silence once again.

We lie there, our bodies entwined, the sweat beginning to cool on our skin. Everything in me screams against the idea of letting her go, but I know I must. This is our reality—stolen moments in the darkness, whispers of love that will never see the light of day.

Reluctantly, I pull away from her and prop myself on my elbow to look at her face. Her eyes are still closed, lips slightly parted as she struggles to catch her breath. She appears blissful, a soft smile playing on her lips. It's a sight that makes my heart ache with longing.

She falls asleep in my arms.

And for the rest of the night, I allow myself to hold her.

Until I untangle myself from her at the break of dawn, leaving her sleeping peacefully.

31

RAVEN

The dream starts the same way every time. I'm lying in that cold, sterile bed, staring up at the ceiling with its blinding fluorescent lights, the smell of antiseptic burning my nose. My body feels weak, so impossibly heavy. I try to move, but it's like I'm trapped, frozen under the weight of it all.

I hear the beeping of machines, a steady reminder of how fragile I am. A nurse stands at the foot of my bed, her face masked but her eyes sad. I know what's coming before she says anything. I've heard it before. "Your white blood cell count is not good. We're going to start another round."

My heart clenches. Another round. Another wave of poison coursing through my veins.

The room tilts, spinning in a way that makes me feel nauseated, but I'm stuck. I can't get out of the bed. I can't leave. I see my reflection in the window—pale, bald, with dark circles under my eyes like bruises.

I'm not me. I'm some shell of a person I used to know. My skin is gray, my lips cracked. I look like I'm already dead.

An instant later, I'm in the chair for chemo. The IV drips, and with every drop, I feel the toxin eating away at me. My hair falls out in clumps, and my bones ache like they're breaking from the inside out. The taste of metal on my tongue, the sickening churn in my stomach. I want to scream, but no sound comes out. It never does.

Faces blur in and out—doctors, my mother, friends I haven't seen in years. Their mouths move, but I can't hear them. It's like I'm underwater, drowning in silence, while they watch me fade away. My heart pounds, but it feels too slow, too heavy, like it could stop any second.

Any second now, it's going to stop.

Then there's the darkness.

It's all black. Empty. And in that moment, I'm sure I'm dead. Gone. But something pulls me back, yanks me out of the void. The beeping returns, faster now, and I'm gasping, clawing at the air, trying to breathe, trying to fight for something—anything. My chest heaves, but my lungs feel like they're filled with lead.

And then that crackly, female voice. "Remember..."

"What do I need to remember?" I try to call out, but my voice catches in my throat. Only a hoarse whisper comes out.

"Remember, Raven..."

A face. Blurred, hard to make out. But I can see gray hair tied up in a bun. It's familiar, comforting... But I can't figure out who it is.

I reach out to see if I can see the face more clearly, but I'm yanked back to the hospital room.

I feel a hand on mine, warm and gentle. My mother's hand. I'm back in the hospital bed, but this time it's different. This time, I hear the doctor's voice.

"You're in remission."

The words echo, but instead of relief, fear washes over me. What if it comes back? What if this nightmare never ends?

And who is the woman with the blurry face? What does she want me to remember?

I wake up for real then, soaked in sweat, heart racing, and the darkness of my room closes in around me. It's over. It's done. I'm alive.

But the dream always finds me.

The sheets are soaked with my sweat.

Where am I?

Yes, my room at Mom and Dad's.

The room where Brick Latham was killed.

I came here.

I came to Vinnie.

Vinnie!

I slide to the other side of the bed.

"Vinnie?"

Where did he go?

I jump out of bed.

I look around.

No sign of him.

Even his tuxedo, which was thrown over a chair when I came into the room last night, is gone.

I throw on the T-shirt I was wearing, grab an old pair of lounging pants out of my closet, and make my way to the kitchen.

My father and Jared are having a cup of coffee.

I expect them to say something about the fact that I was in the room with Vinnie, but neither does.

Good. I'm twenty-nine years old, after all.

"Where's Vinnie?" I ask.

My father raises his eyebrows. Does he think Vinnie told me where he was going?

"He called a car early this morning. He said he has business back in Austin. I'll be joining him there later."

"What business do you have with Vinnie?" I ask.

Dad brings his mug to his lips. "Nothing you need to be concerned about."

I shake my head, sighing. "Everything about this concerns me, Daddy. I love Vinnie. And I love you."

"I love you too, sweetheart." He takes my hand. "And I need you to stay here. Your mother and Robin are coming home this morning. Your mother needs to know you're safe."

"What? Did you think I was going to run after Vinnie?"

"No. Jared has his orders."

I shake my head. "Fine. You win, Daddy. You and Vinnie and Jared, you all win. I'll stay here like a good little girl. But I need you to do something for me."

"And what's that, Raven?"

"If you love me, Dad, and I know you do, please do everything in your power to protect the man I love. Please protect Vinnie."

32

VINNIE

My parents' housekeeper—*my* housekeeper—Phyllis, meets me at the door when I return home by nine a.m.

"Mr. Gallo," she says, "it's good to have you home."

"Where's Daniela?" I ask.

"She's upstairs with our guest." She thins her lips. "Miss Serena had a rough night."

"I'm sorry to hear that."

"She's not ill or anything, but she slept fretfully," Phyllis says. "The nurse will be here soon. She texted me to tell me she had caught traffic and will be a little late."

"See about finding a live-in nurse," I tell her. "Serena is elderly, and she has been treated poorly. I believe she needs round-the-clock care. I don't expect Daniela to do all of that."

"Daniela is quite good with her," Phyllis says, "but I understand."

The intercom buzzes by the door.

"That's probably the nurse," Phyllis says. "Would you like me to take care of it?"

"Yes," I say. "Send her up. I'm going to go up and see how Serena is doing."

I ascend the curved stairway to the second floor.

This is the home where I grew up. Where I spent my first eighteen years, as the older son of Vincent Gallo Senior and his wife, Caroline Bianchi Gallo.

Funny. I've been back for a couple of months now, and I still feel like a stranger here. I spent nearly half of my life out of the country, away from this home.

I knock softly on the guestroom door where we've settled Serena.

"Yes, come in." Daniela's voice.

She looks up when she sees me. Serena is in her rocker. She looks good. Still too thin, and her face is wrinkled, but her eyes brighten when she sees me.

"Vinnie," she says in her crackly elderly voice. "I'm so glad to see you."

This is the second time she's called me Vinnie. She's making progress, no longer calling me Mario.

"Good to see you too, Serena. I have a surprise for you. You're going to have round-the-clock nursing care."

She frowns. "I don't need that. I'm perfectly fine."

"Serena, you were held captive for over fifty years in Colombia. The doctor says you're in decent health, but you're weak, and you need care."

She swallows, her eyes sullen. "Only the first couple years were bad, Vinnie. After that, they left me alone. They fed me."

"They kept you locked in a room."

"Yes, but believe me. I learned to be grateful for that." Her breath hitches. "Especially after those first years."

"I'm not going to ask you what they did to you." I turn to Daniela. "Did you know she was in your father's home?"

"No, I didn't. I was just a kid for most of that time."

I rub my forehead. "Right. Sometimes I forget you're only seventeen years old. You seem much older."

"I was forced to grow up quickly," she says.

I don't press her on that. I know too well what she's been through.

God, both of these women have been through so much.

"Has she been able to move by herself today?"

Daniela crosses the room and takes Serena's hand. "Yes, she can walk, but it's difficult. She's going to require a lot of physical therapy to strengthen her bones."

I'm not sure how much a physical therapist can do for an eighty-year-old woman who's been kept in captivity for God knows how long, but we can hope.

Phyllis stops at the open door, and behind her stands a young woman wearing dark jeans and light-pink scrubs.

"This is Renée Erickson," Phyllis says. "The nurse."

"It's good to meet you, Mr. Gallo," Renée says, holding her hand out.

I shake her hand quickly. "This is your charge. Serena."

Renée enters the room and walks to Serena's chair. "It's wonderful to meet you, Serena." She holds out her hand, and Serena takes it in her bony one.

"You look like a lovely young woman," Serena says, "but I don't need nursing care."

"Well, I'm here, and my services are being paid for," Renée says cheerily, "so let's get to know each other."

Serena cracks a small smile. "I'd like that. I won't say no to company."

"Why don't I get the two of you a snack?" Phyllis says.

"That would be great, Phyllis," Daniela says. "Thank you."

Phyllis leaves, and I make sure that Renée is situated well with Serena. Then I nod to Daniela. "I have some business to attend to in my office. That's where I'll be if you need me."

"Thank you. I understand."

I haven't yet told Mario that Serena is here. I was able to get her home without Mario knowing. My first call is to my attorney.

"Morgan and Fort," the receptionist says.

"Hello, this is Vincent Gallo Junior. I'm calling for Brian Morgan."

"Of course, Mr. Gallo. One moment please."

I hear her typing and pressing buttons on the phone, and then the ringer goes again.

"Vinnie," Brian Morgan says into the phone.

"Hi, Brian."

"What can I do for you? I'm not sure why you're calling a divorce attorney."

"There's a simple answer to that. I need a divorce."

"What?"

"Actually, an annulment would be my preference. I've only been married for about two weeks, and the marriage hasn't been consummated. She's not yet eighteen."

"Please tell me she's at least seventeen."

"She is, and we were married in Colombia with her father's permission. She's not an American citizen. But as I said, the marriage hasn't been consummated, and it won't be consummated. It was all part of a...deal."

"Understood. I won't ask too many questions. The less I know about any of your deals, the better." I hear papers shuffling and keys clacking in the background. "Here's the deal. In Texas, there are several potential grounds for getting an annulment. The key point is the non-consummation of the marriage. In Texas, that alone is a solid ground for annulment. Since you're telling me that you haven't had a sexual relationship with your wife since the marriage, we can use this as the primary basis for your annulment request."

"Great. And the fact that she's underage isn't an issue?"

He pauses. "Assuming that parental consent was given for the marriage in Colombia, which complicates things slightly, it doesn't remove your right to an annulment based on non-consummation."

"Great. Let me know what else you need from me."

"Just the certificate of marriage. Send it over when you can. I'll get the paperwork filed. I'm pretty sure we can get this moved along pretty quickly."

"Good."

"But about your wife... If you're not married to her, she won't be able to stay in the country."

"Wait... What?"

"When a marriage is annulled, it's legally treated as if the marriage never existed, which could have implications for any immigration benefits she may have been seeking through that marriage."

"Shit. A divorce then?"

"Immigration law isn't my specialty, Vinnie."

"She wanted to come here. That's part of why I agreed to the marriage. She's an intelligent young woman, and she wants to go to culinary school. She doesn't have those opportunities in Colombia."

"They don't have culinary schools in Colombia?"

"No. It's not that. Her...family. They don't believe a woman should be doing anything except pushing out babies to seal deals with other families."

He pauses again. "I see."

"How can we get her legal status here in the US?"

"Does she have another form of legal immigration status? Like a work visa or student visa?"

"No. This all happened very quickly. I brought her here as my wife."

"A divorce may be a better option for you, then. Though immigration status could still be affected. We have an excellent immigration attorney here at the firm. You should probably talk to her. I think maybe your best bet is to wait until she turns eighteen, have her apply for residency and a green card. Then instead of an annulment, get a divorce."

"Crap."

"What's the issue? So you wait a year or so."

I rub at my temple with my free hand. "The issue is that I want to marry someone else."

He pauses again. "That is a problem. But if you're not sleeping with your wife, you can still have the relationship that you want. I'll confer with my partner, and we'll find a solution for you."

"Much obliged."

I end the call and sigh. That throws a kink into things.

But I don't have time to dwell on that right now. I call Mario.

"Hello...son," he says into the phone.

His voice makes me want to throw up. "I'm not going to call you Father. Or Dad."

"Grandfather's fine," he says.

"I don't like that either. None of it is true. I've decided I'm going to call you Mario."

He chuckles sardonically. "Have it your way. I got word from Agudelo in Colombia that you disappeared. With his daughter. Without sealing the deal."

"Yeah. About that... When were you going to tell me that Diego Vega wasn't dead?"

"There was no reason to."

"Who the hell is buried on the Bellamy property?" I demand.

"There's a reason why Diego was demoted," Mario says. "It's not something I can talk to you about over the phone."

"Good. I need you to come to my parents'"—I clear my throat—"I mean *my* house. I'm sure you'll want to meet my lovely bride."

"McAllister's not happy."

"McAllister doesn't need to worry. I'm working on getting Daniela legal status so she can stay here, and then we'll be divorcing."

"Are you sure? She's a lovely little thing. Tight, I bet."

God, he makes me want to puke. What a dirty old man. I have half a mind not to tell him about Serena. He might know anyway, if he's spoken to Agudelo. Besides, I'm convinced Serena is the real reason he sent me. Mario couldn't care less about Puzo's deal.

"You're disgusting. I haven't slept with her. I don't sleep with children. I don't plan to. This marriage is one of convenience only."

"You may as well take what's yours, Vincent."

"She's not mine. She's a person. She's not an object."

HELEN HARDT

"Did she refuse to sleep with you? She doesn't have that right."

"To the contrary, Mario. She didn't refuse. She offered herself to me up on a platter. I'm the one who said no." I grit my teeth. "But for your information, she *does* in fact have the right to refuse to sleep with me. Or anyone else, old man."

He scoffs. "God, your father ruined you."

"Yes, he certainly did," I grit out, hoping he understands what I mean.

"So what is it you need me to come over about?"

"I believe you already know," I say. "And we have a lot to talk about."

33

RAVEN

My mother and Robin arrive about an hour later. Robin comes in to the guestroom where I'm staying.

"Raven, last night couldn't have gone any better. Have you heard how much money we made?"

Wow. I haven't even thought about that with everything else that went on.

"I assume it was pretty good."

She pulls out her phone and scrolls through it. "From the donations that we received and the silent auction receipts, we're at about two and a half million dollars already. That doesn't even count the three thousand dollars a plate the people paid to go to the gala."

"But it doesn't take into account our expenses," I say dryly.

She raises an eyebrow. "Don't get too enthused."

She's right. Our expenses were nothing compared to receipts so far, and there's no price on the awareness we raised.

I regard my sister. Though we're not identical twins, we look a lot alike. Her facial features are a bit harder than mine, and of course she has a beautiful head of hair. Our eyes are nearly indistinguishable, except her lashes are longer.

Mine will be again, I keep telling myself.

The nubs are growing. I did like how I looked with false eyelashes on last night.

"We made more than enough to rent office space and hire a skeleton staff to get things started," she says. "Then the money you and I are putting in from our trust funds gets us a good start on helping to fund research and giving grants to people in need."

"It's all going to be fundraising, isn't it?" I ask.

"That's kind of what nonprofits are all about, Ray. Surely you thought this through when you went through all of it."

"I did." I rub my eyes. "Don't mind me. I'm just exhausted."

She pats my hand. "Of course you are. You're still in recovery mode. That's why Emily and I are doing all the foot-work. Right?"

"Yeah, right."

I hate lying to my sister.

I hate lying, period.

"So where did you go last night?" Robin asks. "You were gone for a while."

I swallow. "I just...needed to get away from the crowds. You understand."

"I do." She nods. "We all think it's amazing that you took this on. Right after coming out of recovery."

"I'm fine. I'm cancer free, as they say."

"You're in remission, Ray."

"Potato po-tah-to. Whatever."

"I'll let you get some rest." Robin gives me a quick hug. "You planned a great gala."

"*You* planned it."

"All right. But it was your idea." She grabs my hand, squeezes it. "This is your brain child, Ray. You need to take some credit for yourself. That gala was amazing. Your speech brought people to tears."

"Thanks, Robbie."

She leaves the room, closing the door behind her.

I grab my purse and pull out my cell phone along with the burner phone that the fake Uber driver gave me.

I read through all the texts.

The texts on my phone, threatening me.

And the texts on the burner phone, warning me.

Then I pull out the velvet box that contains the pendant I won in the silent auction.

I turn it over, rub my fingers over the engraving, reading the message once again.

Even the raven can't fly forever. Sooner or later, it comes home to die.

I should be more frightened than I am.

But right now, all I want is to fall asleep again.

Even though I was plagued again by nightmares last night.

At least I was in Vinnie's arms.

Until I woke up, that is. And he was gone.

I could call him.

But he won't answer.

I know what he thinks, and I know he's right. But I've seen enough miracles in action to believe in them. I've seen myself go from a sick bag of bones to a healthy woman again.

I believe that Vinnie will come back to me.

I have to believe it.

I look toward my door when I hear a knock.

"Yes?"

The door opens, and my father stands there.

Sometimes when I look at my father, I wonder how we all came from him. His skin is fair, his hair blond, his eyes blue.

We all have darker skin and dark hair like our mother. Only Hawk got his blue eyes.

But I do see similarities between him and me.

When he smiles, I see my own smile reflected back at me. There's a certain crinkle around his eyes that I've been told I have, a shared laugh that cuts through the silence on quiet days.

At times, my reflection in the mirror is like looking into a mural of our family's history—a blend of my mother's Mexican roots and my father's Northern European lineage. My eyes are a deep dark brown almost identical to my mother's.

My father has always been a quiet man, the silent observer in most situations. He speaks when necessary and when he does, everyone listens. His voice is deep and resonating, a stark contrast to his fair complexion. His wisdom seeps through every sentence, every word carefully chosen and spoken deliberately.

Hawk takes after him in that regard. Much like our father, he is reserved, content in his solitude. He shares similar interests with our father—fishing on weekends, reading countless books on history and architecture, and a deep sense of what's good and right.

"What is that?" he asks, pointing to the pendant I'm still holding.

Why not?

I hold it out to him. "Turn it over," I say.

He does, and his cheeks turn red as his jaw goes rigid. "Where did you get this?'

"At the auction. I won it."

He squints at it, tracing the engraved letters with a calloused finger. "This..." he begins, "this was your grandmother's."

My jaw drops.

I think back. My grandmother only died a little over a year ago. I was too sick to go to the funeral, but all those years before, she was a big part of our lives. I don't ever remember seeing her wear this bird pendant. Birds are our mother's thing. They were never our paternal grandmother's.

"It was?"

He nods. "Your mother and I got it for her when you and Robin were born."

That explains the bird motif. "I never saw her wear a pendant like this."

"She didn't wear it much. You know your grandmother. The only jewelry she ever wore were pearls. Your mother and I tried to change that. We got her a Falcon pin when Falcon was born. Then the pendant when you girls came along. After that, we gave up."

"But how did it end up in the silent auction?"

Dad shakes his head gravely. "I have no idea. After your grandmother died, we placed her jewelry in a safe deposit box." His hands tremble. "Someone must have taken it out and gotten it engraved."

I place a hand over my mouth. "I didn't make any bids. I thought it was kind of a conflict of interest, you know? So when they called my name…" I shake my head.

"You didn't know this was in the auction?"

"No. I really only knew about the big-ticket items. Robin and Emily made most of the arrangements for the silent auction. I figured this item was just something that had fallen through the cracks. But Daddy…"

"What, sweetheart?"

"This isn't the first time I've gotten this message." I grab my phone, pull up the requisite text, and show it to him.

He glares at it, his hands curling into fists. "Now do you understand why I want you here? Safe?"

I gulp as I nod.

"Damn that Vinnie Gallo," Dad says. "He's been nothing but trouble."

I don't respond.

I don't know how to.

I love Vinnie. I love him with all my heart and soul. So much that I'm not sure I can ever love another man.

I'm destined to become an old spinster.

Eventually moving back home with my ageing parents.

Hell, I'm here already.

I can't let my life become this.

"I want to go home, Daddy."

"Raven, not an hour ago, you said you would stay."

I sigh. "Yes, and I will. I don't want you and Mom worrying about me. Doesn't change the fact that I *want* to go home."

"I understand, sweetheart." He puts the pendant back in the box. "I need to take this. Have my investigators look at it. See if we can pull any fingerprints off of it."

"Sure. Of course. I didn't pay for it."

"Somebody did and put it in your name. Did you happen to see what the final bid was?"

"I didn't look. Since I technically won it, I didn't have to check out. They all know I'm good for the money. It's my nonprofit, after all."

"I need to look into this," he says. "Is there anything I can get you?"

"How about—"

"An Orange Crush?" he finishes for me.

I sigh, nodding. "Yes, please. I could use a drop of sunshine right about now."

34

VINNIE

I'm still in the office when Phyllis peeks through my cracked door. "Mr. Gallo? Your grandfather is here."

I rise from my desk, shuffling a few papers around. "Thank you, Phyllis. I'll be right out."

I draw a deep breath, getting myself ready.

Inside, my guts are in turmoil. I feel like I need to run for ten miles to take the edge off. But there's no time for that.

I look outside my office window into our backyard. The pool house stands in the distance, the sparkling blue water beckoning me.

About twenty-five laps would take the edge off too.

Maybe this evening.

I walk out of the office, down the hallway, and into the living area where my grandfather sits.

"Vincent," he says.

"Mario," I return.

"What the hell did I need to come all the way out here for?"

"It's a fifteen-minute drive from your office, Mario. This wasn't a hardship."

"My own daughter's house," he says, looking around. "Paid for with my money. And you know I was hardly ever invited here."

"I'm not surprised, given what I know now."

He glares at me. "Family is family, Vincent. You'll do well to remember that."

"Will I?"

"You will. Blood is thicker than water, as they say."

I laugh, shaking my head. I learned so much during that time I spent in the Buddhist temple in Tibet. One thing I'll never forget is learning the true meaning of the old cliché *blood is thicker than water.*

"I agree," I tell Mario. "Blood *is* thicker than water. In the original meaning of the phrase, 'blood' refers to bonds formed by choice, such as those forged in friendship or battle, while 'water' refers to family ties, as in the amniotic fluid of the womb. Do you know what that means, Mario?"

"I know it's bullshit," he says.

"You're short-sighted," I tell him. "I learned the true meaning from the wisest man I've ever met. Bonds made by personal commitment or shared experience can be stronger than those formed by birth or family. And in my case, that's certainly true."

"Bullshit," he says again.

I can't help a smile. "Look it up. The first version is always the correct version."

"So family means nothing then?"

"Family can mean everything," I tell him. "But when you

treat your family the way you've treated them, Mario, family has *no* meaning."

He sniffs. "I'm not going to justify myself to you or anyone else. I'm over eighty years old. Now what the hell am I doing here?"

"Fair question." I nod toward the stairway. "Follow me."

Once we walk up the stairway, I head toward the room where Serena is staying. I knock on the door.

Renée opens it. "Yes, Mr. Gallo?"

"Is she doing all right?"

"Yes. She's resting. She enjoyed her snack."

"I'm glad to hear that. Would you mind stepping out for a moment? I have a guest who wants to meet her."

"Yes, of course. Is there anything else I can do for you?"

"Just give us about an hour. I'll call for you if we need you."

"Absolutely." Renée exits the room, widening her eyes a bit as she spies Mario, and then she goes down the stairs.

I open the door. "Mario, I brought you a gift from Colombia."

Mario walks in and then stops, nearly losing his footing.

I instinctively put out a hand to steady him.

"I'm not the monster you think I am," he says softly.

I have no idea what he's talking about, and I don't rightly care.

He walks slowly toward Serena. Her eyes hold no recognition, but she does not look frightened. We've made her feel safe here.

"My God," Mario says. "Serena, my love."

Serena tilts her head, her elderly eyes sunken. "Who are you?"

"It's me, my darling. Mario."

Serena's eyes dart from Mario to me. "No... You..."

I clear my throat. "When I found her in Agudelo's attic, she thought I was you. Apparently I look a lot like you did when you were young."

Of course there's no doubt about that, unfortunately. I've seen the photos. I'm a dead ringer for my biological father.

How can I not be? I'm the product of him and his daughter. No other genes had a chance.

Mario closes the distance between him and Serena and kneels—actually kneels—before her.

I've never seen Mario kneel before.

He takes her wrinkled hand in his own.

The years have been kinder to him then they have been to her. Of course, he's lived a life of luxury. She's lived life as a prisoner, subject to torture.

"I never believed I would see you again," he says.

"Mario?"

"Yes, it's me."

"You... You look different. You're an old man."

Mario smiles. Actually smiles, and it seems sincere. "And you're an old woman, my love, but still as beautiful as ever."

Serena hasn't aged well, but underneath the wrinkles, the sunken eyes, the thin white hair, I can see that she possessed true beauty at one time.

Mario brushes her hair gently away from her face, his eyes gleaming with unshed tears. He studies her, looking at every wrinkle, every line that time etched on her face. His fingers trembling, he traces her cheeks, her jawline.

"You were always so strong, my love. Even now, I see it in

your eyes," he whispers, his voice thick with emotion. "You've had to endure so much."

Serena's eyes are wet with tears. Mario's touch, Mario's voice has unlocked something within her.

"Her suffering was my doing," Mario says, lifting his gaze to meet mine.

I open my mouth to... To what? To agree? He wasn't the one who took her, tortured her. But it was because of his love for her that she was taken, tortured, held captive all those years.

The same reason Raven is in danger now because of me.

"Dear Mario," she says. "I never blamed you."

Mario's eyes well up with brimming tears as he looks back at her. "I have carried that guilt, Serena," he whispers. "Every day, thinking I'd lost you forever."

Serena pats his hand gently, her own eyes reflecting a deep sorrow. "Life is cruel, my love, but we mustn't let it control us."

Mario returns his gaze to me. "How? Where?"

I widen my eyes. "I thought you knew. Somehow you knew. She's why you sent me to Agudelo."

He gulps, shaking his head. "I didn't. I swear to you."

"I don't believe you. Why would you care about some stupid deal Puzo was trying to close? You—"

He narrows his eyes. "That deal was important, Vincent. The fact that you left things hanging has us in a precarious position. And the fact that you took his daughter—"

"He gave her to me. He knew I'd take her out of her country."

Mario opens his mouth to offer a retort, but then shakes

his head. "I don't care. I don't care about any of it anymore, Vincent. Where did you find her?"

Did he truly not know? "She was being held in Agudelo's attic," I say. "Daniela helped me rescue her and bring her home."

Mario shakes his head again. "Agudelo didn't mention Serena."

"Maybe he doesn't even know she's gone," I say. "It's possible. Daniela was able to turn off the security. But her caretakers would have noticed..."

"It doesn't matter." Mario wipes his eyes. "All that matters is that she's here. That she's alive after all these years. Thank you."

I scoff. "You think I did it for you? I did it for *her*. She's innocent in all this. Her only crime is that you fell in love with her."

"I was also in love with him," Serena reminds me.

I look at the old woman, just a shell of the beauty she must have been. Even now, she seems to have no regrets.

Mario was once human.

Maybe Serena will help him remember that.

"I do not regret loving him," Serena whispers, her voice wavering. "Even if I knew everything that would befall us, I would have chosen to love him still."

Mario places his other hand over the one Serena is patting. His eyes are bright with tears he refuses to shed, his expression one of gratitude and anguish. "We were so young..."

"Innocence can be a form of blindness," Serena murmurs. "However, love can also provide clarity."

Mario simply nods, visibly moved by Serena's words. He

buries his face into her frail hands for a moment. "I should have protected you better."

"It wasn't your fault," I interject solemnly, surprised at my own words.

Serena traces Mario's face with her free hand. "We were both victims, my love," she says softly.

The scene is surreal—the hardened criminal kneeling at the feet of this fragile woman he once loved, his face etched with regret and sorrow.

Mario lifts his head from her hands and looks deep into Serena's eyes. A flicker of hope laces his gaze. "Perhaps it's not too late for us," he murmurs.

Serena shakes her head slowly, her eyes radiating a gentle sadness. "We are both so old now, my love. We have lived our lives, however painful they may have been."

Mario's expression shifts into a grimace. He glances at me, his eyes pleading for something. Understanding? Forgiveness? Absolution? All things I'm not sure I can provide.

"We have a lot to discuss," I say. "A lot to discuss, *Father*."

"SHE CAN'T KNOW," Mario says once we've left Serena in Renée's capable hands and retired to my home office. "She can't know what I've become."

I take a deep breath, sitting down behind my desk and gesturing for him to do the same. He does so reluctantly, looking out the window at the sun setting in the distance.

"She must know something," I reply, keeping my voice steady. "She isn't stupid. She's survived this long."

Mario closes his eyes, leaning back into the chair and

rubbing his temples. "I wouldn't have wished this life on her." His voice is raw, stripped of any pretense. "She deserved better than me."

"But she chose you," I remind him.

He opens his eyes to look at me, his expression unreadable. "Just as I chose her."

Silence again. I watch him. What thoughts are swirling through his head?

"I didn't choose this life," he finally says. "I fell into it because of circumstances beyond my control."

I raise an eyebrow at him, not entirely convinced. "Bullshit. I only exist because you raped your own daughter before her wedding. To assure the continuation of your line. You've made millions off drugs, and now you're set to move toward human trafficking in alliance with the McAllister family."

"That deal probably won't happen since you welched on marrying Belinda," he says.

"Do you think I care? It won't matter because I have a plan, Mario. A plan that lets you and Serena live out your golden years in peace...while I bring this fucking madness to an end."

His eyes bore into mine, the flicker of desperation replaced with a hardened resolve. He leans forward and rests his hands on the desk. "And what if it costs you everything? What if it costs you Raven?"

I swallow hard at the mention of her name, my heart pounding. "I'm aware of the risks." I manage to keep my voice steady and my tone firm. "But I won't let anyone else suffer. Not like Serena had to."

Mario is silent for a moment. Then he slowly nods,

perhaps seeing something in my determination that he respects or understands.

"You're more like me than you realize," he finally says.

I'm not sure whether it's a compliment or an insult.

"There's one difference between us." I lean back in my chair and cross my arms. "I won't allow my love for Raven to be her downfall."

Mario nods. "Then it's time you learned the truth about her father."

"I'm way ahead of you," I tell him. "I know Bellamy isn't the saint he's cracked up to be. But he won't harm his children. Especially not Raven."

"You are aware, aren't you, that he was instrumental in his son serving time?"

"I've come to that conclusion, yes. I just don't know why."

"It's a long story. One only he can tell you in its entirety."

"I've been pushing."

"Push harder."

"I will," I respond firmly. But my thoughts are whirling. How deep does Bellamy's treachery go? And why does it involve his own flesh and blood?

"I have much to make amends for," Mario says, dragging me back. "Starting with you."

"You can't undo the past," I say, my voice colder than I intend it to be.

"No, but I can attempt to rectify some of its consequences." He meets my gaze squarely. "I understand if you hate me for what I've done."

"Hate is a strong word, Mario," I reply evenly, swallowing back my emotions. "It's also a wasteful one. I'd rather spend my energy ensuring that the cycle ends with me."

35

RAVEN

fter dinner, I find myself thinking about ways to sneak out of my parents' home. Get a car. Drive to Austin to see Vinnie.

But he's told me to stay away.

Besides, he's married now.

I don't for a moment believe he loves Daniela. In fact, I believe him when he says they haven't consummated the marriage.

My thoughts go to Belinda, the lovely little girl who Vinnie is supposed to marry when she turns eighteen. The little girl who is pleading for help.

I wish I could do something for her.

But here I am, trapped.

Though I beat cancer, and I'm no longer trapped in the hospital, I am no less trapped.

Jared, of course, is hovering.

My mother's out on the deck having a glass of wine. Robin has left to go to her own home.

I decide to go outside and sit with my mother.

Jared follows me, of course.

I turn to him. "I'd really like to talk to my mother alone."

He nods. "I'll go out of earshot." He walks off the deck, toward the pool house, where he takes a seat on one of the Adirondack chairs near the entrance to the pool.

And he watches.

"He's driving me slowly into madness," I say to my mother.

Mom reaches over to my shoulder and squeezes it. "That doesn't matter, Raven. What matters is that you're safe. And Falcon, Leif, and your father believe you need Jared."

"Yes, I know."

She takes a sip of her wine. "I've seen one of my children go to prison. Another nearly lose her battle to cancer. And now this." She shakily takes another sip. "I don't know how much more I can take."

I sigh. Then I stand, walk over to the outdoor bar, and pour myself a glass of the red wine my mother's drinking. Yes, I'm still on medication.

And I don't fucking care.

I take a sip.

And it's delicious.

It's nothing fancy, just a Côtes du Rhône from France, but it's been so long since I let myself have a drink of wine. I return and sit next to my mother.

"You shouldn't be drinking," she says.

"Maybe not," I say. "But one glass of wine isn't going to change anything. You remember our trip to wine country?"

She nods. "Yes. I was supposed to go with Falcon."

I gaze out toward the pool. "And you got stuck with me."

"Oh, Ray. That's not what I meant and you know it."

"Yes, you're right. I shouldn't be so defensive. I'm just so tired of all of this." I scoff. "I went and fell in love with a fucking gangster."

"You wouldn't fall in love with someone who isn't a good man."

"I know that. And I know he loves me. That's why he left me. He doesn't want me in danger. Yet here I am in danger anyway. With a bodyguard. Being forced to stay with my parents." I let out a sarcastic laugh.

Mom takes another sip of her wine. "I can't lose you, Raven."

"You're not going to lose me, Mom."

And damn it, I mean those words with all my heart. I didn't let cancer get me, and I'm certainly not going to let some mafia hit get me.

"But I *am* going to live my life," I add.

"I know. You've lost too much of it already." She pats my hand gently. "You and Falcon had years of your life stolen through no fault of your own."

"So you never thought Falcon was guilty."

Mom steels her face. "I know he wasn't. Falcon's one of the good men. He and Leif were supposed to join the Navy SEALs together after college. They'd been talking about it for a good decade, since they were teens. He was twenty-two years old. He knew how to handle a gun better than your father did. And that's saying a lot because your father's an excellent shot. So am I, for the record, so I know what I'm talking about. I've watched all of you learn to shoot a gun, and I know which one of you is the best at it. Falcon. My oldest. And there was no way he would've accidentally shot anyone. He was too careful for that."

"So you've always known."

"That he was protecting someone? Yes, I have. He was protecting Hawk."

"Hawk?"

"Yes, he and Hawk were outside doing target practice. Who else could it have been? Who else might've been using Falcon's gun?"

I take another sip of my wine. Do I tell my mother the truth?

"He had to take the blame for it," Mom continues. "You know Hawk. His sense of justice. He couldn't have handled being labeled a criminal. What I don't understand is why Hawk didn't confess. His conscience should have made him."

Funny how my mother can't see the truth in front of her eyes. If Hawk had shot that cop, he *would* have confessed. That's who Hawk is.

"Mom," I say, "Hawk is as good a shot as Falcon is. And Robin and I are pretty good as well. The one who never took to it...was Eagle."

Mom blinks. "Eagle is good with a gun."

"I'm not saying he's not. I'm just saying he's not as good as the rest of us. And...he's the most erratic of the five of us."

Mom says nothing.

Until, "Eagle wasn't there, Raven. Only Hawk. So it must've been Hawk who Falcon was protecting."

Oh God. My mother really doesn't know what's going on. But I'm not going to be the one to tell her. I can't be the one to tell her that her baby—my baby—is the one who shot an innocent young police officer.

"Falcon swears it was him," I say, robotically.

"Yes, I know." She lays a hand over her heart. "But a mother knows."

She's right about one thing. Falcon didn't shoot the police officer. But neither did Hawk. So a mother really *doesn't* know. Maybe she's just fixing the scenario in her mind in the way that makes sense to her.

"Did you know your father taught me how to shoot?" she says.

"No, you never said that."

"I was a natural. But I grew up the daughter of Mexican-American immigrants. They didn't believe in guns. They'd seen enough of them during their childhood in Mexico. When I married your father, though, he insisted that I know how to defend myself."

"And you are okay with that?"

"I was more than okay with that. My parents' philosophy never made sense to me. If they came from somewhere dangerous, why wouldn't they want to exercise their right to defend themselves?"

I nod.

"So I let him teach me. He was a good and fair teacher."

"I know. He taught me."

"He and I both felt that all of you kids should know how to defend yourselves. We also taught you gun safety."

"Yes. You did."

"But the lessons seemed to fall short with Hawk."

I regard the woman who gave me life. She can't really think what she's thinking about her second son. Hawk is one of the best men I know, and an excellent shot.

"Whatever happened, it was an accident."

"Yes, I suppose—"

I jerk.

No!

A gunshot.

We're talking about guns and a fucking gunshot!

Jared jumps up from his chair in the distance.

Mom is gasping, screaming.

I turn toward the door.

The sound came from inside the house.

36

VINNIE

"Why did you bring her here?" Mario asks.

"She was suffering."

"Yes, but you hate me. You knew bringing her here would make me happy." He looks into my eyes—really looks into them. "So I'm asking you, Vincent. Why?"

Clearly I was mistaken about why he sent me to Colombia. So I'll use this to my advantage. "She's a gift. And I'll ask for a gift in return."

"And what is that?"

"You and Serena take off. I'll get you new IDs, a wonderful place to live out your final years. In return, you turn control of everything over to me."

His jaw tightens. "So that's what this is about."

"I would've rescued Serena no matter what," I say. "Because I have empathy. I have feelings. I don't think anyone should be held against their will, especially not a woman in her eighties."

"I see."

"The only difference is I wouldn't have told you about it. I would've taken care of her, made sure she lived out her last years in comfort and riches."

He wrinkles his forehead. "So why involve me at all?"

"You know why. You wanted me to take over eventually anyway. You were just waiting to see whether you could trust me. I've done everything you've asked, Mario, other than complete the negotiations with Agudelo. I thought getting Serena out of there was more important, and I think you agree with me. Now it's your turn. I've earned the right to take over this family, to run it the way I see fit."

He scowls. "You'll run it into the ground."

"And what if I do? Would it matter? You'll be with the love of your life. If you're lucky, you've got ten years left, and you'll get to spend them safe and sound with Serena. Without watching over your shoulder all the time. Without knowing that in an instant, it could all be over if you piss off the wrong person."

"I've pissed off many people in my life." He crosses his arms defiantly. "No one's taken me out yet. I have the best security in the business."

"And wouldn't it be nice *not* to have that? Wouldn't it be nice to live alone, somewhere tropical maybe, only you and Serena?"

He sighs. Pauses a moment. Then, "I don't know that she wants that."

I have to stop myself from laughing. Is Mario Bianchi actually concerning himself with what another person might want?

He really *does* love her. He never stopped loving her. As hardened as he became, as many horrible things as he did, inside he always loved Serena.

"She should be given a choice," he continues, his voice barely a whisper. "She deserves that much."

My God, who is this man? He never gave *me* a fucking choice. He never gave my mother a choice. Not Mikey either. Savannah's the only one who got a choice, and I had to return so she could have it.

I think the original version of "blood is thick than water" is making sense to Mario now.

I look into the eyes that are so like mine. God, I'm a dead ringer for him. This is what I'll look like in fifty years.

Where before I saw only malice, now I see fear. It's an emotion that Mario Bianchi has never allowed himself to show, not even to his own family. But it's there now, swirling in his eyes. Fear of losing control. Fear of losing Serena. Fear of the future he thinks I might build, one that could erase every trace of his rule.

I'll be damned.

This man, the terrifying patriarch of our family, is afraid of me. It's a sobering thought, but also an empowering one.

"Mario," I tell him firmly. "This isn't about my power or your fear. This is about Serena and what's best for her. You know as well as I do that she belongs with you. She always did."

He scowls at my sentiment, not bothering to respond. An uncomfortable silence settles between us. In the stillness, I see the gears in his mind turning, indecision pawing at him like a stray cat at a closed door.

Very quietly, so quiet that I can barely hear him, Mario murmurs, "And if she doesn't want me?"

I raise an eyebrow. I didn't expect this question from him. "What?"

"If she doesn't choose me, what then?" He's looking down now, his gaze fixed on the floor.

His vulnerability is palpable and shakes me to my core. This is not the man I've known and feared my entire life. This is someone else. Someone I don't recognize.

I pause before replying, considering my words carefully. "If she doesn't choose you," I begin, my voice somber but steady, "you'll walk away. You'll give her the freedom to live her remaining years as she sees fit. I swear to you she'll be well cared for."

Mario doesn't answer immediately. He sits there for what feels like an eternity, immobile except for the rise and fall of his chest. His gaze remains fixed on the floor.

Eventually, he looks up at me, age evident in his weary eyes. The years of ruling our family with iron fists seem to have caught up with him in this single moment.

"I've done a lot of things in my life that I am not proud of," he begins, his voice hoarse with emotion. "But losing Serena was and always has been my biggest regret."

His words hang in the air.

His biggest regret?

Not his violation of me? Of Mikey? Of our mother?

Not all the merciless killings?

But at least he's showing *some* emotion.

I swallow down my bitterness and manage a nod. "Then don't make the same mistake again. If she chooses you, you'll both get your happily-ever-after in some tropical paradise. If not, then at least you gave her the respect of a choice."

"What about you, Vinnie?" he asks, dragging his gaze from the floor to meet mine. "What do *you* get out of it?"

My heart clenches. What do *I* get? A kingdom built on

blood and violence...and the chance to make it into something better.

"I get a chance," I reply, "to prove that the Bianchi family can be more than its past."

A slow, reluctant smile tugs at the corners of Mario's lips. His eyes glimmer with a mixture of pride and resignation.

"I always thought you had potential," he admits. His gaze never leaves mine, the somber resignation in his eyes slowly replaced by a flicker of hope. "I just hope you're ready, Vinnie."

"Ready for what?" I ask, raising an eyebrow at him.

He smirks at me, the ghost of the man I grew up fearing coming back to life in that fleeting smile. "For everything that comes next. You think you can handle it?"

The question hangs in the air between us, heavier than any silence we've shared tonight. It's not just about running the family business anymore. It's about proving myself, changing decades' worth of tradition and expectation.

I lift my chin up and meet his challenging gaze with determination. "I can handle it."

37

RAVEN

Jared rushes toward us, gesturing, his gun in his hand. "You need to stay put," he commands.

"Austin!" Mom yells.

"Quiet, Mrs. Bellamy," Jared says. "Just keep your mouth shut. Move out. Move out into the yard. Now!"

I grab Mom's hand. "Come on. We need to do what Jared says."

"Austin!" she yells again.

"Mom," I say. "You heard Jared. Be quiet." I pull her across the deck, to the stairs, out into the yard. "Let's go to the pool house. We'll be safe there."

But she yanks my hand out of hers and runs back toward the house.

"Mom, no!"

But she's gone, out of my grasp.

I have no choice but to follow her. I can't let my mother be in any kind of danger.

She rushes through the French doors and into the house. "Austin!"

I follow her, grabbing her arm. "Mom, please."

She yanks free again. "Don't you understand? There's no one home. No one but us."

Shit.

She's right.

Which means...

"Jared!" I yell.

I follow my mother as she frantically searches every room, finally getting to my father's study.

The door is open, and Jared is standing behind Dad's desk.

My heart nearly stops.

On the floor...

Seeping into the hardwood...

Redness.

Sticky redness.

I should know.

I've had enough of it drawn out of my body, enough transfusions to last a lifetime.

It's blood.

"Raven, Mrs. Bellamy," Jared says, his voice a monotone, "you need to get out of here. Now."

But my mother rushes toward Jared, and then she lets out a bloodcurdling scream.

I gulp as I walk toward them.

Jared is holding Mom, and I cast my gaze to the floor.

Nausea crawls up my throat, inch by inch, sticking its talons into my flesh.

A body.

My father's body.

Next to it.

A gun.

I try to speak, to scream, but the words die in my throat as I stumble back, smashing into a bookshelf. The room spins, my vision blurring. I can hardly make out my mother's figure slumped against Jared's chest as she sobs.

But I don't need to see. The metallic scent of blood fills the room, cloying and thick. I fall to my knees, the world tilting around me. Daddy? Dead?

Jared is saying something, but his voice is distant and warped, like he's speaking underwater. He sounds calm—too calm for what has just happened.

A chaotic jumble of questions claws at the edges of my mind. What happened? Who did this? And most importantly, why? But I can't ask. Not now.

I squeeze my eyes shut against the tears pricking at their corners—hot, burning tears of shock and grief.

Then I open them and I walk toward the gun.

"Don't touch it!" Jared warns. "Leave everything exactly as it is."

"Yes, yes. Of course," I hear myself saying. "Daddy? Is he okay, Jared?"

But the words are ridiculous. He's not moving, and blood is seeping out of the side of his head.

He's not okay.

More than not okay.

I fall to my knees next to my father. "Daddy! Daddy, wake up!"

I touch my hand to his neck. His flesh is clammy but...

"He's got a pulse! There's a pulse! Call 911!"

"I already called them before you got here," Jared says. "They're on their way. But Raven, he's bleeding out."

"No, no, no," I shake my head, tears welling and spilling over. "He's got a pulse, Jared. He's still alive."

Jared kneels beside me, his hand on my shoulder. "I know," he says softly. "But we need to stop the bleeding. Can you do that?"

I nod, wiping my tears away. "Yes, yes," I echo to myself and fumble with my trembling hands to open the drawer of the nearby desk.

There are towels there. Dad always kept some in case he spilled his coffee while working late nights. He was so meticulous about everything, never leaving anything to chance.

I grab one and press it against my father's wound, wincing at the sticky warmth spreading through the fabric.

"Keep pressure on it," Jared instructs me.

Mom continues to sob softly from where she's collapsed against the desk, her body shuddering with each hiccupping breath.

"Keep pressure on it. Pressure..." I chant in my head like a mantra, forcing myself to focus. I need to keep the blood from pouring out, need to keep my father alive until help arrives.

Outside, a siren wails, growing louder as it approaches our house.

"I'll go flag them down," Jared says, standing abruptly.

My heart sinks as he leaves the room, leaving me alone with my mother's sobbing and my dying father.

The towel is quickly becoming saturated, so I grab another one from the drawer. Each second feels like an eternity.

The sirens grow louder and then stop altogether. The front door bangs open and I hear distant voices shouting commands at each other.

"Jared! Jared, he's bleeding out!" I scream at the top of my lungs, my voice cracking under the strain of my terror.

Mom's sobs turn into wails, loud and piercing.

Footsteps echo through the hallway, coming closer and closer until two paramedics burst into the room.

"I've got a pulse," one of them says after examining Dad. "But he's lost a lot of blood."

As they begin to work on my father, I'm pushed aside, relegated to a corner where I can do nothing but watch. Jared comes back into the room, his face drawn. He looks at me, and in his eyes, I see the same helplessness that gnaws at my own heart.

The paramedics move quickly, their hands a blur as they try to stabilize my father. They speak in medical jargon that only seems to heighten my growing panic.

My mother is led out of the room by one of the police officers who have arrived, her frail form shaking with each sob. The sight of her falling apart rips my heart into pieces.

Here we are in another nightmare.

How many are we supposed to endure?

Chaos reigns in the once-peaceful study. The paramedics operate with a controlled frenzy that is both reassuring and terrifying.

Then a loud beep.

"I'm losing him!" one of the medics yells to his partner who is frantically pumping at a bag connected to an oxygen mask on my father's face.

"No, no, no," I whisper under my breath, my hands clenched so tight they hurt.

Then I know.

I know what to do.

I leave the room, grab my phone, and I call Vinnie.

38

VINNIE

My phone buzzes, and I pull it out of my pocket.

It's Raven.

I don't think she would call without having a good reason.

"Go back in there with Serena," I say to Mario. "I'm taking care of everything. If she agrees, you and she will be out of here by morning."

"But I have to alert the—"

"If you're gone, I'll alert everyone. They'll have no choice but to do as I say."

"Vincent—"

"I have to take this call. I'll be back."

Mario relents and goes back in with Serena. I close the door of the room and answer the phone as Renée comes back up the stairs.

"Raven?" I say.

"Oh my God, Vinnie," she sobs. "I don't know what to do."

My heart lurches. "Raven, what happened?"

"It's my father," she gulps. "Someone shot him. In our own house."

"What?"

That doesn't make sense. He has the best security out there.

"Who? What happened?"

"I don't know. Paramedics are taking him to the hospital now. He has a faint pulse, but the shot was in the head, Vinnie."

Damn. A shot to the head would take him out. It must've just grazed his skull or something. But God, the blood. Head wounds are the worst because of the many vessels close to the skin's surface. Part of my so-called education when Mario was grooming me to join the family business.

Who the hell would have done this?

Then again, he's working with some dangerous people. Perhaps Bellamy got in over his head.

"Raven," I start, carefully choosing my words. "You need to get out of there now. We don't know if they're coming back."

"But Vinnie, I can't just leave him. He's my father. I have to go to the hospital with him."

"You could be in danger there. Let the police handle this."

"My mom is going in the ambulance with him. I'll follow in the car." She sobs even harder, her voice breaking. "Vinnie...I'm scared."

"Raven, do not go to the hospital. Please. Stay put. I'm sending someone for you."

"All right." She gulps. "All right, Vinnie."

As I hang up the phone, my mind races, spinning different theories and outcomes. Bellamy is no saint. Any number of people could have done this, but doing it in his own home? That takes a lot of balls.

I open the door to the room where Mario and Serena are waiting. Mario instantly sits up straighter.

"What is it?" he asks.

"It's Bellamy," I say, straightening my jacket and turning for the door. "Someone took a shot at him."

Mario's eyes widen in surprise. "A shot? At Bellamy?"

"Yeah. I have to go."

He narrows his eyes. "Your loyalties lie elsewhere, Vincent."

"Damn it!" I nearly pull my hair out. "I'll do my duty. I'll take over the organization. You're free now to be with your love. I've given *my* love up, but I have to protect her, Mario. I won't let her end up like Serena."

I leave then, hastily making a call to Elmo. "I need you to get on the horn and call your best man," I tell him. "Closest to the Bellamy ranch. He needs to go pick up Raven. Then meet me at the secure location in San Antonio."

"I'm on it."

A moment later, I'm in the car with Fred and Elmo. "All set?" I ask.

"All set. Slade is on his way to her."

"Slade?" I cock my head. "You sent someone named Slade?"

"He's the best. He'll get her there quickly and safely."

"Good."

"What's up?"

"Someone took a shot at Raven's father. Right in his own home. The cops are swarming right now, and I don't have a clue who may have done this. All I care about is Raven. Getting her out of there."

"I understand."

My mind races as the car swerves through traffic.

"I hope Slade gets to her before the police lock everything down," I mutter.

Elmo looks at me, a grim understanding in his eyes. "Don't worry, Vinnie. Slade's never let us down."

Despite Elmo's soothing words, my heart pounds like a jackhammer. Time seems to stretch and warp, every second crawling by at an agonizingly slow pace.

Eventually, we pull up to the secure location—an inconspicuous three-story building tucked away in a run-down part of town. From the outside, it looks abandoned—part of its disguise. Inside is a state-of-the-art security system and enough firepower to hold off an army.

As I step out of the car, Elmo reaches for his phone and reads a text. "Slade got Raven. They're en route."

Relief washes over me, but it's short-lived.

"She safe for now, Vinnie," Elmo says, clapping a hand on my shoulder. "Slade won't let anything happen to her."

I nod, trying to focus. We have to prepare for what comes next. Whoever shot Bellamy won't stop there.

We enter the building and head straight for the operations room. Screens display live feeds from various locations around Austin while some show news channels reporting about Bellamy's shooting.

"Anything?" I ask, scanning the screens.

"Not yet," Elmo replies, his brow furrowed. "I'm monitoring police scanners and all of our sources. Nothing concrete so far."

"Keep looking," I tell him, pacing back and forth like a caged animal.

Hours pass with no break in the tension. Every minute seems like an hour, until finally—

"Vinnie."

I turn.

Raven. Two men flank her.

She runs into my arms.

39

RAVEN

"Anything?" Vinnie asks the men at the monitors as I hold onto him for dear life.

"Something's coming in." One of the guys adjusts his headset. "It's... Repeat that please?"

Pause.

"You sure?" Another pause, and he turns to Vinnie. "Report is coming in that Bellamy's gunshot wound to his head was...self-inflicted."

My heart plummets to my stomach. My pulse was fluttering so fast, but now it feels like it's not beating at all.

Surely I didn't hear those words. My father would never harm himself. Never shoot himself. He'd never leave Mom. Or me. Or my brothers and sister.

"Confirm that, please," Vinnie says.

"I need confirmation," the man wearing the headset says.

Pause.

The man pushes his headset into his ears for a moment before turning to us. "Confirming. The trajectory shows that the bullet's entry point was consistent with self-harm. Bellamy...shot himself."

A wave of nausea rolls over me, and I grip Vinnie tighter, as if he can shield me from the harsh reality. The room spins around me. I want it to stop. I need it to stop.

Vinnie wraps his arm firmly around me, a steadying force in my whirlwind of despair. "Reconfirm," he demands, his voice steady despite the tumultuous news.

"We've received images from local security cams. Forensics have already processed them," the guy at the monitors says. His face is pale beneath the fluorescent lights. "It's definite."

The words ring hollow in my ears, playing over and over like a broken record.

Self-inflicted. *Self-inflicted.*

"No." The denial rips from my throat before I can stop it. "No!"

"Easy, Raven," Vinnie says. "We need more information."

"Prognosis looks pretty good," the man with the headset continues. "He just grazed his skull. Missed major arteries. He's unconscious but stable."

Unconscious but stable—those words don't offer the comfort they're meant to. Instead, they bring a new wave of fear that crashes over me, threatening to pull me under its icy depths.

My father. The most grounded, rational man I know tried to kill himself. And if he wasn't successful this first time, who knows if he'll try to do it again?

Why would he do a thing like this?

He couldn't. He simply couldn't. There must be another explanation.

"I'm sorry, Raven," Vinnie says. "It seems you weren't in any danger after all."

I pull back and punch Vinnie in the upper arm. "How can you say that? I'm in danger of losing my father."

"He's stable," the man repeats.

"Stable. My father's a great shot."

"Not everyone is a great shot when they're aiming the weapon at their own head," the man replies.

Vinnie shoots the guy a glare. "Can you work on your bedside manner a little bit? Christ."

He then leads me out of the communication room.

"I'm so sorry," he says. "I thought this was related to the pendant, to the messages you've been receiving. I just assumed someone shot him."

"Someone did!" I scream. "My father would never try to harm himself. There was so much blood, Vinnie. So much blood."

"I know, Raven, I know." Vinnie leads me to a quiet corner. His grip on my arm is firm, but not unkind. He knows I need the support right now, both physically and emotionally.

We find a vacant room with an untouched sofa and an old coffee table scattered with outdated magazines. He guides me to sit on the soft leather couch, whispering comforting words that I barely hear over the sound of my own thunderous heartbeat.

"I don't believe it." I shake my head. "He was a rock, Vinnie. Always there for me. When I was sick, he fought for me when I was too weak to fight for myself."

Vinnie kneels in front of me, his hands holding mine. "I know."

But in his eyes, I see the uncertainty that matches my own.

I grab his face, pull him to me. "Kiss me, Vinnie. Please. Kiss me."

Without a word, he complies. His kiss is gentle, a soft press against my trembling lips. It's not a passionate kiss born out of desire, but one of comfort and assurance. He pulls back too quickly, his gaze locked onto mine.

"Raven," he says softly, "We *will* figure this out."

He's holding onto hope for both of us. But the world feels like it has crumbled around me. A part of me wants to believe him, but the stronger part—the part that saw the life ebbing out of my father—refuses to.

"Can I go see him? Can I go to him?" My voice sounds small and distant even to my own ears.

Vinnie hesitates for a moment. "I need to make sure it's safe."

"You just said it has nothing to do with—"

He touches his fingers to my lips. "I said no one else shot him, Raven. But if he felt desperate enough to try to end his own life, something big is going on. Something he doesn't want your mother, or you, to know about."

I rub at the sides of my head. I can't think of this right now.

"Take me away from this, Vinnie. I need you."

He kisses me again. This time hard, raw.

A moment later, he's on top of me, grinding his erection into me. "God, Raven," he grits out. "The thought of losing you. I can't... I just can't."

He kisses me again, one hand cupping my breast, the other sliding beneath my waistband.

"Are you sure?" he whispers.

This must be what he felt like when his mother was in the hospital, before she died. When we fucked hard in the hospital cleaning closet.

I have no idea where we are. Who can hear us. But I don't care.

"Yes," I say to him. "Yes, please. Love me, Vinnie. Love me."

He pulls me close, his mouth descending on mine again, hungrily, anxiously. His hands are all over me, slipping under my clothes, tracing the contours of my body. I'm desperate to consume him and be consumed by him in return.

The cool air hits my skin as he pulls my shirt over my head. He kisses my neck as I gasp and dig my nails into his back through the fabric of his shirt. The familiar feel of him drives away the pain, if only for a moment.

His hands are on me again, sliding over the expanse of my bare skin. Fingers gently brushing against curves and valleys. A soft moan escapes my lips as he reaches under my bra, thumbing my nipple until it hardens.

I can hardly breathe, every single touch electric and raw. I arch into him, wanting more, needing more. His breath is ragged against my skin.

Vinnie tugs at my bra until the clasp unhooks, freeing my breasts. He skims over my bare flesh, making me quiver. He lowers his mouth to my left breast and teases the nipple with his tongue. His hot breath makes me squirm beneath him.

"Vinnie!" I gasp out his name like it's a prayer.

I need him in ways I can't articulate. The taste of his lips on mine is like my favorite wine, intoxicating and dizzying in equal measures.

He trails down my sides to the waistband of my jeans and unbuttons them.. The world outside fades away as he lays me on the sofa, slides my jeans and underwear down my legs. I kick them off and pull Vinnie back to me. I crave him, his touch, his scent. He's all that keeps me sane in this moment.

He slides his hands down my body, leaving a trail of fire in their wake as he reaches between my legs. His touch is light, almost reverent, but it's enough to make me gasp in pleasure.

"Vinnie," I whisper again, my voice shaky with need.

"Shhh," he murmurs against my ear. "I've got you."

He slips his fingers between my folds. I buck my hips against his hand as a moan escapes my lips. He groans in return.

I reach for the buckle on his belt. His pants follow, and within another moment he's inside me, thrusting, thrusting, thrusting...

Our bodies move in perfect rhythm, his thrusts matching my gasps, creating a symphony of unsaid words and pent-up desires.

"Raven..." He breathes my name into the crook of my neck.

I dig into his back and pull him closer. His hips grind into mine again and again. Each stroke of his hard length inside me is a brand, marking me as his.

His lips find mine again—rough, passionate, needy. They taste like desperation and promise.

A moment later, he stiffens and buries himself deeper within me with a low grunt. Heat floods me as he spills into me while I cling onto him tightly, my body convulsing around him.

And for just this moment, I have everything I need.

40

VINNIE

God, I love this woman.

I know in this moment that our lives will be entwined forever. No matter how hard I try to push her away for her own safety, we always return to each other.

And maybe that isn't such a bad thing.

While I'd like to stay embedded in Raven forever, I force myself to get to my feet, giving her a gentle kiss on the forehead before I do. I dress and tell her she must as well. Then I leave her in the capable hands of Slade and two others and I head to the communications room.

I need answers.

If this doesn't have anything to do with whoever is threatening Raven, then what *is* it about? Why would Austin Bellamy try to take his own life?

He's hardly a saint.

Maybe he *has* truly bitten off more than he can chew.

Thank God he'll survive.

And now that Mario has agreed that I'm in charge of the family business, I can take care of this.

Austin Bellamy will live.

Diego Vega will not.

Jacinto Agudelo will not.

Declan McAllister will not.

The plans are already set. I put them into motion when I was driving to the airport in Bogotá.

They go down within forty-eight hours. As soon as Mario and Serena are safely out of Austin with their new identification.

So many unanswered questions regarding Austin Bellamy's role in this whole thing.

And I still don't know who the hell is buried underneath his old barn.

Whoever it is, Eagle recognized him as Diego Vega all those years ago.

Hawk and Falcon wouldn't have known the difference.

The only other people who can answer any questions, besides Bellamy himself, are the two men who were with Vega that night. The two men who escaped, were apprehended at the border, and never heard from again.

I haven't told Raven about her father's role. That he was the one who hijacked her Uber app. That he's the one who's been sending the warning messages on that burner phone. I'm not sure about the pendant, but he might have had something to do with that as well.

As for the threatening messages, I have my suspicions that they've been coming from the McAllisters.

There's only one way to find out.

Declan McAllister will be dead within forty-eight hours. If the messages stop after that, I'll know.

Taking down my father's cartel won't be simple, but I have enough clean money through the coffee business that I can make sure all of the best men are taken care of. They'll live out their lives with their loved ones and all their needs will be met.

I'll take down the men who are controlling the cartel my mafia family is involved with. Jacinto Agudelo and Diego Vega will go down in Colombia. McAllister will go down in Austin. Several others will go down at the same time in various places. It will be bloody, but silent. The plan is already in motion, and it will be carried out while I'm here in Austin with an ironclad alibi.

And they made fun of my peanut butter plot.

In Bogotá, Jacinto Agudelo will be entertaining one of his lavish parties twenty-four hours from now. I attended one of his get-togethers while I was staying at his home. He spares no expense, be it on booze, drugs, or women. Around midnight, he'll disappear from the party after all his friends have taken an escort to bed. He'll lock himself in his study, where he'll indulge in vintage Scotch and Cuban cigars alone. There, my man Rodrigo will strike. Rodrigo is an expert at blending in the crowd. The waitstaff for the company catering his events is regularly replaced, and Agudelo won't recognize Rodrigo as a new face. He will poison Agudelo's Scotch without a hitch.

Diego Vega is a different breed entirely. He shuns luxury, preferring to handle things on his own turf—on the streets of Bogotá where he grew up and built his empire from scratch. This rugged reality makes him more guarded and difficult to reach, but not impossible. Vega's unwavering loyalty to his roots is where I'll get him. The local soccer match he attends every Sunday without fail. Manuel, a local street vendor known for his empanada stand near the soccer field, will ensure that Vega's usual order is laced with a lethal dose of cyanide baked carefully into his favorite beef empanada.

I have found that McAllister in Austin is a man of meticulous habits, predictably punctual and consistently cautious. His morning routine consists of an early jog along Lady Bird Lake and then a vanilla latte at the same coffee shop he's patronized for over a decade every morning at precisely eight-fifteen.

At that precise time tomorrow morning, Sofia, who has been working at the coffee shop for the last week, will serve McAllister his daily brew. Sofia has an uncanny ability to make herself forgettable, a trait that makes her perfect for this job. She'll poison his morning drink flawlessly.

McAllister won't suspect a thing. He'll raise his cup to his lips and not even notice the slight bitterness masked by sugar and warm milk. By the time he realizes something is wrong, it will be too late. He'll clutch at his chest, gasp for breath and collapse right there in that quaint little coffee shop. It will look like a heart attack. I've already paid off the coroners at the local hospital in the likely event that an autopsy is ordered. Once his staff is notified of his demise, Natalie will take Belinda to social services, where a contact there has agreed to allow me to take guardianship of her until she turns eighteen.

Once Daniela is eighteen and she gets her green card, she and I will divorce and I'll send her to culinary school on my dime and make sure she has everything she needs. It's the least I can do, since I'm having her father killed. His assets will be seized by the cartel, and there won't be anything left for Daniela. I will make sure she's set for life.

I will be in Austin at City Hall tomorrow morning, presenting a hefty check to the local school district, shaking hands with politicians, and making speeches about how we need to invest more in our children's education. Lots of witnesses to solidify my alibi.

At least that's where I'm supposed to be.

Bellamy's suicide attempt has fucked up those plans. I'm not leaving Raven alone.

"Get information on Austin Bellamy first," I tell Sam, my hacker. "I want to know his prognosis."

Sam hacks into the hospital computer and scans the screen.

"Looks like he's going to make it. They stitched him up. Gave him a transfusion for the blood loss. He's in ICU for observation, but the prognosis is good."

I heave a sigh of relief for Raven.

For me? I'm convinced Bellamy has plenty to hide, and though he may think he has his children's best interests at heart, I'm not so certain that he does.

"Any news from Bogotá?" I ask.

He shakes his head. "Not yet."

I nod. Not that I was expecting any. Nothing will go down until tonight.

"What about Mario and Serena?"

"Their documents are in their hands, and they're boarding a flight to Dubai tonight."

I nod.

John and Marla Perkins, as Mario and Serena will now be

known, will live in a villa situated in a quiet gated community in Emirates Hills that offers security and privacy. Their home is close to high-end amenities and an excellent healthcare facility. Mario has enough clean money to live comfortably with Serena for the next twenty years.

I'm confident in my plans to keep them safely hidden away for the rest of their days. After all, I escaped from my own family's watchful eye for seventeen years. I can certainly give Mario and Serena ten or so.

I leave the communications room to check on Raven.

"Please," she begs when I go to her. "I have to see my father. I have to, Vinnie."

She's not asking for a lot. But, "I just checked with the hospital, Raven. His prognosis is good. He's going to be okay."

"I'm glad of that. Thrilled, actually. But I still need to see him. Please."

When she looks at me like that, with those brown eyes pleading, I can't deny her anything. Nothing could have kept me from my mother's side when she was in ICU.

I can't deny Raven the same.

"All right. I'll get Elmo and Fred to take us. Jared too."

41

RAVEN

Today is Daddy's birthday.

I'm the only one of the five of us who remembers his birthday. Eagle is too little, and maybe Hawk too, so I guess they get an excuse. But Falcon is older than I am, and Robbie is of course the same age as I am.

I guess some people are just better at remembering birthdays.

I got up early and made him blueberry pancakes all by myself. Our housekeeper offered to help me, but I wouldn't let her. I want Daddy to know that I made these from scratch.

They came out pretty well. A little burnt. But it's my first time. Daddy will still gobble them up. He loves blueberry pancakes. He'll especially like them if he knows I made them for him.

I make a big stack of pancakes on a plate and place a big square of butter on top. I'm serving the syrup on the side, because that's the way they do it in restaurants. I also poured him a big glass of orange juice. I don't like orange juice, but Daddy does. I prefer my Orange Crush. Mommy says it's bad for me, but I learned in school that it has less sugar than regular orange juice. Mommy didn't think it was funny when I pointed that out.

I checked when I woke up to see if he was still in bed. He wasn't. Daddy usually gets up early to check things out on the ranch, but today he's taking the day off for his birthday. He's probably in his study, so I'll bring his breakfast in there.

I put the plate of pancakes, the container of syrup, and the glass of orange juice on a tray and carefully carry it to his office door, making sure the orange juice doesn't splash everywhere.

The door is closed, but I can see that the latch isn't in place, so I'll be able to open it up with my hip.

I walk inside, beaming.

"Happy birthday, Da—"

Daddy isn't alone. There's a man in his office. His skin is tan, he has dark hair, and he looks...just a little slimy.

Daddy looks at me and widens his eyes. "Raven!" he yells. "Get out of here! Can't you see I'm in a meeting?"

I drop my jaw. Daddy doesn't ever yell at me.

I want to leave, but I'm frozen in place. The tray in my hands feels like it weighs a hundred pounds.

"Raven, did I stutter? Leave!"

I drop the tray. The plate under the pancakes shatters into a million pieces, as does the glass of orange juice. The syrup and the juice splatter everywhere, and the pancakes I worked so hard on all by myself are ruined.

I burst into tears and run out of the office.

"Raven. Whatever is the matter, darling?"

It's my grandma. She came over to help Mom with the preparations for Daddy's birthday party tonight.

I run into her arms, bawling.

"Honey, what is it?"

I wipe my eyes. "Daddy yelled at me. I came into this office to surprise him with breakfast. And he was talking to someone and he got mad at me for interrupting."

Grandma strokes my hair. "Oh, sweetheart. I'm so sorry."

I look up at her. "He's never yelled at me like that. And I've accidentally interrupted him before. Normally he's calm."

Grandma takes a deep breath in. "Raven, my angel. I've got a secret for you. Something that every child must learn eventually. Promise you won't tell?"

A secret? What is Grandma talking about?

"I promise."

Grandma gives me a smile, but her eyes are sad. "Grown-ups make mistakes. And your father has made a big one."

"He has?"

She nods slowly. "He has. He thinks I know nothing about it, but people tend to underestimate old women. We know a lot more than people think we do."

"Is Daddy going to fix his mistake?"

"I sure hope he does, sweetie." Grandma looks out the window and lets out a sigh. "I'm not sure if it will happen in my lifetime, but your Daddy is a good man. But he has...his own secrets. Every grown-up does."

"They do?"

"Yes. And I'm sure you have secrets too, right?"

I wipe a tear from my cheeks. "Sometimes I sneak the dog scraps from the table. Especially if it's something I don't like."

Grandma chuckles. "Of course. Remember that, Raven. Remember that everyone has little secrets. And sometimes you're better off not asking questions you don't want the answer to."

～

I JERK myself out of my daydream. I'm in the car with Vinnie. His people are driving us to the hospital.

That voice from the dreams, the one telling me to remember something...

It's my grandmother. It's a memory from the day I walked in on my father in his office talking with that strange man. The strange man who looked like he was up to no good.

She told me to remember that everyone has little secrets.

I haven't thought about that day in forever. I always just thought that my father was in a bad mood and overreacted.

But now, in the light of his attempted suicide, I can't help but wonder.

Is Dad involved with something bad?

I TRY NOT to cry when I see my father in the ICU bed, hooked up to all kinds of monitors. So many times he had to look at me like this.

It must have been awful for him.

My mother sits next to him. Robin, Falcon, Hawk, and Eagle are here, but they're in the waiting area with Vinnie and Jared. The staff doesn't like more than two visitors in the room at a time.

I sit in the hard, uncomfortable chair near the window as I watch my father sleep. I let the silence of the room wrap itself around me, the steady beep of the heart monitor the only sound that breaks through. I trace the weathered lines on his hands.

My mother's face is a mask of calm, but her eyes betray her fear. She squeezes my father's other hand gently. "How could he do this?" she asks, but I don't feel like she's talking to me.

She's talking to the universe.

A nurse walks in, her face impassive behind her sterile mask. She checks my father's vitals and gives us a curt nod before leaving. Her detached professionalism does nothing to ease the tension in the room.

I squeeze his hand. "Daddy," I whisper. "You have so much to live for. How could you?"

His eyes flicker open. "Ray," he croaks out.

"I'm here. Mom's here."

"I need to see Vinnie," he says.

I raise my eyebrows. "Vinnie? Why?"

"Is he here with you?"

How would my father know that? "Yes, he's here."

"Please. I need to talk to him. Before I fall asleep again."

"Okay. I'll get him."

I walk back out to the waiting area and grab Vinnie's hand. "He says he wants to see you."

My brothers all raise their eyebrows, though not one of them speaks. They're still all in shock.

"Why me?"

"I don't know. I didn't ask." I wipe a tear from my cheek. "I just want... I want whatever he wants."

Vinnie nods. "Of course. I'll go."

He follows me down the hallway to my father's room.

Dad's eyes are still open, and Mom is wiping his forehead with a cool towel. His head is bandaged.

"I'm back, Daddy," I say. "Vinnie is with me."

"Thank you." Dad tries to clear the hoarseness from his throat. "I need to talk to Vinnie alone."

HELEN HARDT

"Daddy..."

"Go, Raven." He looks at Mom. "You too, Star."

"I'm not going anywhere," Mom says.

"Please," Dad says. "It's only for a minute. Please."

Mom stands, gulping. She looks at me, her forehead wrinkled, her eyes sunken and sad. Is she looking for reassurance? I have none to give.

"Come on." I take Mom's hand and lead her out. "Everything will be okay."

Mom grabs a tissue and dabs her eyes. "How could he do this, Ray? Why would he do this?"

I don't reply.

Because I have no answer.

276

42

VINNIE

Bellamy's skin is pale, but he otherwise looks strong. His physique is still muscular, and but for the bandage over his head, he looks okay.

"I'm here, Austin," I say.

"Thank you, Vinnie."

"For what?"

"For what I'm about to ask you to do."

I raise an eyebrow. "And what's that?"

He grits his teeth. "Finish what I started."

I drop my jaw.

Did I hear him right? He just asked me to kill him?

"Before you say no," he continues, "I know all about you. I know what you've done. What you will do."

There's no way he knows about the plan in the works for Agudelo, Vega, McAllister, and the others.

So what the hell is he talking about?

"Yes, you've made it clear you're aware of my past. But the answer is no. And you knew damned well it would be no."

"It's the only way I can save my family," he says.

"Look. I know what you've gotten yourself into. You may not have had a choice. You may *have* had a choice but got seduced by the money."

"Money has no value to me," he says. "My mother left me more than I could spend in four lifetimes."

"Then why?"

"I could say it started eight years ago, but it started much earlier than that."

"But eight years ago was when Falcon—"

"Yes," he interrupts me. "It was. I used it to my advantage, but I was also protecting my son."

"Falcon?"

He shakes his head. "Eagle, actually. The kid's a loose cannon. Always has been. Star and Raven babied him something awful. He grew up entitled, and you know what happens to entitled rich boys."

"I'm afraid I don't."

He wrinkles his forehead. "You grew up rich."

"I did. But you know where my money comes from. And you know damned well I wasn't entitled. If you knew anything about my grandfather—"

"I know." He weakly raises a hand to quiet me. "You didn't have it easy. I didn't mean to say that you did. Hawk, Falcon, the girls, they all grew up the same way. But Eagle was the baby. None of that really matters now. What matters is that they're better off without me."

"I don't think *they* believe that."

"Please, Vinnie. Finish it off. I know you have access to anything you need."

I shake my head. "I won't let you put me in this position. I love your daughter, and she would never forgive me if I was ultimately the one responsible for her father's death."

He closes his eyes.

"There are things," he says. "Things that, if my family found out, they'd turn their backs on me anyway."

I've only just begun to scratch the surface of what's going on with Austin Bellamy.

"Tell me this, Austin," I say. "Are you my friend? Or are you my enemy?"

Bellamy opens his eyes, looking straight into mine, yet his gaze feels distant, unreachable.

"Vinnie," he says, "I am neither a friend nor an enemy. I am a desperate man. I have done things—horrible things—and now, I can't see a way out."

"You could face it," I say, "Face the consequences."

"A luxury I don't have," Bellamy replies with a bitter smile. "Not with my children at stake."

There's something profound in the silence that follows. A heavy weight of a father's love and guilt mingle together in the room. It drowns every other sound, leaving just the whispering wind outside the window to break the silence.

He reaches out and takes hold of my hand with an unexpected strength. His grip is like iron, the desperation seeping out of him so tangible I can feel it clenching my heart. He locks his gaze onto mine.

"Your love for Raven..." he starts. "It's real, and I trust it. But it's her love for me that worries me. That's why you cannot tell her about any of this."

I pull my hand from his grip, a cold sense of fear creeping up my spine.

"I won't be your executioner, Austin," I say firmly. "But I can help you find another way."

He stares at me, silent and inscrutable. I can't tell if he's considering my words or simply resigned to his fate.

"Vinnie," he finally whispers. "I've dug myself too deep to climb out. There's no other way."

"You're wrong," I argue. "There is always another way. You're just trying to take the easy way out. This is really about deciding whether you're strong enough to take it."

His eyes search mine. I see a flicker of something in those blue irises, but it's quickly concealed behind a wall of resignation.

"You don't know the full story, Vinnie," Bellamy says. "Once you do, you'll understand why I'm asking this of you."

The prospect of uncovering Bellamy's secrets makes my stomach churn with unease. But despite the dread seeping into my bones, I know that I have to hear him out.

"Then tell me," I press on, my voice steady in spite of the tremor threatening to break loose inside me. "Tell me everything."

Bellamy draws in a long breath, his chest rising and falling with an audible sigh. "Just protect them. Please. Protect Raven."

"With everything I have. But she can't weather the loss of her father. Neither can the others. You have to heal. And then you have to face what you've done."

He closes his eyes.

I wait.

A moment passes.

And then another.

I stare at the clock, watching the second hand.

Minute by minute by minute by minute.

Has he fallen asleep?

"Austin?"

No response.

I grab his hand and squeeze it. "Austin?"

Still no response.

I nudge his shoulder. Again no response. "Austin!" I shake both of his shoulders. I don't want to shake them any harder because of his recent head trauma.

I rush out of the room. "I need a nurse, please."

"What is it?" A nurse comes bustling in.

"We were talking, and then he closed his eyes. When he didn't open them back up, I thought he'd fallen sleep. But I can't rouse him."

"Mr. Bellamy?" The nurse puts the stethoscope into her ears and listens to his heart. "His heart sounds good. The monitors are all good." She nudges him. "Mr. Bellamy? Can you hear me?"

"What's going on?" I demand.

"I'm not sure. Let me get a doctor."

A moment later, a doctor in a white lab coat comes in. She takes all of Bellamy's vitals again.

"Odd. Looks like he may have fallen into a coma. He may have a hematoma that we missed during the first scan." She turns to the nurse. "We need to check for brain activity. Order another CT and MRI. Stat."

"I'm going to need you to update his wife and children," I say. "They're outside in the waiting area."

The doctor cocks her head at me. "You mean you're not family?"

"I'm a...friend," I say. "He asked to speak to me alone."

She rolls her eyes. "Great. I've just violated HIPAA." She whisks out of the room.

I follow.

As she explains the situation to Raven and her family, I listen with one ear.

No need to get freaked out until we have his test results back.

Maybe he's just in a really deep sleep. He is healing from a massive injury, after all.

Raven falls against me. "Oh, Vinnie."

"It will be okay, sweetheart." I kiss the top of her head.

She pulls back a bit. "Oh, how can I be so selfish? You just lost your mother. And all I'm thinking about is me."

"That was a month ago, baby. I'm okay. It's okay to lean on me."

God, I love her. I love her so damned much.

Does her father have any idea what he asked me to do?

If I did what he asked, Raven would hate me.

And that I cannot bear.

43

RAVEN

After what seems like an eternity, we finally have news from the doctor.

"Thank you for your patience," the doctor begins. "The good news is, we've done extensive scans—MRIs, CTs—and there's no sign of any major brain damage. His brain activity looks normal, which is reassuring. The bullet missed any critical areas, and there's no significant swelling or bleeding that would typically explain why he's in a coma."

I pause for a moment, letting that sink in as I grasp Vinnie's hand with desperation. My mother's face is impassive. It's all too much for her to bear.

"However," the doctor continues, her voice softening, "despite those promising signs, he's still in a coma, and at this point, we're not entirely sure why. His body is not responding in a way we would expect, given the scans. There's no clear medical reason for this level of unresponsiveness. It's not unheard of, but it's rare, and we need to explore all possibilities, including metabolic or chemical imbalances, or even psychological factors. Sometimes, after trauma, the brain can react unpredictably, almost as if it's protecting itself, even when physically, everything seems stable."

I swallow. My throat hurts. My head hurts. My heart hurts.

Psychological factors? I guess Dad would have to be in a bad place mentally to want to kill himself in the first place.

God, I hate this.

My mind keeps wandering back to that day years ago when I made him pancakes. The slimy-looking man in his study. Grandma telling me to remember that grownups make mistakes. That grownups have secrets, and sometimes it's better not to know what they are.

Does that have anything to do with this?

"Right now, we're monitoring him closely," the doctor continues. "We'll keep running tests, and we'll do everything in our power to understand what's going on and give him the best possible care. For now, what's most important is that his condition hasn't worsened, and that's a positive sign."

We all stare at the doctor in silence. She's offered some comfort, but the big question—will our father wake up?—is still hanging in the air.

I can tell by the sympathetic look in the doctor's eyes that she's seen all this before.

She takes a deep breath and nods to each of us in turn. "All I can offer is patience. Recovery in cases like this can be unpredictable, but we won't give up. We'll take this one step at a time."

I collapse back in Vinnie's arms.

He runs his hands up and down my back. "It's going to be okay, baby. We'll get through this together."

I look up at him. "Did you just say what I thought you said?"

He raises an eyebrow. "What do you mean?"

"You said *we'll* get through this together. You and I. Together."

He squeezes me. "I didn't misspeak."

"So you're done with this *stay away from Raven for her own safety* bullshit?"

He cracks a tiny smile. "I suppose I am."

I wrap my arms around him, squeeze him as tight as I can. "Oh, Vinnie. I love you."

"And I love you too, baby."

And in this moment, perhaps the darkest my family has ever faced, there's a small glimmer of something beautiful.

Hope.

44

VINNIE

A *week later...*
Everything is complete.

Mario and Serena are settled in Dubai.

I've received confirmation that McAllister and Agudelo are in their graves. No news yet on Vega, but I'm confident that my plan worked with him as well.

I've cooperated with law enforcement, handed over tainted funds to the Feds, and cleared our coffee import business of all illegal activity.

Belinda and her governess, Natalie, are getting settled in my home, and Daniela is thrilled to have a little sister.

But Bellamy is still in a coma.

He's not on life support. He's breathing on his own. But he won't wake up.

～

THREE MONTHS LATER...

Daniela now has legal status in the US, and our divorce

286

will be finalized in another few months. She's living in one of my guestrooms, and she'll begin culinary school soon.

Belinda is doing well. She's in therapy to deal with her father's abuse, but she finds solace in her music. I've hired a college piano professor to teach her and bought a nine-foot grand piano for her to practice on.

I haven't heard anything from Mario and Serena, but that's expected. I assume they are happily enjoying their time together in Dubai. I've begun the process of getting my father released from prison. It will be a long road, but my attorneys think it can be done.

Austin Bellamy is still in a coma, and the physicians don't know why. He shows brain activity, so pulling the plug isn't an option. He's been moved to a facility here in Austin, and Raven—who has moved in with me—visits with him every day. Her other time is spent working at Raven's Wings, which is thriving.

I'm now CEO of the Bianchi Coffee Imports—a totally legit company, and a successful one. I have enough money to live out my life in luxury and support Daniela, Belinda, and any children Raven and I may have together.

And it's clean money. So clean it squeaks.

I did what I set out to do, and though I was victorious, I had to become everything I despised about Mario. Unlike my money, my hands *aren't* clean. I had to use evil means not to bring about ruin, but to achieve victory.

Victorious vice.

Victory came at a price. When you're fighting darkness, you don't walk away unscathed.

I have to live with that.

"Hey, babe!" Raven knocks on the open door of my study with that smile that still makes my heart pump faster.

"How is he today?" I ask.

She sighs. "The same." Then she smiles again. "But I just heard Belinda working on a new piece. It sounds amazing. And she was smiling, Vinnie. Smiling!"

I nod. Belinda started smiling a few days ago. It was a huge thing for all of us, but especially for Raven. She's grown to love the girl like a daughter.

In my desk drawer is a five-carat diamond engagement ring.

I haven't yet popped the question to Raven. I want to, more than I want my next breath. But technically I'm still married to Daniela, though my attorney assures me the divorce will be final soon. And we'll arrange an alimony agreement to make sure she's taken care of as she pursues her culinary dreams.

But Daniela is not the real reason I haven't proposed yet. I don't need to be legally divorced to get engaged.

Part of me still feels unworthy of Raven. She is goodness and light personified, and I...

Well...I'm not. Plus, I'm a genetic nightmare—the product of a father and his daughter. I even had my DNA tested, just in case Mario was lying to me.

He wasn't.

Raven's cheeks are rosy and they've plumped up, and her hair is now in a stylish dark pixie cut that she tucks behind her ears. Her latest scans and blood work were perfect.

She deserves everything life has to offer.

"Vinnie..." she says.

"Yeah, baby?"

She wiggles the fingers of her left hand toward me. "When are you going to make us official?"

I raise my eyebrows. Has she been reading my mind?

I rise and walk to her, taking her in my arms. "I officially love you, Raven. You know that."

"And I love you. We're safe now. You took down the Bianchi empire. You're a legitimate businessman. And you're a wonderful human being."

I don't reply.

"How can you not agree with me?" she asks.

"I didn't say I didn't."

"Yes, you did. By not saying anything." She shakes her head. "Look what you've done for Belinda. For Daniela. For Savannah and Falcon. You're everything, Vinnie. I want you to be *my* everything."

I kiss her then—a raw, open-mouthed kiss—because what I'm about to tell her may send her running for the hills.

I break the kiss. "I love you so fucking much."

"I love you too, Vinnie."

I grip her shoulders. "I have to tell you something."

She bites her lower lip. "You can tell me anything."

God, I hate keeping secrets from her. She still doesn't know the extent of her father's involvement with the cartels. Hell, I don't even know the extent, since Agudelo is now dead. Only Bellamy himself knows...and he's not talking from his coma.

But one secret remains that Raven has to know before she consents to a life with me.

"I found out something right after my mother died," I say. "Something that rattled me to my bones. But in an eerie way, it made sense."

She bites her lip, her eyes wide. "You're scaring me, Vinnie."

I cup her cheek. "Don't be scared. I don't want you to ever feel fear again, Raven."

"All right." She swallows. "Just tell me. You can't tell me anything that will make me stop loving you."

I hope she's right. "I'm just going to say it." I draw in a breath. "Vincent Gallo Senior isn't my biological father. Mario Bianchi is."

She drops her jaw. "Then who's your mother?" Then she gasps. "Oh my God..."

I nod. "Right. My mother is my mother. I'm a product of incest, Raven. And I don't blame you for being disgusted. I know I am."

"Oh, Vinnie." She wraps her arms around me. "I'm not disgusted. Not by you. Maybe by how you came about, but that's not your fault."

"You should know that I've talked to a DNA expert and to my personal physician. They say that because I don't have any genetic abnormalities from inbreeding that any children of mine probably won't either. But there's always a possibility, Raven. You need to go into this with your eyes open."

She steps back. "This is... This is..."

God. I can't lose her. Not after everything we've been through to be together.

But I'll let her go if I have to.

If this is a dealbreaker for her, she certainly won't be able to handle all the other skeletons in my closet as they reveal themselves.

I've already let her go once, to keep her safe while I was taking down the family business.

"I understand if you want to break it off," I say quietly.

Then she lunges toward me. "No! I'm not leaving. I don't even know if I'll be able to have children after all the poison that's been pumped into my body. But if I can, Vinnie, I want to have *your* children. And however they come out, they'll be perfect and we'll love them."

And in that moment, the room gets a little brighter. Maybe the sun is peering out from behind a cloud, or maybe Raven is just that fucking radiant.

I crush my lips to hers in a devouring kiss.

"God, I love you," I say against her lips.

"And I love you."

I break away for just a moment to retrieve the ring from my desk. Then I drop to my knee in front of her, opening the black velvet box. "Be my wife, Raven. Make me the happiest man in the world."

She holds out her left hand, a single tear streaming down her cheek. "Absolutely, Vinnie. There's not a doubt in my mind."

I slide the ring on her finger and kiss her again until she jerks backward.

"You okay?" I ask.

"Yeah." She giggles. "It's just my phone. It's buzzing in my pocket because I have it on silent. I'll ignore it."

"It's okay," I say. "It could be important."

She nods and retrieves her phone, looks at it, and her eyes go wide.

"What is it?" I ask.

She swallows. "It's my mom in the group text. My father. He's awake."

THANK you for reading *Victorious Vice*! I hope you loved reading Vinnie and Raven's story. The romance, intrigue, and mystery continues with Hawk's story in *Cryptic Curse!*

She escaped hell. Now it wants her back.

At just eighteen, Daniela Agudelo has already lived through more than anyone should. After fleeing Colombia and the men who stole her childhood, she lands in Texas with a dream of becoming a gourmet chef and a desperate need to stay invisible. But everything shifts when she meets Hawk Bellamy.

The middle son of the Bellamy billionaire ranching family, Hawk is used to being overlooked. Trapped between a hero brother and a reckless one, he's the family fixer, the one who follows the rules—until Daniela crashes into his life with her intense beauty and haunted eyes.

Their connection is magnetic. Dangerous. She's too young. He's too jaded. Too bound to secrets and responsibilities he never asked for. But need has a way of ignoring the rules.

Until the first cryptic message arrives—and the hell Daniela thought she left behind doesn't feel so far away.

And Hawk? He'll break every rule in the book to protect her.

One-Click CRYPTIC CURSE now!

Want to stay in the know? Sign up for my newsletter! https://www.helenhardt.com/newsletter-sign-up

I appreciate you helping to spread the word about my books. Reviews help readers find books! Please leave a review on your favorite book site. You can also join my reader group: https://www.facebook.com/groups/hardtandsoul

Visit my website: https://www.helenhardt.com/

MISSING BRIDGERTON? You'll love the sensual world of the Sex and the Season Series. One-click Lily and the Duke now!

READY TO GET in your feels? She's lost in the dark. He's the storm that might lead her home. Colleen Hoover meets Ana Huang. "Literally perfection." One-click My Heart Still Beats now!

ACKNOWLEDGMENTS

Thank you so much to my editor, Eric J. McConnell; my beta readers, Karen Aguilera, Linda Dunn, and Serena Drummond; my cover artist, Amanda Shepard of Shepard Originals; and my audio narrators, James Sydney and Kaileigh Riess.

ALSO BY HELEN HARDT

Bellamy Brothers

Savage Sin

Sweet Sin

Seductive Sin

Vengeful Vice

Volatile Vice

Victorious Vice

Cryptic Curse

Chaotic Curse

Captivating Curse

Aces Underground

Spades

Diamonds

Clubs

Hearts

Vampire Princess Diaries Duet

Princess Fallen

Princess Redeemed

Follow Me Series

Phoenix

Amethyst

How to Marry a Billionaire

Enticing You

Captivating You

Seducing You

Claiming You

Sex and the Season

Lily and the Duke

Rose in Bloom

Lady Alexandra's Lover

Sophie's Voice

The Perils of Patricia

Steel Legends

I am Sin

I am Salvation

Broken Dream

Healed Heart

Steel Brothers Saga

Craving

Obsession

Possession

Melt

Burn

Surrender

Shattered

Twisted

Unraveled

Breathless

Ravenous

Insatiable

Fate

Legacy

Descent

Awakened

Cherished

Freed

Spark

Flame

Blaze

Smolder

Flare

Scorch

Chance

Fortune

Destiny

Melody

Harmony

Encore

Non-Fiction

got style?

Cooking with Hardt & Soul

ABOUT THE AUTHOR

#1 *New York Times*, #1 *USA Today*, and #1 *Wall Street Journal* bestselling author Helen Hardt's passion for the written word began with the books her mother read to her at bedtime. She wrote her first story at age six and hasn't stopped since. In addition to being an award-winning author of romantic fiction, she's a mother, an attorney, a black belt in Taekwondo, a grammar geek, an appreciator of fine red wine, and a lover of Ben and Jerry's ice cream. She writes from her home in Colorado, where she lives with her family. Helen loves to hear from readers.

Please sign up for her newsletter here:
https://www.helenhardt.com/newsletter-sign-up
Visit her here:
http://www.helenhardt.com